Ghost
of a
Chance

Ghost of a Chance

a novel

Kerry Blair

Covenant Communications, Inc.

Covenant.

Cover illustration by Josh Yamamoto.

Cover design copyrighted 2007 by Covenant Communications, Inc.

Published by Covenant Communications, Inc.
American Fork, Utah

Printed in United States of America
First Printing: January 2007

13 12 11 10 09 08 07   10 9 8 7 6 5 4 3 2 1

ISBN 1-59811-157-6

Acknowledgments

Acknowledging all the people I could (and should) thank would take more pages than are in the story. That said, thanks to Linda Prince, Hilary Blair, Kat Gille, and many more for peerless proofing, Jessica Warner for another wonderful cover, Medic Scott Blair for research into what corpses do and do not do (Ick!), Margaret Turley and Jeri Gilchrist for wading through the rough draft, Melissa Dalton for yet another fabulous Mystery Dinner (and a whole lot more), Six Writers (and a Frog) for the friendship, wisdom, and support I've found in their bog, Shirley Wolfe (my mother) for feeding my family on days I don't get around to it, Cheri Crane for patiently luring me out from under the bed with promises of a Chili's run, and Gary Blair for continuing to be, day in and day out, a man after whom a romantic hero can be patterned!

As always, appreciation, kudos, and love to the remarkable, renowned, irreplaceable Angela Eschler!

Finally, everything I know about ghost hunting (which is really quite a lot) I owe to Jake Blair—talented writer, confirmed skeptic, horror movie aficionado, and one of the most truly interesting and intelligent people I've ever known.

To Valerie Holladay.
There wouldn't be an eighth book
if there hadn't been a first,
and there wouldn't have been a first
if it hadn't been for you.

There needs no ghost, my lord, come from the grave to tell us this.
Hamlet, William Shakespeare (1564–1616)

Though this be madness, yet there is method in 't.
(Ibid.)

Chapter 1

"I ain't afraid of no ghost," I told my stakeout partner, hoping it was true.

Outside the windows of our hearse, the crumbling remains of the San Rafael Mission seemed to glow under the ochre spell of a late-October moon. Built by Catholic friars in the days when Arizona was claimed by Mexico—and Mexico by Spain—it had once been an architectural marvel, towering over the vast and barren Sonoran Desert. But in the last two centuries, Phoenix and its suburbs had grown up around it. Now San Rafael crouched in a barrio, its adobe walls profaned by graffiti and overrun with thorny bougainvillea. Even so, the mission looked beautiful. It looked ethereal. It looked . . . haunted.

I quit looking.

"You ain't afraid of ghosts, either," I assured my partner with a pat on her velvety head. If Clueless noticed that my hand shook a little, she was too polite to mention it. I waited for a witty comeback, but although the Weimaraner is about my age in dog years (twenty-three) she must have missed *Ghostbusters* growing up. Or maybe she wasn't into lighthearted banter. She'd wanted to go home about the time we ran out of snacks.

"Just a little longer," I promised as I picked up the crossword puzzle I'd been working.

My partner sighed and lowered her head to lick crumbs of powdered sugar from my lap.

Maybe I should introduce myself. I'm Samantha Shade, interim head of Nightshade Investigation and a rookie detective who is hopelessly addicted to crossword puzzles and powdered-sugar donuts. The first is pretty benign as vices go, but the second is bad. So bad, in fact, that now it's giving me nightmares.

Just the other day (I work nights, sleep days), I dreamed I was Batgirl: black spandex unitard, yellow knee-high boots—the works. I'd draw you a more vivid mental picture but, believe me, you don't *want* to imagine me in spandex astride a Bat Cycle. In the dream I tore back to my Fat Cave in humiliation. I'd let the bad guys *have* Gotham City before I'd let the citizens get a gander at my love handles.

I've always dreamed of being a superhero. I think that's what makes me so self-conscious about my figure. I mean, can you name one member of the Justice League with thunder thighs? No, Superman doesn't count. Name a *female* member who doesn't look like Angelina Jolie. Think about it. I'll wait.

My point exactly.

Remembering the nightmare, I frowned down at my supposedly slimming black pants and sucked in my tummy. Nothing moved.

Clueless lapped at the crumbs of sugar on the seat. (Powdered-sugar donuts are not only fattening, they're messy.) "Enjoy it while you can," I told her. "It's carrot sticks for us from here on out. As of this second, I am on a diet." Clueless snorted. Or maybe she sneezed. Whatever she did, it meant the same thing. I'd threatened to diet before, but this time I'd do it. I'd lose those love handles if it meant eating rabbit food for the rest of my life.

I turned in my seat and leaned against the door to make myself more comfortable while I divided my time between working the puzzle, watching the old mission for signs of a ghost, and daydreaming of a more wraithlike me. In the meantime, Clueless explored the floorboards for any remaining atoms of powdered sugar.

I was staring at the mission and contemplating what a great setting it would be for a horror flick when somebody tapped on the window behind my shoulder. If I'd been a snake I'd have shed my skin. As it was, I set a new world record for long jumping across the bench seat of a hearse. Clueless—alert now that she'd been alerted—let out a shrill bark from the safety of my lap.

"Sorry, Sam," a deep, familiar voice said through the window. "I didn't mean to scare you."

"You didn't scare me!" I croaked. (It was a froglike croak, not an expired-on-the-spot kind of croak, though my heart *had* considered it.) I scooted out from under the dog and back over to the driver's side. Then I rolled down the window with one hand and pushed my partner back with the other. I had to keep pushing her because there's something about Thomas Casey—the handsome young police detective who'd almost given me a coronary—that attracts female attention, apparently even that of the canine variety.

"You shouldn't be out here alone," he said. Thom tends to be short on small talk and long on advice.

"I'm not alone," I said. "I brought a partner."

"Your partner's a dog."

I stroked the Weimaraner's velvety muzzle. "Don't you like dogs?"

"I like dogs fine."

I was glad to hear it. I was glad to hear anything I didn't already know about Thom, what with him being the new love of my life and all. "Do you have a dog?"

"No," he said. "I have a cat."

"What's its name?"

"Mr. Mistoffelees."

"A tomcat!" I said, hoping he would admire my quick wit.

"She's female."

"But I thought you said *mister*."

"The name is from T. S. Eliot's *Old Possum's Book of Practical Cats*."

"Oh," I said. "I've been planning to read it." I said it as if it were on my nightstand atop volumes of H. G. Wells, e. e. cummings, and other notable men of letters Thom admires. In reality, I don't have a nightstand beside my bed, let alone any of those authors lying around. I fudged a little because Thom is a police detective by profession, but he's a literature professor at heart. It wouldn't surprise me to learn that he has stockpiled more books than the Mesa bishops' storehouse has grain.

I was about to change the subject from T. S. Eliot to *anything* else when a to-die-for dimple winked into Thom's cheek—something that happens when he frowns—and he changed the subject himself. "There was another murder."

I told you he was short on small talk.

"Where?"

"The body was found a few blocks from here. It's on the way to the morgue now. The victim was probably shot last night, but the corpse was dumped within the last couple of hours." He pulled a PDA from a jacket pocket. "You've been in the neighborhood. Can I ask you a few questions?"

I nodded. *A few. A dozen. A hundred. A thousand.* "Come in and sit down," I offered.

Thom's gorgeous gray eyes slid along the side of my uncle's hearse with something less than appreciation.

Some people. The hearse is a classic—a 1963 Superior Caddy in mint condition. It's easy to see why it's one of the earthly joys of my uncle Eddie's life. It's teal green with *Nightshade Investigation* in bold, black letters on the sides. Within the large letters is a smaller, greenish script that, like the print on our business cards, glows in the dark. (Very appropriate for a place that's open from 8 P.M. to 5 A.M., don't you think?) It might not be the ideal vehicle for an ordinary stakeout, but what's ordinary about trying to catch a ghost?

"Where's your car?" Thom asked.

I sighed. I love my little black V-dub almost as much as Eddie loves his hearse. "You know how I told you the other day that she was going *thwip-ping, thwip-ping?*" I asked Thom. When he nodded tentatively, I said, "Well, then she started going *thwup-pong, thwup-pong.* And then she finally went *thwip-thwup-pong-thwup-ZOING.*"

"Uh-huh," Thom said. He had no idea what I'd said, but he didn't ask for more information. He circled the hearse's long, sleek hood as he headed for the passenger side. As he passed in front he stopped for a second to run his hand over the silver raven hood ornament. (This might be an apt time to slip in that Edward Shade—my uncle, the stake patriarch, and the founder and owner of Nightshade Investigation—is a tad . . . um . . . eccentric.)

"You have to get in back," I told Clueless as I unlatched the sliding panel that separated the driver's seat from the formerly casket-bearing part of the vehicle. I slid open the small door and wrinkled my nose at a faint odor that wafted into the front. Clueless whined, but I pushed her into the carpeted, wood-lined compartment anyway. "You'll be fine," I assured the dog while I motioned for Thom to open the door.

"It smells like a hearse," he observed when he had opened it.

"It's your imagination," I said. "There hasn't been a corpse in this thing for thirty years."

Thom looked dubious, but he got in anyway and closed the door behind him. Then he cracked the window.

"Delano took it in to be detailed," I explained. "We want it to be perfect when Uncle Eddie gets back from Europe this weekend. The car-wash people must have used something stinky to clean the paneling."

Clueless whined again and stuck her head out between me and Thom.

"I'm with you," Thom told her.

"It's not that bad," I insisted, but I left my window down. "Tell me about the murder. Was it the same killer?"

"Same M.O."

Thom didn't have to elaborate. I already carried a grisly picture in my mind. I'd heard about it often enough. There wasn't a news affiliate in the city—or in the country, for that matter—that wasn't covering the story of the "Marigold Murderer." In the last nine days there had been three murders. All the victims were young Latin American males. All were found within blocks of one another. All had been executed by a single gunshot to the fore-head, but that wasn't the ghoulish part. After they were killed, each man's tongue had been removed. Then the murderer carefully cleaned the blood from the victim's face and inserted the slim stem of a marigold between the lips. Finally, in the middle of the night, the creep left the corpses where they couldn't be missed, lying faceup with arms folded serenely over their chests.

Thinking about it, I struggled to keep down the donuts I'd so recently eaten. "That's awful."

Thom stared out the window toward the mission.

I studied his handsome profile and felt a rush of sympathy for a guy who'd clearly rather read *Death of a Salesman* than investigate one for the Phoenix PD. Still, I knew it was his sensitivity and intelligence that made Thom so good at his job. Uncle Eddie has a description of the quintessential detective hanging on the wall at Nightshade. It says: "Down these mean streets a man must go who is not himself mean, who is neither tarnished nor afraid." (It's from Raymond Chandler's *The Simple Art of Murder*—if you haven't read this classic 1939 detective novel, trust me, you should.) That is *so* Thom. He'd left academia to please his terminally ill father, a captain with the LAPD. He'd been promoted to detective recently and already he was assigned to homicide on the trail of a serial killer. Then again, *every* detective in Phoenix and the surrounding areas was probably working that case.

"I'm sorry," I said softly, knowing as I did that the words wouldn't make any difference.

To my surprise, he gave me a grateful smile. "Thanks, Sam."

Have you ever been so in love with somebody that hearing your name fall from their lips gave you goose bumps? That was me.

And Thom is so observant that he noticed the gooseflesh even though he was oblivious to the cause. He thought I was creeped out over the serial killer. "I'm sorry too," he said. "But I do need to ask you those questions." He pulled the stylus from his PDA. "How long have you been parked here?"

"Uh . . . " There's no clock on the dashboard of my uncle's hearse. There isn't even a radio. What's more, the battery in my watch is as dead as my dearly departed Volkswagen. "Let's see," I said. "I've worked one crossword puzzle, that takes me about forty-five minutes, but I've also walked Clueless, reviewed my Sunday School lesson, and—"

"What time did you leave Nightshade?" he interrupted while I was still trying to do the math.

"A little after midnight."

"It's almost three now."

"No wonder Clueless wants to go home!" I exclaimed. At the sound of her name, the Weimaraner whined. "She hates to miss *Twilight Zone.*"

"I've been of the impression that's where you live."

Okay, so Thom didn't say that, but I know he thought it. And I couldn't blame him. The first night we met I'd had him arrested. The next time we were together I lost a priceless Egyptian mummy (yes, a real one) and he got the back of his head bashed in. The very next night I demolished his patrol car. In the days to follow I almost cost him his badge, got him sprayed by a skunk, and was the reason he was lured into a potential death trap at an old planetarium. (Yes, it *had* occurred to me that our relationship might be off to a rocky start, but I still had hope. Who was it who wrote that the path to true love never does run smooth? Thom would know.)

Thom said, "So you've been here at least a couple of hours?"

"Yes."

"Any unusual activity?"

I looked at San Rafael and sighed in resignation. Or maybe it was relief. "No," I said. "No ghost."

"No kidding." Thom tapped his PDA. "I'm asking about the *un*natural, Sam, not the *super*natural."

"You don't believe in ghosts?"

"I believe in the Holy Ghost," he said. "And in resurrected beings. And I believe in the occasional pseudo-physical manifestation of a spirit currently abiding in another sphere appearing with God's approbation."

"Is that a yes or no?"

He smiled. "To quote H. G. Wells, 'It will take a very tangible ghost to frighten me.'" (What did I tell you about H. G. Wells? Do I know Detective Casey, or what?)

Well, that made it unanimous. None of us in the hearse were afraid of ghosts. But Father Pedro Rodriguez, under whose jurisdiction the abandoned property fell, *was* afraid of a ghost. Of course, he didn't believe in ghosts, either; what he feared was the gossip and alarm that haunted his parish. He'd already given in to a group of his parishioners—superstitious people newly arrived from small Mexican villages—and performed an exorcism. The supposedly undead monk who was said to walk the halls of San Rafael hadn't shown up for the rite. But he (or someone or something) had been active since, as evidenced by the strange lights and low moans that continued to plague the mission.

I'd toured the condemned building with Father Rodriguez—in the daylight and wearing boots and a hard hat because of the building's disrepair. There were ample signs of rats, feral cats, and other four-legged trespassers—and some signs of partiers, mostly of a previous generation—but no indication of pranksters or live-in vagrants as I'd suspected.

For a week now my coworkers and I had taken turns staking out the mission for several hours every night. Knute and Delano and I had changed times, vehicles, and places we'd parked. Either the ghost was more observant of us than we were of him, or our timing was lousy. Nothing unusual happened on any of our shifts, but when we returned to the neighborhood the next night, we'd almost invariably hear that we'd missed a "haunting" by an hour, sometimes less. The phantom reportedly showed up one or two nights a week. We showed up five or six, but never at the same time.

"Anyway," Thom said, breaking into my thoughts, "I'm looking for somebody a whole lot less ethereal—and far more dangerous—than your ghostly friar."

I nodded somberly. I wouldn't change places with Thom for all the world and a new pair of skates besides. Give me a phantasmal phantom over a maniacal murderer any day.

Clueless read my mind and whined her agreement. Or maybe she still had her mind on the odor and/or the lack of donuts.

"Did any vehicles pass by while you were parked here?" Thom asked.

"Yes." Before he could ask for a description, I added, "But I didn't look at them, Thom. I'm looking for a ghost. Ghosts don't drive lowriders."

Anybody else would have said, "What *do* they drive?" but not Thom. He merely frowned and extended an elbow to block Clueless's full frontal assault on the passenger seat. He was unsuccessful. I wondered what was wrong with that screwy dog. I was still wondering it when Thom resumed his interrogation around the beast. "Did you see any pedestrians?"

"Only the usual gang," I said, meaning it literally. "The ones with the orange bandanas. Six of them."

When Thom looked up, the worry-born dimple was back in his cheek. "You shouldn't be in this neighborhood alone, Sam. I can't believe Knute and Delano let you— "

"Until Uncle Eddie gets back, *I'm* the boss at Nightshade," I interrupted. My cheeks grew hot. "This is my *job*, Thom!" I paused to count to ten and got as far as four before I lost my temper. (For me that's pretty good.) "And I'm *good* at it. You've said so yourself."

I pushed Clueless aside so I could better glare at Detective Casey. Rather, I *tried* to push her aside, but the hound wouldn't move. Instead, she held her ground, raised her muzzle toward the moon-filled windshield, and let out an ear-piercing howl.

As bad as that was, what followed was worse. Two hundred yards away in the spooky, supposedly deserted mission, someone— or something—answered with a bloodcurdling cry of terror.

Chapter 2

The scream that came from the old mission lasted less than two seconds and ended so abruptly that it was as though somebody had pushed the pause button on a CD of *Spine-Tingling Halloween Sounds.* If every single hair on the back of my neck hadn't been standing at attention, I might have wondered if I'd heard it at all.

Two seconds is longer than it took Thom to pull a radio and a service pistol from beneath his jacket. "Stay!" he told the dog as he opened the door of the hearse. Or maybe the command was directed at me. Regardless of who he was ordering around, neither of us obeyed him.

Talking into the radio as he ran, Thom headed toward San Rafael.

Yelping as she ran, Clueless headed in the opposite direction. I stood between the two of them while my head whipped back and forth, my legs momentarily paralyzed by indecision.

A siren blared a block away and came closer. Clueless loped down the middle of the street. (We don't call her Clueless for nothing.) I knew that when the squad car rounded the corner, there was no way it would miss her.

"Clueless!" I yelled, running after the dog. "Come!"

I might as well have commanded her to fly. Despite the fact that she possesses a nicely framed diploma from obedience school, Clueless has retained only one thing from her eight weeks of training—a great fondness for training treats.

I searched my pockets as I ran and came up with half a stick of wintergreen gum. The Weimaraner was most of the way down the street. Judging by the shrieking siren, the car was almost to the corner. "Clueless!" I shrieked louder than the siren. "Do you want a treat?"

Don't tell me dogs don't understand human vocabulary. To Clueless, *duyuwannatreat* is the most beautiful word in the English language. She stopped so fast her claws probably left long scratches on the asphalt.

"Do you want a treat?" I called again, waving the gum.

She wanted it all right. She plowed into me at the same moment the car careened around the corner and sped past the spot Clueless had occupied seconds before.

From my new position, on my rear on the sidewalk, I hugged the dog's neck in relief. Then I wrapped my fingers securely around her collar to keep her from getting away from me. "You almost got yourself killed," I scolded.

Yeah, yeah, yeah, she panted. *Where's that duyuwannatreat you promised me?*

I extended the gum sheepishly.

Clueless sniffed it. Then she licked it to make sure her nose hadn't deceived her. Then, I swear, she frowned. *That's not duyuwannatreat,* she said very clearly with her soft blue eyes. *I think it's that nasty . . . medasun . . . the vet gives me for worms.*

"I owe you," I told her sincerely. I stuck the gum back in my pocket and tried to pull her and myself up at the same time. Only one of us rose. "I'll give you the treat when I take you home. I promise."

She wasn't convinced. By the time I'd managed to drag the reluctant Weimaraner back to the hearse, I didn't have the heart to close her up in it. But I did reach inside for her leash so I wouldn't have to walk the rest of the way to the mission hunched over like Quasimodo.

More cops had arrived by now, and that's an understatement. Judging by the cars and sirens, half the Phoenix PD was already there or en route. I ignored the uniformed officer on the side-walk, but Clueless had the courtesy to sniff his shoe as we passed.

"You can't go in there," he said.

"It's okay," I replied over my shoulder, tugging at Clueless's leash to keep her moving. "I work there."

"Whattaya talking about?" In two shakes of a dog's tail the officer caught up to me and yanked my elbow to slow me down.

You'd have thought my trusty companion would object to this rough treatment, but she didn't. Despite their reputation as women's best friends, some dogs have a difficult time forgiving and moving on. Besides, when it came to that spooky mission, Clueless was still of a mind to retreat rather than advance.

"I do work there," I told the cop.

"Yeah, you look like a nun," he said sarcastically.

Clueless sat down and rooted for local law enforcement.

"I'm a private detective." I motioned toward the hearse. "I work for Nightshade Investigation. That's *our* ghost in that mission."

Maybe I should have left off that last line because the policeman rolled his eyes. "Go home, lady."

"I will not go home!" I yelled. In my defense, I *had* to yell to be heard over the police helicopter hovering overhead. Besides rendering the people in this part of town partially deaf, it bathed the area in blinding light. In the squalid apartment complexes nearby, dusky faces disappeared from the windows. I wondered how many families were prepared to flee with only the clothes on their backs if this turned out to be another raid on illegal immigrants.

I yanked my elbow free of the officer's grasp. Then we spent the next little while engaged in a farce that would have done discredit to a Leslie Nielsen comedy. I stepped forward. The policeman stepped in front of me. I moved to my right. He moved to his left. I tried a duck-and-feint maneuver. He didn't fall for it. I tried to distract him by yelling, "Serial killer!" and pointing toward the street, but he didn't fall for that either. I finally darted around him and broke into a sprint. He caught up and grabbed my elbow once again. (I might have made it if I hadn't been dragging that dog. I may not be exactly lithe, but I'm quick.)

The officer and I were locked in a fierce stare-down when a second man approached. "Is there a problem here?" he asked.

I turned to the older man, determined to prove how much of a problem I can be when I don't get my way. He was almost bald, middle-aged, and had enough of a paunch to necessitate wearing his belt three or four inches below his waistline. Although not in uniform, he was clearly in charge.

"She's a private detective, sir," the uniformed officer said. "She says it's her ghost in there."

The older man's eyes strayed from me to Clueless and stayed there. He laughed out loud. "Well, if it isn't Scooby-Doo and his faithful sidekick . . . "

I figured he didn't finish the sentence because he couldn't think of any more of the *Mystery Inc.* characters. That was probably a good thing for him. If he'd called me Velma I'd have kicked him in the shin. As it was, I graciously overlooked the snide remark and went through my pockets one by one until I came up with a snazzy, white-on-black business card. "Samantha Shade," I said, extending the card. "Nightshade Investigation. We've been hired by Father Rodriguez to investigate the possibly paranormal activity in San Rafael."

The guy ignored my card but said, "I'd heard that the crazy old padre went to you after all the real detectives in town laughed him out of their offices."

I straightened my shoulders, gripped Clueless's leash a little tighter, and hoped I looked as though I'd known all along that Nightshade was the priest's last resort. For sure I *should* have known it. It was virtually the story of our lives. "Then I'll go to work now. Excuse me."

"I'll excuse you to move that monstrosity of yours off the street," he said, meaning the hearse. (At least I hoped he meant the hearse and not my derrière.) "Now."

I kept my cool—something for which I am not exactly renowned—and tried another tack. "I'm with Detective Casey."

"Tennyson?" he said, raising one eyebrow.

"No, Casey. Thomas Casey. We're . . . together." Not thirty minutes before, we had been sitting in the very same hearse, so my claim was true in a manner of speaking.

When the man smiled it was apparent that he would benefit from fewer cigarettes and more mega-whitening toothpaste. "Yeah," he said. "Now that you mention it, I'd heard that, too."

No surprise there. Ever since my last case, The Mystery of the Missing Mummy, made it onto a nationally syndicated talk show (long story—read the book), Thom and I were practically famous.

Before I could reply, a muffled voice spoke from within the breast pocket of his jacket. He reached for the radio, but said to me, "I'll give Tennyson your regards if I see him again. Now beat it."

If he saw Thom *again*? My eyes cut toward the mission. Did they think the serial killer was holed up in there? My question was answered when a SWAT van screeched to a stop behind my hearse. I looked in awe at the firepower exiting the vehicle. They were prepared to take on a deranged serial killer and a largish band of international terrorists besides.

The guy with the paunch finished barking orders into his radio and looked back at me. "I thought I told you to beat it."

Forget that. If there was an "if" involved in Thom's return from the mission, I would hold my ground in case he needed me. What if he was hurt? What if he'd confronted the killer alone? What if the SWAT team had been called in because he was a hostage?

Judging by the beads of perspiration on his shiny scalp, the middle-aged cop was as nervous as I was. (Or maybe he was just hot and bothered.) "Look, Ms. Shade—"

"Want a piece of gum?" I fished in my pocket for the square Clueless had rejected. True, it wasn't much as bribes go, but you work with what you have. Besides, a little wintergreen wouldn't exactly have hurt his breath any, if you know what I mean.

"That's it!" he said ungratefully. "I'm gonna—" I didn't find out what he'd intended to do to me because he cut himself off at the sight of a giant striding toward us.

The first thing I noticed was that none of the officers tried to stop *him*. That might be because my associate is about seven feet tall and half that wide. (If I'm exaggerating, I swear it's not by much. In dimmer light, Knute Belanoff might be mistaken for Frankenstein's monster. Come to think of it, in dim light he *has* been mistaken for Frankenstein's monster.)

"Glad you're here, Belanoff," the plainclothesman said by way of greeting.

Again I wasn't surprised. Knute has worked the Phoenix streets for more than forty years. Almost everyone in local law enforcement knows him.

I looked back at the detective and decided he was hot and bothered, but not necessarily in that order. He said, "I can't seem to make this girl understand a simple two-word directive to *get lost.*"

"Listening isn't her greatest strength," Knute agreed, his dark face crinkling into a wink aimed my direction. He extended his sledgehammer of a hand. "How you doing, Detective Lasovik?"

"Been better," the detective said as they shook. "Got a real psycho on the streets."

I don't think he meant me.

"So I've heard," Knute said. "Anything I can do to help?"

"Yeah," the detective said. "You can take Nancy Drew and Toto back home to Kansas."

Lasovik had mangled his metaphor (Nancy's dog is Togo and they live in River Heights), but he'd made his point and I was offended. Only the timely arrival of Knute's hand over my mouth forestalled a response that would have landed me in the back of one of those dozen patrol cars.

"Come on, Sam," Knute said. When I only sputtered, he practically picked me up off my feet. "You know Eddie's number-one rule is to never interfere with law enforcement."

I did know that, but I also knew that Knute and Delano had modified this rule to "Never interfere with law enforcement . . . when they're looking." I glanced around. They were looking. Knute released me and I followed him reluctantly back to where I'd parked the hearse. Though I looked up and down the street, I didn't see his car.

"They've closed off the area for two blocks in every direction," he explained. "I parked on Guadalupe and walked in when I heard what was going down." As I circled the hearse with Clueless, Knute opened the door and attempted to fold his large frame onto a passenger seat designed for an average-sized human being. When he was mostly successful I started the engine. "Don't," he advised. "Make somebody walk all the way over here to tell us to move the vehicle."

I switched off the ignition without mentioning that I'd *already* been told to move it—several times. "Thom's in there," I said.

Knute picked up on the tremor in my voice. "He's okay."

He had no way to know that. Thom might be a hostage. He might be hurt. He might be . . . I couldn't finish the thought. Accepting Knute's platitude was probably the way to go. "I should have gone in with him," I said. "But . . ."

(This time the ellipses are the part where I filled Knute in on everything that had happened since Thom had tapped on my window.)

When I'd finished my story, Knute stroked the dog's muzzle with his finger. "You made the right choice, Sam. Going after Clueless is what Eddie would have done."

That wasn't a platitude, it was the truth. Eddie's tender heart is the reason our modest offices are downtown over a flower shop—squeezed in between a funeral home and a kosher deli—instead of uptown in one of the ritzy glass-and-steel skyscrapers favored by much of our competition. (On the other hand, it might be where it is because Uncle Eddie is tremendously fond of pastrami, and because the florist has reminded him of all fifty-two of his and Aunt Elise's anniversaries.) For sure his charitable nature is the reason we work for so many underdogs like Father Rodriguez.

I couldn't take my eyes off the mission. Pinned in place by a spear of white light from above, it was ringed by the SWAT team plus perhaps a dozen more Phoenix PD officers. I watched as two of the heavily armed sharpshooters knocked bits of adobe brick from the historic walls in their ascent toward the bell tower. "They think the serial killer's in there," I told Knute.

"Well, it's a safe bet they're not after our ghost."

"Thom hasn't come out," I worried aloud. "It's been a long time." I wished the hearse had a clock so I'd know *how* long. I'd have guessed a week, but since the sun hadn't risen a single time I would probably have been a little off in my reckoning.

"He's okay," Knute said again. "Despite the dog-and-pony show, they're not acting like it's a hostage thing."

"What *are* they acting like?"

"They're acting like cops with a serial killer on the loose and no leads. Think about it, Sam. Lasovik has a terrorized city and harried politicians breathing down his neck." He pointed through the windshield at the most recent news copter to arrive. "I'd bet at this point he's doing PR. He wants Joe Q. Public to wake up to the morning news and see Phoenix's finest hard at work making the streets safe again."

I frowned. "If that guy is their *finest,* heaven help us."

Knute grinned. "Then you'd better pray harder, Sam. He's the best they've got. The best they could get, in my book."

"Seriously? That old bald guy?"

"Seriously," Knute said. "That 'old bald guy' is a former FBI agent out of Philadelphia. They don't come any better trained or more dedicated than Ivan Lasovik. He's a great chief of detectives."

"He doesn't even know Thom's name!" I protested. "He called him . . . some dead poet."

"Tennyson," Knute supplied.

"How do *you* know that?" I exclaimed, thinking again that Knute Belanoff must be the best PI in the business. The way he picks up on things is positively clairvoyant.

"Thom told me."

Okay, so maybe *clairvoyant* wasn't exactly accurate in this case, but he really is good.

"Why does he give Thom such a hard time?"

"He's old-school," Knute said. "Hard-nosed. Thom's gonna have to earn the chief's respect and prove he didn't get the job riding on his father's coattails."

"Thom's already proven himself," I pointed out. "He exposed a sleazy city councilman."

"He had help." Before I could glow with pride over my part in the bust, Knute pointed upward. "Besides you, he can thank that wishing star of yours, Sam. More than once he lucked into being in the right place at the right time."

"More like the wrong place at the wrong time," I said, "considering that he was almost killed twice over." Frankly, people with Thom's kind of "luck" should never buy raffle tickets. "Besides, a wise man once told me that fifty percent of the best detective work is luck."

Knute chuckled. "And I'd have sworn you never listen to me."

Once again we sat in silence and watched the police. At this point even I could have told you they were just milling around. Several squad cars had already pulled away. Mostly only the SWAT guys were left, and they seemed to be conducting training maneuvers. I figured it was because once you're up and dressed and armed to the teeth you have to work off all that nervous energy somehow.

Garbled words from the police scanner in Knute's hand confirmed our suspicions. He raised the scanner to his ear. "Thom's on his way out."

Sure enough, a minute or two later Detective Casey and half a dozen more men appeared. I reached for the door handle, but Knute shook his shaggy head. I stayed put and watched Thom brush dirt and cobwebs from his broad shoulders as he approached his boss.

I couldn't make out the chief's words from where we sat, but it was clear he shouted them. For sure it couldn't have been a conversation because Thom never responded. The longer Lasovik yelled, the lower Thom's chin sank toward his chest. At last Lasovik threw his hands in the air, turned, and walked away. Thom looked after him, then glanced toward the street and saw us. He hesitated a second or two before walking over to the hearse and squatting beside Knute's open window.

I gripped the steering wheel to keep my hands from shaking. That man has the strangest effect on me. Whenever he approaches, some kind of electromagnetic current sends a jolt from his eyes to my heart.

"Bad night?" Knute said to Thom.

Thom nodded. "I'm the one who called this in. A hundred man-hours and fifteen thousand dollars later we didn't even catch the wild goose."

"You did what a good cop does," Knute said.

"Tell that to Lasovik. He thinks I'm hallucinating." He ran a dirty hand over his eyes. "Looks like I'll be teaching school before long."

I leaned over Clueless and Knute to be closer to Thom. "I heard the scream too," I said. "It was horrible. It sounded like somebody being tortured."

"It was a cat fight."

I shook my head. "Cats don't sound like that."

"There's nothing else in there."

"There is!" I insisted. "Or there *was*. There *had* to be."

Thom shrugged. "Then I guess it was your ghost."

My eyes strayed back to the mission. Smeared with crimson bougainvillea blooms, it looked bloody—and almost as haunted as the look in Thom's eyes as he turned away.

Chapter 3

I went into Nightshade reluctantly the next night. It was Delano's turn to stake out the mission. Knute was handling one of our new cases. All I had to look forward to was a drawerful of payment-due notices. While my partners were on the city streets risking life and limb, the only danger I faced was from a paper cut.

Due to the time of year, we had more new cases than usual. Not that there's generally more mayhem in the fall, but the potential clients who do walk through Nightshade's front door in October are charmed by our "seasonal décor" and are thus much more likely to hire us. Not that we decorate. Nightshade looks the same in early April as it does in late October (it's looked the same for fifty years, in fact), but things like the mechanical fortune teller in the front office next to the receptionist, and the faux electric chair in Eddie's office seem to be more socially acceptable at Halloween than they are at Easter.

Go figure.

Anyway, while Delano and Knute had all the fun, it fell upon me as temporary CEO to balance the checkbook and pay the bills. As blood chilling as the scream was the night before, I'd have traded assignments with Delano in a heartbeat. It was almost the end of the month and it seemed as though every bill was due—or past due—at once. Seated at Uncle Eddie's desk in his vintage *Maltese Falcon*-esque office, I pushed aside a stack of reports I needed to read/revise/file/shred before the real boss came home and stared at the figures in the ledger. I stared until my eyes crossed.

Then I picked up a wooden pencil (they taste better than carrot sticks if you ask me) and gnawed away, wondering what a nice detective like me was doing in a bookkeeper's purgatory like this.

Like many of you, I grew up reading the new adventures of Nancy Drew, and the old adventures of Sam Spade, and watching every detective show rerun on cable TV. Thus had I been led to believe that private investigators do the most fun, exciting, glamorous, fulfilling work in the whole world. Boy, have we been misinformed! What you don't read between the lines of books or see between the commercials on television is that professional private investigation is work—fact-filled, endless, glum, unfulfilling *work*. Nancy Drew and Jessica Fletcher never filed a report in all their frothy little lives. I don't know who paid Sam Spade's phone bill, but I'd bet it wasn't him. Columbo and Mr. Monk wouldn't spend more than two prime-time minutes on a stakeout, and *none* of them—not one—had worked with somebody like Chaiya.

For those of you who haven't met her, Chaiya (pronounced like *kayak* without the last *k*) is Nightshade's part-time receptionist. She is also my cousin and my roommate. She's unconventional at best, and a little Chaiya goes a long way—and I happen to have a whole lot of Chaiya in my life. It's a wonder I still have my hair.

The old-fashioned intercom buzzed for the fourth time in ten minutes. "Sammy," she said from the reception area, "do we have an encephalon?"

Ignoring her never works, so I reached for volume one of Uncle Eddie's 1920 set of dictionaries to see if I could figure out what she was talking about this time. We keep the lexicons within easy reach because they're our only hope of communicating with Chaiya. My cousin is a firm believer that it pays to increase one's word power, but she wields that power with impunity and almost total inaccuracy. In other words, while she's compiled a massive vocabulary list in her brain, she's hazy on the definitions.

I flipped pages until I found the misused word-of-the-moment: *encephalon: the vertebrate brain.* "Some of us have one," I told my cousin, wondering what it was she really meant. "Not you."

"Can I borrow yours? I need to look up *apotheosis* for my class."

Cue the light bulb. "You need a *dictionary*," I told her (and not for the first time) "not an *encyclopedia*." I stuck my finger in the *E*s and headed for the *A*s. "*Apotheosis* is deification," I reported. "What does that have to do with cosmetology?"

"I don't know. What?" Chaiya said.

"I don't know! You're the one who's going to beauty school and looking up *apotheosis* for class."

She sighed. "That was so last week, Sammy. I dropped out of beauty school. All those mirrors gave me the willies. Now I'm taking a creative writing class. I'm going to be a novelist." After a pause, during which my head began to throb, she added, "But my teacher says I need to learn how to use an apotheosis first."

"Apostrophe?" I guessed.

"Okay," Chaiya said, unaware that she drove me crazy one syllable at a time. "What's an apostrophe?"

"Look it up in the encephalon," I said, using my free hand to grab the intercom's cord and rip its plug from the wall. When I turned back in the dictionary to withdraw my finger, my eyes fell upon another definition. *Encephalasthenia: extreme mental fatigue due to emotional stress.* I wrote it down on a notepad so the doctor who found me slumped over Uncle Eddie's hopelessly messed-up ledger would know what to write on my death certificate.

Disabling the intercom was a stroke of genius. It was almost twenty whole minutes before I heard from Chaiya again. This time she appeared in the open doorway.

"Mr. Meyers is here," she said. "I told him we wouldn't pay the rent until he has the wiring fixed in this old building. The intercom quit working. That's in-excruciating."

"For sure," I said. "But not inexpedient." (I learn a lot of mostly useless vocabulary myself by working all those crossword puzzles.) "Send Sully in, Chaiya."

When Sully Meyers entered, I rose at once to offer him a chair. His few remaining wisps of hair stood on end, and he looked almost as pale as his clientele. (Sully is the undertaker who owns all three buildings on our little block. He is the embalmer and director of Rest in Peace, the funeral parlor to our east.)

I smiled tentatively. "Are we so late with the rent that you've come to collect in person?" Not that he has a lot of rent to keep up on. His sister, Sally, owns and operates Forget-Me-Not, the floral shop downstairs, and his twin brother, Sol, is the proprietor of Eat, Drink, & Be Merry, the deli to our west.

Sully sank onto the faux electric chair in the corner and my smile faded. Nobody with any presence of mind sits there— except for Knute, who is too big to sit anywhere else. But Sully looked like he thought he belonged in an electric chair and would welcome a lethal jolt besides.

I took the elderly man's arm, pulled him up, and urged him toward Uncle Eddie's desk. When I pulled out an Oriental black-lacquer chair, he sat numbly on it with his elbows on his knees and his chin in his hands. I waited for him to speak, but he was as inanimate as Quoth, the large, stuffed raven that would perch forevermore on the grandfather clock across the room.

"What's wrong, Sully?" I asked, perching myself on the edge of the desk and reaching across it to push the intercom button to ask Chaiya to bring in a cup of water. I pushed the button three times, but nothing happened.

"Won't work," Sully mumbled. "The whole building's wiring is shot to—"

"Oh!" I said, remembering at last that I'd pulled the plug. "No, I—"

Before I could explain, Sully continued, "Building's falling down around my ears. My life is over, Sam. You're witness to the final scene. Everything I worked for. Everything I accomplished. My father's good name. All gone." He raised his arms over his head and waggled his fingers as if urging the building to fall faster. "Bury me, already!" he urged some heavenly demolition team. "Get it over with!"

I looked up at the cracked, molded plaster. Despite empirical evidence to the contrary, I said, "Sully, the building's fine."

"Then strike me with lightning," he suggested to the heavens. "It's the least you can do."

I probably don't need to come right out and tell you that Sully has a bit of a Tevye complex, right? But since I'd known him all my life, I knew that tonight's theatrics were a little extreme, even for him.

He finally lowered his arms, but his eyes drifted toward the window. "If I jump, will I die?"

"Sully, what's the *matter?*"

It was almost a minute before he replied. Then he whispered, "Samantha, I lost a client."

I rolled my eyes. "Is that all? I've lost clients almost every day that Uncle Eddie's been gone, and you don't see me jumping out of windows." (I'd considered it once or twice, but the window is only on the second floor.) It took a horrible, strangled sound in his throat to finally make me understand. I gasped. "You mean you lost a *client? A dead* client?"

Since his mouth was now covered by both his hands, Sully could only nod.

"When?" I asked. "How?"

"I don't know when, Sammy," he mumbled through his fingers. "As for how . . . it must be the devil's handiwork! I, Sully Meyers, am a cursed man."

I didn't believe the cursed part, and I sincerely hoped he'd incorrectly identified the culprit as well. "When did you discover that the cadaver—"

"Please don't say *cadaver,*" he interrupted. "Please, Samantha, *kevod ha-met.*"

I nodded. I had still been a little girl racing around Uncle Eddie's offices with my cousins when Mr. Meyers taught us the meaning of *kevod ha-met*—respect for the dead. Though it had once been one of the premier mortuaries in town, Sully's business had changed with the demographics. As the affluent took their deceased with them to the suburbs (you understand what I mean by that, I hope), he found even greater satisfaction serving the mostly destitute inner-city families who were left behind. Regardless of their station in life, every person who received their last earthly services from Sully Meyers was treated with honor and respect.

"I refer to them as *clients* or the *dearly departed*," he reminded me.

"I know. I'm sorry." I tried again. "Well, then. When did the, um, client . . . depart? I mean . . . depart again. I mean . . . leave your place of business."

"I don't know!" Sully said. "The vigil service at his parish was this evening. Since he could not be there in person because of the state of his body, I went back after supper to sit *shemirah* with him." He leaned onto Eddie's desk as if needing more support than the chair and I were providing. "In the morgue I thought to myself, 'Sully, Mr. Batista should not be alone in a locker on this occasion,' so I opened it up and—poof!—the client was gone."

"Corpses don't go 'poof,'" I said, scarcely believing I was in a conversation where it *could* be said.

"This client went poof!"

"Spontaneous human combustion?" I guessed aloud. I'd heard of that, but couldn't remember if I'd come across it in one of my father's medical journals or seen it on the *X-Files*.

"Mr. Batista did not combust," Sully insisted. "He poofed."

"Before your eyes?"

"Certainly not!"

Thank goodness for that. "Could you have . . . misplaced . . . him?"

Sully again raised his hands toward heaven, but this time I think he was praying for patience. When at last he dropped his hands, he said, "I do not misplace clients, Samantha, though I did check the other lockers, of course. He is nowhere. If he did not poof, then he was kidnapped."

"Corpse-napped? Do the police have a unit for that?"

"Police!" Sully's hands flew back to his lips.

"You've called the police," I said, knowing by his face that he hadn't.

He shook his head. I had to lean farther forward to hear what he said through all those gnarled fingers. "I didn't know *what* to do, Sammy! I walked the streets for hours, asking God for guidance."

I couldn't fault him for that. As first steps go, petitioning God is always the best.

"God sent me to you."

"He did not!" I cried, aghast.

"He did," Sully said, crossing his arms over his sunken chest. "Am I here, or am I not?"

I opted to lean back rather than fall face-first on the floor. He'd been sent to the wrong girl. I'd lost a mummy on my first case, and I hadn't yet found the ghost that haunted my second. Obviously, working with dead people was not my forte. I would *not* take on a third case to look for a departed corpse, dear or otherwise. I crossed my arms and hoped I looked half as stubborn as Sully did. "You have to call the police."

"God sent me to *you*."

"That's so I could send you to the police." I reached for the phone and Sully reached for his heart. I paused with the receiver in my hand and watched the blood drain from his face. "How about if I phone a friend?" I said. If there was a better answer, I didn't know what it was. "He's a detective with the Phoenix PD."

"That soft-spoken patrolman who loves Chaim Potok?" Sully asked hopefully. The death grip on his rib cage loosened.

"Uh, sure." I hoped Chaim Potok was a writer rather than the new counter help at Eat, Drink, & Be Merry. "Thom Casey. He's a detective now. He can help you more than I can."

Apparently, anybody who loves Chaim Potok is okay in Sully's book. When he nodded, I closed my eyes and prayed that Thom would forgive me for involving him in The Case of the Kidnapped Corpse so close on the heels of The Secret of the Screaming Specter and The Mystery of the Missing Mummy.

Okay, you caught me. Maybe I *do* have a little Nancy Drew in me, at least when it comes to naming cases. But I've got one thing for which Nancy would trade Togo, Ned Nickerson, *and* her shiny little sports car. *I* know a gorgeous guy who reads Chaim Potok.

* * *

"The thing is," Thom said to me and Sully Meyers about an hour after I'd called and begged for his help in locating a missing corpse—and thus forestalling the imminent suicide of a certain overwrought mortician I knew and loved—"I'm assigned to homicide. I've run the info you gave me. Antonio Batista died of a drug overdose. In other words, he killed himself, if accidentally. Since the missing body isn't evidence in a murder investigation, I can't get involved."

"How do you know it was an overdose?" Sully countered. "There was no autopsy. Suspicious, yes?"

"No," Thom said kindly. "Batista died at home in front of witnesses. He had needle marks on his arms. The coroner's office did a simple blood test on the scene and found enough drugs in him to kill a horse. There was no reason to autopsy."

"Ah ha!" Sully said. "I cleaned and dressed the dearly departed myself, Detective. Those needle marks were old scars. Very old. No new shoot-up killed that boy."

Thom looked skeptical, but I tended to believe the mortician. After all, Sully saw a whole lot of needle-scarred arms in the clientele he served.

"It *could* have been murder," Sully insisted. "You do not know beyond a shadow of a doubt it was *not* foul play."

"The point," Thom continued, "is that unless there is probable cause to suspect a homicide, I can't help you. I'm sorry, Mr. Meyers, but it's out of my area."

"Even the police specialize!" Sully complained to heaven. But this was the last of his tenuous bravado. The next second he crumpled into a heap of discouraged old man and whispered, "When word of this gets around, I am ruined."

I watched Thom close his eyes. There had been a lot of prayers offered that night. Sully, me, and now Thom. At last he pulled a PDA from his pocket and said, "Tell me everything you can about Batista and his family. Don't leave anything out."

When Sully raised grateful, tear-filled eyes, Thom cautioned, "This isn't official. I'm not on duty."

"But you admire Chaim Potok," Sully said.

At first Thom looked puzzled. Then he smiled. "Yes."

Sully told us everything he knew, and Thom filled in the rest from the police report. Antonio Batista was a Mexican national who had come to work in the U.S. on a green card. He'd recently returned to Mexico to bring his mother and sister to Phoenix. About twenty-six hours after coming back over the border, he died of an overdose in his own apartment. After his body was released from the medical examiner's office, Antonio's family had sent it to Sully. They offered what little payment they could and, of course, Sully told them it was more than enough.

Rest in Peace had received the body Monday morning. Sully had taken it in himself and put it in a refrigerated locker until the burial because the family couldn't afford embalming. It was now Tuesday night, so Batista's remains must have disappeared sometime the night before, after the funeral home was closed and the employees had gone. There had been no break-in, and nothing else was missing or disturbed as far as Sully could tell.

I rubbed my temple and craved powdered-sugar donuts. Discounting spontaneous human combustion and translation, poofing looked like the only explanation.

"Who has keys to your building?" Thom asked.

"Samantha," the mortician began.

"I do not!" I said so quickly I probably appeared to have a guilty conscience.

"Surely you do," Sully said. "I gave them to Eddie years ago. Good neighbors watch out for each other."

I frowned, hoping that "watching out for each other" didn't mean that if he was ever away we were expected to take in the newspaper and tend the clients.

"Employees?" Thom prompted.

"I have two assistants," Sully said. "Marty Poe and Roderick Harte."

Sully and I waited for Thom to write this down, but the stylus didn't move. At last Thom said, "You're joking." (If your literary IQ is higher than mine, perhaps you'll find this as ironic as Thom seemed to.) Finally convinced that Sully wasn't pulling his leg, Thom wrote down the names. Roderick, I soon learned, was the tall, dark, depressed man I'd seen driving Sully's hearse and attending the door at nighttime viewings. He assisted with funerals and worked in the front office. Marty was the Napoleon Dynamite look-a-like who occasionally helped out in the morgue.

The only other employee was Veronica Chavez, a young beautician who went in to arrange clients' hair and apply makeup before the viewings. She was the only one of the three I knew, and that was because she was also an instructor at Chaiya's beauty school—her former beauty school, I mean—and the granddaughter of one of the residents at Shady Acres, the assisted care center my mother owns. While I mostly ran into Veronica when she was visiting her grandfather at Shady Acres, she'd occasionally drop by Nightshade to chat with Chaiya after finishing a job next door. It was she who had convinced Chaiya to give beauty school a try in the first place.

"The police will want to talk to them," Thom told Sully as he closed his PDA.

The old man was gazing out the open window. I walked over and closed it as a precaution.

Thom knelt in front of Sully and laid a sympathetic hand on his shoulder. "Mr. Meyers, they'll interview you while forensics goes over the morgue. It would be a good idea to have somebody you trust watch the investigation—for insurance purposes, if nothing else." He paused as if hating to say the next part. "And if you have an attorney, now would be a good time to call." Sully looked as if Thom had punched him in the stomach. "I'm sorry," Thom said, "But . . . " His words trailed off when the mortician raised his eyes toward the cracked plaster overhead.

"All my blood. All my sweat," Sully told the ceiling. "Come to *this?*"

"It'll be okay," I said, joining Thom at Sully's side. But tears had come to my eyes as well. Even if Sully didn't lose his license, this could still force the closure of Rest in Peace. That would be a tragedy on many levels. Sully's broken heart aside, what would the desperately poor people in the area do without the services of this gentle, generous man? "It *will* be okay," I repeated.

"It will be what it will be." Sully squared his shoulders. "Mr. Casey, thank you for volunteering to supervise the police while they are at my parlor. It is a comfort to know my clients will be in your capable hands." Before Thom could recover from his surprise appointment as guardian of the dead, let alone protest it, Sully added, "And I will take your advice and call Mick Farrell."

Thom looked stunned. I would have been more sympathetic if Sully hadn't just handed me a metaphorical "get out of this mess free" card. My contrition was overcome by my elation.

But my relief was premature. Instead of reaching for the phone to call the lawyer, Sully reached for my hand. "Keep this month's rent check as your fee, Samantha."

"Fee?" I didn't like the sound of that.

"I certainly don't expect you to work for free. The funeral is tomorrow morning at eleven. I'll need Mr. Batista back in his casket by ten."

"But—"

"You're right," Sully said. "Nine would be better."

Instinctively, I looked up at the grandfather clock. Seconds ticked by before my brain could process that the big hand was on the eight and the little hand neared the eleven. That meant I had ten hours and twenty minutes before the deadline.

Plenty of time to find the guest of honor.

If I were Green Lantern, maybe. Even *I* know I'll never be a full-fledged superhero. What I didn't know was that by the time the big hand made it all the way around the clock I'd be halfway there—I'd be green.

Chapter 4

It might have been my imagination, but standing on the plush, jade carpeting in the foyer of Rest in Peace, Thom looked a little green himself. No matter how many times he punched the buttons on the control panel, the lights never grew any brighter than a twilight glow. But the lighting wasn't what he was trying to change.

"Does anybody know how to turn off that music?" he asked me, Delano (who had just come in from the stakeout), and the two uniformed officers who had responded with a CSI team to Thom's call. Since the intercom was turned to the track Sully plays for his Christian clients, strains of "Amazing Grace" wafted through the heavy, floral-scented air.

"I once was lost, but now am found . . ." a tenor sang.

"Maybe it's prophetic," I said optimistically, thinking of the missing corpse.

"Maybe it's annoying," Delano said. He scratched his red Brillo pad of a beard and considered the panel. He turned a knob and pushed another button. "Got it."

Sure enough, the music changed. Now a soprano sang: "Rock of ages, cleft for me, Let me hide myself in thee."

"That's appropriate too," I said, thinking of my latest case and wishing I had a rock to hide in.

"Never mind," Thom said. "Maybe we won't be able to hear it in the back.

I froze at the thought of what *was* in the back. "I should stay with Sully," I decided aloud.

"Isn't Mick in there?" Delano asked.

I shook my head. "He's a morning person. He sent that new guy who works for him, Kitandkaboodle—or whatever his name is. Besides, since it's our case, we ought to be there to hear Sully's official statement, don't you think?"

Delano nodded and moved toward the door marked "Director," where Sully and his new attorney awaited the police. "I'm all over it."

"But—"

"You've already heard what Sully has to say," Delano pointed out. "Let's see what I pick up, and then we'll compare notes."

I'd have thought it was good investigative procedure myself except for the fact that I would have to leave the eerie foyer to go into the mega-eerie morgue—a place I'd hoped to never have to personally take my body. But given the choice of going in there or confessing my fears to Delano and Thom, I went.

Thom led the way down a long hall and paused before an open door. I knew the voices I heard in the next room were the CSI duo that had arrived a few minutes earlier. Looking into the room, I was glad I'd gone with Thom after all. Half the duo was young, female, and very pretty.

"You okay?" Thom asked when he saw me peer apprehensively into the morgue.

"Of course I'm okay," I said. Didn't he see the smile plastered on my face? It was designed to make me look as though I routinely tour embalming chambers in the middle of the night and think nothing of it.

"You're grimacing," he observed.

"I'm *smiling*."

"Oh," he said, as if he didn't see anything to smile about. Then he motioned politely for me to precede him into the room.

There are times when chivalry isn't called for, and this was one of those times, but I stepped into the room in front of Thom nevertheless. I didn't step very far into it. In fact, Thom had to urge me forward so he could get all the way past the door frame.

As we entered, the gorgeous member of the team turned toward us, a newly lifted fingerprint clasped in her hand. Even through the plastic glove I could see her beautifully manicured nails. Her red hair was short and stylish, and her makeup looked as freshly applied as any actress's on TV.

Looking from the CSI babe to her large, lumbering bear of a partner and back again, I felt like a member of a studio audience at the taping of a *Law & Order* show. Unfortunately, I was a tourist who had spent too long on the tour bus and was now on the frowsy side. As a precaution, I remained rooted in front of Thom, even though I knew he could probably see just fine over the top of my head.

The CSI cutie shrugged the strap of a leather case from her shoulder—she was so slender she could as easily have hung it from a hip bone—and slipped the piece of evidence inside.

"Thanks for coming," Thom said to her.

"My pleasure," she cooed as though he'd invited her there on a date.

I didn't move. If Thom wanted to be closer to her he'd have to push me aside.

He didn't push. He said to the man, "Anything?"

"Hard to say," Bear replied. "Nothing out of place that I can see." His face twisted into a rueful grin. "On the other hand, you wouldn't expect a cadaver to put up much of a fight over being abducted."

The glamour girl of Phoenix Forensics had turned her attention to the storage lockers on the far wall. To my horror she opened one and began to pull out a long, steel tray.

You've seen this on television, I told myself quickly. *Chill.*

I chilled, all right. I couldn't have moved if I'd wanted to. I watched as the first foot of tray came toward me. I'm sure I blanched at the sight of the lumpy plastic bag that lay atop it. Fortunately, being frozen and all, I didn't scream.

Pretend it's TV, I reminded myself as she reached for the zipper on the bag.

It wasn't TV. Once the bag was open and I glimpsed the naked, pasty-gray corpse, the view screen swung slowly to the right, then to the left, then abruptly upward.

After that it went black.

* * *

When I awoke some time later, I was hunched over on a cold cement floor with my ears between my knees. I couldn't remember what I'd been doing before this, but judging by my position I thought it must have been yoga. I tried to raise my head, but Thom Casey's warm hand held it in place. Even in my befuddled state I knew he knelt in front of me. Every nerve in my body told me he was close. Very close. Closer than he'd ever been to me anywhere but in my dreams. I felt suddenly faint.

I mean fainter.

"I love you, Samantha," Thom said. He pulled me into his arms and kissed me tenderly.

Okay, that might not be exactly the way it happened. It might have been more along the lines of him saying, "Take a deep breath, Sam," and putting his hands on my shoulders to keep me from toppling forward and breaking my nose on the concrete. But he *was* close—and I *was* delusional—so I took advantage of the situation by leaning into him and nestling my cheek against his solid, comforting chest. Being almost in Thom's arms was heady. Heavenly. I prayed we could stay this way forever—or until I remembered where we were, whichever came first.

"I love you too, Thom," I murmured.

I think I really said it, but I might not have because Thom's response was, "Take a deeper breath, Sam."

Hearing him say my name made me tingle all over. I nodded blissfully, snuggled closer still, and drew a breath full of content-ment and hope and Thom's aftershave. Too much aftershave. I wrinkled my nose. Then I made a face. He smelled like my sophomore biology teacher. I bolted upright. "Thom, you stink!"

"I think that might be this embalming fluid," Bear said from a couple of paces away. He screwed the lid back on a noxious bottle and returned it to the cabinet.

Embalming fluid? I closed my eyes and tried to sort out where I was and what was happening to me. I think I also tried to lean back into Thom, but he moved me the other direction. Things were clearer by the time he had me propped against the wall. I looked up into his amazing gray eyes. The little crinkles around the corners were a clue they were smiling, but to his credit they were the only part of his face doing it.

"Sit quietly and keep breathing," he said. "Your brain will clear and you'll be okay in another minute."

The strong whiff of chemical had already cleared my brain, but I was *not* okay. I was lucid. As Thom rose, my eyes darted around the room. I remembered everything. The lockers were closed now, but one had been open and I had fainted at the sight of the cadaver within it. Since nothing hurt, Thom must have caught me as I fell, then lowered me to the floor. When I finally came to, I had fawned all over him and said—

Pass the embalming fluid. I'm going to die of mortification.

On the other side of the room, the young woman who could probably examine a body without batting a single perfect eyelash placed a final plastic evidence bag in her case, closed the case, and shrugged it onto her shoulder as she looked at Thom.

I swiped at the hair plastered to my sweaty forehead, tried to suck in my tummy, and wondered how long I'd been unconscious. Pretty long if they'd finished their whole investigation in the time it took me to faint dead away, fantasize about Thom while semi-conscious, and publicly humiliate myself upon coming to.

"That's it, Detective," she told Thom with a smile that led me to believe I might not be the only one who fantasized about him. "I'll take this in tonight, but don't hold your breath for the results. With the Marigold Murders taking top priority, the lab's backed up four ways from Sunday."

Thom nodded and returned her smile. "Thanks, Amber."

He knew her name? Her *first* name?

"Strange deal," Bear said, following his partner to the door. "You've got to wonder who would want a corpse . . . and why."

"I'm not going to wonder about it," Amber said. "I want to sleep tonight." She looked down at the stylish and fully operational watch on her graceful wrist. (I bet her car worked, too.) "What's left of tonight, that is."

* * *

I knew I had to say something to Thom about what had happened between us in the morgue thirty minutes before. (Or rather what had happened between me and my overactive imagination.) All I needed was the right opening.

I wasn't going to get it. The uniformed officers had finished their investigation and left by the time we returned to the foyer, but the attorney was still there with Sully and Delano. "Shall We Gather at the River" played on the intercom. I wished we had gathered at a river so I could drown myself.

At the same time we entered from the back, Chaiya breezed in the front door. "Do you know what time it is?" she demanded of me. (Of course not. No watch, remember?) "I was supposed to get off work two hours ago, but I can't leave Nightshade desecrated."

"Deserted," Delano supplied with a grin. He thinks Chaiya is adorable. For such a smart man, you'd think he'd notice that she pays more attention to the Chia Pet on her desk than she does to him.

Before I could decide whether to apologize or point out that she *had* deserted her post, Chaiya's internal man-o-meter clicked on. Now, I know everybody comes to Earth with certain gifts and abilities, but I've seen few that match Chaiya's. Not only does she routinely speak in tongues and write Post-it notes in reformed Egyptian, she can also recognize the presence of an attractive, single, LDS guy before setting eyes on him.

This is how it works. First, two invisible antennae pop up from beneath her raven-dark hair. They vibrate for a second, swivel around the room, and lock on target. In the next second her green eyes go neon and, if you stand close enough, you can hear the hum of her pulse as it accelerates. This activates the current that powers her 100-watt smile. Truly, it's a sight to behold.

This time Chaiya's antennae had picked up the slight, swarthy form of LeVar Zabloudil, formerly of Navajo County's public defender's office, and now Mick Farrell's newest associate.

Delano rolled his eyes as Chaiya introduced herself to LeVar. (I'd tried concertedly to get Delano to ask my cousin out himself, but so far he'd never caught her between dates. This probably wasn't his fault. Catching Chaiya between dates is about as likely as me morphing into Amber the CSI goddess upon consumption of my six-hundredth carrot stick.)

"LeVar Zabloudil," Chaiya repeated, giggling over the way the name zinged around her brain cavity and tickled her tongue on the way out. "I love it!"

"It means he-who-keeps-his-master's-most-favored-sheep-in-a-sheltered-and-secure-place," the bespectacled young man told her.

"Wow," Chaiya said. "I've never dated a *shepherd!*"

Zabloudil's dark brows drew closer together. Clearly he wished he had a little flock waiting for him in the parking lot or a lamb in his briefcase. "I'm an attorney," he said by way of apology.

"Well . . . " Chaiya said, "I guess that's okay. I sometimes date attorneys."

While I had been watching Chaiya in action, Thom had been talking to Sully about the investigation. "They'll do their best," he assured the poor man.

Overhearing this, Zabloudil saw his chance to prove that attorneys are almost as useful in modern America as shepherds. "I hope so," he interjected. "But they might not consider it a felony since a felony consists of the theft of an item worth more than $500."

"What's a dead body worth?" Chaiya asked with genuine interest.

"For trace materials," Delano said, "about ninety-eight cents." When I frowned at him, he shrugged. "I read it someplace."

"Exactly," LeVar said, unhappy to see there was another alpha-male know-it-all in Chaiya's proximity. "Then you are familiar with the Dr. Handyside case of the mid-eighteenth century?"

Delano shook his head.

"*Campbell vs. Campbell* in the nineteenth?" Apparently, arcane legal knowledge was all LeVar had to show off, so he ran with it.

I could tell that Delano would like to show his fangs—if he had fangs, which he doesn't. His eyeteeth are just more prominent than most people's. You remember I told you earlier that Knute bears a passing resemblance to Frankenstein's monster? Well, think of handsome Lon Chaney Jr. in his classic Wolf Man role, and you'll see Delano. He has a little less hair, but not much.

"These precedents are from the first great legal minds to consider this question," Zabloudil continued as though he was certainly the latest. "It boils down to the question of what is left after death. The soul has departed. What remains doesn't remain long—or static. Basically, it returns to the earth no matter what Mr. Meyers and his ilk might do to it."

Nobody spoke. I don't think Sully *could* speak. Chaiya didn't know what LeVar was talking about. None of the rest of us wanted to engage in the conversation.

"Therefore," LeVar concluded, "dead bodies are not property subject to the state's theft laws, and neither Mr. Meyers nor Mr. Batista's family has a fiduciary relationship with his corpse. There was no breaking and entering. Nothing of tangible value was removed. Therefore—"

"Nothing happened here," Delano finished for him, but scornfully.

"Legally, no."

I looked at Thom for a rebuttal, but he didn't offer one.

"Okay," Chaiya said slowly, "but body snatching is still pretty creepy, right?"

For once Chaiya had nailed it. Felony or misdemeanor or *whatever,* body snatching was still *plenty* creepy.

Chapter 5

"This is the place," I told Thom, frowning. It was Wednesday morning and we stood on a littered sidewalk looking up at the run-down three-story apartment building where Antonio Batista's mother and sister lived. The heap of old brick and crumbling mortar was in almost as bad a shape as nearby San Rafael, albeit 150 years newer. A sign in front read "Abandon Hope, All Ye Who Enter Herein."

Maybe it didn't say that. Maybe it bore whatever name the slumlord had attached to the property, but the other was definitely implied.

It had been about eight hours since Sully Meyers's collapse. Because the funeral director wouldn't stop wailing and entreating the ceiling for the return of his dearly departed, Zabloudil had taken him to an emergency room, where doctors sedated the poor man and admitted him for psychiatric evaluation. I wasn't worried. I knew Sully would be released soon. In the meantime, tranquilizers and a quiet room were no doubt doing him more good than I could.

I could have used a sedative myself. My knees wobbled and my mouth was dry from apprehension. It wasn't the thought of going into the building that scared me. (At least it wasn't *only* that.) I was afraid of what we had to do when we got there. Somebody had to tell Señora Batista, the mother of the missing corpse, why the liturgy and burial planned for that morning would have to be postponed. I wished that somebody didn't have to be *me*. (I mean *us*. Okay, I mean *Thom* since he was the one of us who spoke Spanish.) Nevertheless, Thom had agreed to do it, and I'd promised Sully I would stand there while he did. Frankly, I'd rather have faced another cadaver.

"Do you think Father Rodriguez is here yet?" I asked hopefully.

Thom shook his head. "His housekeeper said he was ill. He'll send somebody, though." He reached for the grimy door handle. "Ready?"

"No."

"Take a deep breath," he advised with a grin that told me he was teasing me about fainting in the morgue. Then he turned and pulled open the door.

I was glad Thom's back was to me now because I felt my cheeks grow warm. *Should I be embarrassed?* I wondered. *What did I say when I first came to?* I wished I could remember for sure. I didn't want anything I babbled—true confession or not—to jeopardize my professional relationship with Detective Casey. If Thom couldn't love me, maybe he could at least respect me. I had to find out just how bad my blathering had been. Since he'd brought it up, this was probably the time to broach the subject and get it over with.

Following Thom into the building, I took a deep breath, as he'd suggested . . . and gagged on it. The air was filled with the accumulated odors of half a century—an overpowering, if invisible, cloud of spice, rancid grease, and other things too icky to name. I clasped a hand over my nose and suspected that in another second I would faint. Again.

"Forget deep breaths," Thom said, forging onward as if he wore a gas mask. "Breathe shallow and through your mouth. You'll get used to it."

"Not in a hundred years." I retreated back to the stoop for a welcome gasp of Phoenix smog. "Let's call them instead."

"No telephone." Thom paused on the first step of a steep, narrow staircase and waited for me to catch up.

I didn't move. "I don't want to do this."

"Me either. Coming?"

"No." But my feet carried me back into the building just the same.

As I followed Thom up the stairs, practically hyperventilating in my effort to get air into my lungs without first smelling it, I considered how to best address my recent morgue misfortune. At least the circumstances were ideal. Anything I had to get out would be easier to say to Thom's back than to his face. "About what I . . . *might* have said last night . . . "

"What?" Thom responded when my words trailed off.

"You know . . . "

"No, I don't. It was a long night and you tend to talk a lot."

Since I couldn't see his face, I didn't know if he was bluffing. "After I . . . um . . . passed out in the morgue," I continued. "When I was coming to I was a little woozy and think I *might* have said . . . something . . . to you."

"Like what?"

"Like . . . "

On the first landing Thom stopped, turned, and leaned against the wall. The grin on his face told me everything I needed to know: I'd said it and he'd heard it. Right there beneath my feet a paradigm shifted. I'd thought Thom Casey was the kindest, most chivalrous man on the planet. I'd been wrong. He was a jerk.

"S-something totally delusional!" I sputtered. "Something I would never, ever have even *thought* if I were in my right mind."

"Oh," Thom said, the grin widening enough to cause my heart to turn over. "That."

I stomped up the stairs past Thom and arrived on the third floor with my heart pounding and my head spinning. (Exertion, anger, infatuation, embarrassment, shallow breathing—it was hard to pinpoint the cause.) Looking up and down the hall, I spotted the Batistas' apartment and knocked on the door before returning to my senses. When it opened abruptly, I took a step back, startled and dismayed.

The woman who appeared in the door frame was my age or a little younger. Her thick, dark tresses were pulled back under a mantilla that fell to the shoulders of her black dress. Her eyes were large and luminous and she spoke rapid Spanish. I understood about three words of what she said—*good, morning,* and *what*—but could surmise the rest. This morning of her brother's funeral was not a good one, and she wanted to know what a gringo like me wanted at a time like this.

As I retreated sheepishly, Thom stepped forward. He pulled his badge from his jacket pocket and extended it with his ID. The girl's mouth went slack, and she took a wobbly step backwards. Before she could flee, a young man joined her in the doorway. He spoke even more rapidly, all the while fumbling through his pockets until he came up with a greenish, plastic-coated rectangle that he extended towards Thom. Then he wrapped his free arm protectively around the girl's waist and glowered at the cop.

Thom nodded at the card but didn't take it. The young man ignored whatever Thom said and continued to wave the card in his face. At last Thom took it to be rid of the distraction, but once it was in his hand he looked a little more closely. A minute later, and without thinking, he folded it into the wallet with his badge and stuck it back in his pocket. I made a mental note to mention what he'd done before we left since the young man hadn't noticed either. He still spoke so quickly and fervently that it was impossible for Thom to reply.

At last Thom raised one hand in what is probably law enforcement's international signal for "I've heard enough. Be quiet." The younger man's words trailed off, but he looked defiant and angry.

I'm not sure what Thom said, but I think it began with an apology for his rusty Spanish—he'd been home from his mission almost six years, after all. The apology wasn't necessary. He didn't seem to have any trouble making himself understood once the pair started listening. The young woman's manner changed abruptly when she understood Thom was not from Immigration. She introduced herself as Marina Batista and her companion as José Gutierrez before at last stepping back to invite us in.

Once inside the apartment, I couldn't believe what I saw. Or didn't see. Although probably cleaner than the apartment I share with Chaiya, this small combination of living room and kitchen had no carpeting, no rugs, no curtains at the windows, no appliances younger than me, and virtually no furnishings. There was one wooden chair and a battered folding table near the gas stove, but the rest of the room's décor was early *Arizona Republic.* By this I mean that somebody had gathered newspapers—dozens of issues, maybe hundreds—stacked them carefully, and then bound them together with odd pieces of twine and bailing wire. These ingenious creations were the Batistas' only "couch" and "chairs."

Marina motioned politely for me to take a seat, but Thom bent close and whispered in my ear, "Don't. Lice."

I stood where I was, fighting the urge to scratch. To distract myself I focused on the scant decorations on the cracked and stained walls: a tattered, unframed picture of Christ, and a large, metal crucifix. Then my gaze wandered and I caught a glimpse of a cockroach skittering along the floorboards. I wrapped my left foot around my right ankle, hoping that having only one foot on the floor would cut in half my chances of a bug running up my leg.

At a few more soft-spoken words from Thom, the young woman went into the bedroom and returned with an older, plumper woman who was also dressed in black. This, Marina said, was her mother, Rosa. It didn't take more than a glance at the poor woman's puffy, bloodshot eyes for me to believe that her son's death had broken her heart.

Tears came to my eyes too. I looked up at Thom and saw compassion overcome the tough police persona he tried without success to project. At that point either the earth moved under my foot or my paradigm shifted back. Thom wasn't a jerk. Or if he was, I loved him anyway.

Rosa Batista knew at once that something was wrong. She sank down on the nearest stack of newsprint and buried her face in her dark, calloused hands.

Despite his caution to me about vermin, Thom sat beside her and spoke quietly. I braced myself for the wailing I knew would follow.

There was no wail when Thom finished explaining that Antonio's body had been taken from the mortuary. Neither Rosa nor Marina let out a sob—or even a sound. Still, the pall that fell over the room couldn't have been called a stunned silence. The glances that passed back and forth between the three were sad. Guilty. Terrified. But Thom and I were the only ones who were stunned. Antonio's family didn't seem particularly *surprised.*

Thom spoke again, but this time I knew from his inflection that it was a question.

When nobody responded, he repeated it.

The Batistas looked to José. "Yo no sé," he said at last when Thom's eyes wouldn't leave his face.

Yo no sé. I don't know, I translated silently. It was about the only thing I'd learned in my high school Spanish class. I had spoken the truth when I replied "Yo no sé" to all my teacher's questions. I wondered if José was being as honest with Thom.

Thom apparently didn't think so. He asked another question, then another.

"Yo no sé," the young man repeated more strongly and stubbornly. His grip tightened around his sweetheart's waist.

I watched the dimple wink into Thom's cheek as the tension in the room increased. He asked yet another question of the young man and didn't look as if he'd accept "I don't know" for an answer this time.

José's arm dropped from Marina's waist. His eyes flashed but he remained mute.

Marina leaned into him and whispered into his ear, apparently entreating him. José shook his head. Antonio's sister turned to Thom. For a moment I thought she would tell the detective something herself, but José's hand tightening on her arm seemed to change her mind. She looked at Thom in despair. Her bright, dark eyes reminded me of a frightened sparrow's. It was almost as if I could see her heart pounding beneath her thin dress.

I don't know what might have happened next if there hadn't been a knock at the door. Since I was standing within a foot of it I reached automatically for the doorknob and pulled it open.

The sharp gasp I heard next could only have come from me, but I clasped a hand to my throat as if to make sure. Despite the apparition in the hallway, I didn't scream and I didn't faint. I merely stood and stared and kept gasping.

It was all I *could* do. It's not every day I see a ghost.

Chapter 6

If I had opened the Batistas' door to Antonio Batista returned from the grave—or wherever his body was at the moment—it wouldn't have surprised me any more than it did to see Carlos Diego standing there live and in person.

Although he must have been equally surprised to see me, Carlos recovered faster. "Sam!" he said. "I don't believe it! My gosh. You . . . " For one horrible moment I thought he would say "grew," but he didn't. He said, " . . . haven't changed at all!"

That wasn't a compliment either. The last time I saw Carlos was the summer after high school graduation. I'd just returned home from a stint as a youth leader at girls' camp. My hair was dirty, my clothes were rumpled, and my face and neck were covered with sunburn and hives. To add insult to injury, Carlos had met me in the church parking lot to dump me. He was nice about it. He said it was only because he was leaving Phoenix to go to school in New York, but I received exactly four e-mails after he left and then nothing. My self-esteem took a major hit along with my pride and perhaps one vital organ—my heart. I'd put myself through a lot because of him. It wasn't exactly easy being a Laurel class president who had a Catholic kid as a high school sweetheart.

Five years later, I stood in the Batistas' home, stared up at Carlos, and rubbed unconsciously at my neck where the hives had been. A lot of time had passed since he'd dumped me in the church parking lot, but it still itched a little.

At last it occurred to me that we weren't the only two people in the galaxy—or even the room. It also occurred to me that

Carlos couldn't have come there to see me. I stepped aside so the Batistas could see who was at their door. When I did, Señora Batista let out the wail I'd expected earlier. Then she held out her hands to Carlos as if she'd fallen into quicksand and only he could save her.

Carlos crossed the room in two long strides, knelt in front of Rosa, and took her hands in his. Before he could speak, Antonio's twice-bereaved mother collapsed into sobs. In the next minute Marina was at his side as well. Even the wary José moved closer.

I considered the tableau in confusion. "That's my boyfriend," I told Thom.

Thom looked at Carlos and his eyebrows rose. I'd like to think he was jealous, but he looked mostly dubious.

Looking closer myself, I noticed for the first time that in addition to the jeans and sweatshirt he'd always favored, Carlos now wore a thick, silver chain with a cross on it. In his hand he held a rosary and book of prayer. Moreover, Señora Batista kept calling him "Hermano Simon." Although we commonly refer to each other as "sister" and "brother" in the LDS Church, Catholics reserve the terms for nuns and brethren of the cloth. Besides, Carlos's last name was Diego, not Simon.

All of a sudden I felt my jaw hinges loosen.

After listening for several minutes to Rosa and Marina babble in unison, Carlos excused himself long enough to rise and extend a hand to Thom. "Brother Simon," he said by way of introduction.

"Thom Casey." He shook Carlos's hand. "I'm a detective with the Phoenix PD. As you've heard, we're here because of the . . . unfortunate occurrence."

"Yeah," Carlos said. He glanced back at Rosa, then looked longer at Marina and José. At length he said, "I need to spend some time here, obviously, but I'd like to talk to you, Detective. Can I meet you somewhere in, say, an hour or so?"

Thom agreed and named a nearby café, then ushered me from the apartment. As we left the building he said, "Are you on your way home, or back to Nightshade?"

As if either was an option I'd consider. "I'm eavesdropping on your meeting with Carlos."

"Then how about I buy you breakfast while we wait?"

It would be more like a bedtime snack, but I quickly accepted and offered a little prayer of gratitude besides. I'd spent the last two weeks praying that Thom Casey would ask me out, and it had finally happened. (This is my book. If I say his offer to pay for breakfast qualifies as a first date, then it does.)

"I hope your 'boyfriend' won't think this is a date," Thom said when we were seated in the restaurant and had plates of food in front of us.

I rolled my eyes. "I meant to say he *was* my boyfriend. In high school. He dumped me after graduation."

Was admitting that stupid or what? Maybe next I could list for Thom all the guys in the singles ward who think my only purpose in life is to take messages for Chaiya. I mean—*gosh.* Suddenly my fruit plate held my full attention.

"I wouldn't take it too hard if I were you," Thom said. "Look who he chose instead."

I looked up. "You mean God? You think Carlos is a priest or something?"

"Something."

I'd thought Carlos Diego was something the first time I met him. Our stake was building a Habitat for Humanity house with the youth of the Catholic diocese. Carlos was their youth leader— dedicated, dynamic, and always smiling. (The fact that he was tall, dark, and handsome didn't escape my attention either.) Although it wasn't love at first sight for either of us, we did seem to hit it off. By the end of the three-day service project I'd told him my deepest secret—that I'd always wanted to be a superhero. He'd laughed at me, of course, but he'd also asked me out.

The only other man I'd ever told my secret to was seated across from me, eating pancakes as though he hadn't a carb in the world. Thom hadn't laughed at my confession like Carlos had, but he hadn't asked me out either. (Well, except for this breakfast—which *counted* as a date.) Thom had all the qualities I'd admired in my first love, plus he had a temple recommend and knew how to use it. This time around I'd found everything I'd dreamed of in an eternal companion.

Everything except my intended companion's wholehearted cooperation in the relationship, that is.

I used my fork to roll a honeydew ball around a piece of banana while I wondered if Thom would think of me differently if I looked more like Batgirl. While I really do believe that beauty is skin deep, I still wish my beauty weren't quite so thick in places.

Noting that I was using my food for recreational purposes only, Thom said, "You're not hungry?"

"I'm starved," I admitted, lost in thoughts of my thighs in spandex.

"Is the fruit bad?"

"Hmm? No. The fruit's fine." To prove my point, I popped a large strawberry in my mouth. A too-large strawberry. *What now?* If I bit into it, the bright red juice would leak out from between my lips and run down my chin. Since I was dressed all in black as always and have naturally fair skin, I'd look enough like a vampire to frighten the little children in the next booth. What to do? I couldn't chew the fruit up and I couldn't swallow it whole. That left only one option. I raised a napkin to my lips and spit it out. It was the kind of dainty gesture you'd expect from a rottweiler.

Thank goodness Thom wasn't looking at me. He was looking toward the entrance to the café. "Brother Simon is here."

I'd managed to wipe my lips and hide the berry in my lap before Carlos slid onto the bench next to me. "Thanks for waiting," he said.

"How are the Batistas?" Thom asked. When Carlos didn't immediately reply, he got right to the point. "There's something strange going on there, Brother Simon. Do you know what it is?"

Carlos shook his head. "I wish I did. I'd like to help. They're good people."

"Good people with bad habits?" Thom suggested mildly.

"You mean Antonio's drug overdose?" Carlos frowned. "I don't believe it. He'd had a problem in Mexico, but he kicked it six months ago. Antonio was a hard worker devoted to giving his mother and sister a better life." He leaned forward. "I met with them on Sunday—the day they arrived from San Luis. I've never seen happier, more hopeful people. Nobody could have been more excited about a new life than Antonio Batista. He wouldn't have screwed that up."

Thom looked skeptical.

"Sully said the needle marks were old," I reminded him.

"I can introduce you to a dozen people who'll say Antonio wasn't a user," Carlos added with a grateful smile in my direction.

Thom frowned. "And I can introduce one toxicology report that says otherwise."

Carlos helped himself to a piece of fruit from my plate. It was like old times. "Could there have been a mistake?"

"I don't see how," Thom said. "All the signs were there. They drew the blood at the scene. When the results came back the coroner ruled an autopsy unnecessary and released the body."

"What was in him?"

"Pure cocaine," Thom said. "High grade and enough of it to drop a horse."

"It doesn't add up," Carlos said around a second bite of melon. "You saw where the Batistas live. Even if we assume for a minute that Antonio wanted to go back to the stuff, where'd he get the money for it?"

"Dealing."

Carlos motioned toward the window where a flashy yellow lowrider was parked at the sidewalk. "Let me assure you, Detective, dealers live a whole lot better than the Batistas."

"You know a lot of dealers?"

"Let's say that I come across more than I want to."

"What do you do, Carlos?" I asked, pushing the fruit plate in front of him.

"I serve in the Franciscan Brotherhood." He picked up my fork and used it to spear a piece of banana. "I joined the order in New York shortly after I got there."

"I thought you went to college."

"I did. My degree is in social work."

"But if you joined an order, that means you're a . . . " My words trailed off because I didn't know for sure what it meant.

"It means I'm a monk," Carlos supplied. "Or I will be when I take my final vows." He grinned. "Real deal, Sam. Brown robe, white-rope belt, the works." He pinched the fabric of his NYU sweatshirt between his thumb and finger. "This is a costume—a secret identity I assume when I'm on the streets doing my superhero gig."

He was probably making fun of me, but his eyes were kind.

"Don't monks live in monasteries?" I asked. (Yes, it might have been a stupid question, but I'm not only blond, I'm a Mormon girl, born and raised. What I don't know about Catholicism fills the Vatican's vast libraries.)

"Some of them do," Carlos said. "Not so many these days. But I'll take the same vow they had in the twelfth century when St. Francis founded the order. Poverty, celibacy, obedience, and service to my fellow man." He leaned back. "Right now I'm on an outreach ministry until the call comes. We all have specialized training. Many of the brethren have degrees in law, medicine, or other social services. We go where we can do the most good. Since I grew up here and am fluent in Spanish, I came back to work with Father Rodriguez."

Once my mind had worked itself around the word *monk*, it all made sense—even why he hadn't written to me. "Wow," I whispered. "And I thought *I* had taken that prayer to heart."

For Christmas during the year we were an "item," Carlos gave me a small statue of St. Francis of Assisi and a copy of the saint's legendary prayer:

Lord, make me an instrument of Your peace; where there is hatred, let me sow love; where there is injury, pardon; where there is doubt, faith; where there is despair, hope; where there is darkness, light; and where there is sadness, joy.

O DIVINE MASTER, grant that I may not so much seek to be consoled as to console; to be understood as to understand;

to be loved as to love; for it is in giving that we receive; it is in pardoning that we are pardoned; it is in dying that we are born to eternal life.

I love those words. (If superheroes have a creed, I'll bet it's similar to St. Francis's.) Still, I'd never succeeded in making it a way of life like some people I knew and had once loved. I looked at Carlos—Brother Simon—with a new sense of admiration.

From the corner of my eye, I saw Thom sneak a peek at his watch and knew he had to be at work before long. As interesting as Carlos's new life was to me, Thom had more on his plate than pancakes.

"And how are you helping Father Rodriguez?" I asked Brother Simon to steer the conversation back toward the reason he'd set up this meeting in the first place.

"I'm working with . . . immigrants," he said with a sheepish glance at Thom. To Thom's credit, the cop didn't ask if the immigrants were of the legal variety. "I help them get settled and learn the system. Point them in the right direction for jobs, education, and medical care—that kind of thing. We involve them in Catholic Social Services, other church programs, government agencies—anybody who can help them beat the poverty, illiteracy, and despair they've known all their lives."

"Not a very popular line of work these days," Thom observed.

I sighed in agreement. Since we'd left high school, immigration reform had become almost as volatile an issue for us as civil rights was for our parents and grandparents. Sitting there at breakfast, I knew that less than twenty miles away, immigrant protestors were marching on the state capitol yet again, while to the south the National Guard and armed vigilantes lined Arizona's border with Mexico.

One corner of Brother Simon's lips rose. "When it's all said and done, Detective, nobody's going to tally up the number of people who loved me. They're too busy keeping track of the number of people I loved."

"Good thing," Thom said, but I saw the admiration in his eyes. Next he asked, "How well do you know the barrio?"

"Pretty well," Carlos replied, "for an outsider. At least I was making inroads before things started to get . . . strange."

"So it's not my imagination," Thom said. "That guy at the Batistas'—José—had issues."

"What he has issues with," Carlos said, "is fear. And it's not only José. Men, women, children—everybody's scared."

"Of deportation?" I guessed.

"No," Carlos said. "Or they're not afraid of the federales alone. The legals are just as spooked."

I leaned forward. "Is it the haunted mission?"

Thom pushed away the remnants of his breakfast. "If *I* were guessing, I'd say it's the serial killer targeting young Latinos."

Oh, yeah . . . him.

"You'd think," Carlos said. "But that's only part of it. Whatever's going down started before the killings. I've been here about three months now. I'd come across nervous people now and then in my first few weeks on the street, but it's fast become a very public paranoia."

"And the root?" Thom asked.

Carlos shrugged. "I hoped you'd tell me. I need help, Detective. These people need help." Catching the dubious look on Thom's face, he added, "You're wondering why I'm asking you. It's because you've got an air of St. Jude about you."

"Excuse me?"

"St. Jude. He's the patron saint of impossible causes." Carlos grinned. "Unless I've read you wrong, you're a person who believes that we were all sent here to help each other. St. Jude syndrome is a rare quality, but you find it in people of every faith. It's what I love about Sam, in fact. St. Jude people . . . *care* . . . even when nobody else does." He laid down the fork. "So, I wanted to tell you what I know about Antonio and make sure you know there's a good reason his body disappeared. When we know that reason, I think we'll know what everybody's afraid of."

Thom nodded, but he didn't look convinced.

"José may be the key. He and Antonio came to Phoenix together. They've been friends since childhood—closer than brothers." Carlos's eyes darkened. "He knows what's going down, Detective."

"But he won't tell you?"

Carlos considered. "I think it's more that he *can't* tell me. He's protecting someone—maybe Marina. Maybe himself."

"I could take him in for questioning," Thom said.

"Except that you don't have just cause," Carlos replied.

"I have this." Thom reached into his jacket for his wallet. Opening it, he showed the green card that lay atop his badge.

I started. The shock of seeing Carlos again had made me forget to remind Thom to give it back. Now I realized that perhaps the detective hadn't been as absentminded as he'd seemed when he took it.

Thom looked down at the card. "I think it's a forgery."

"No way!" Carlos exclaimed. In the next moment he seemed to reconsider. "Or if it is fake, I'll guarantee José doesn't know it."

"I don't need your guarantee," Thom said. "Judging by the way he waved it in my face, I'm sure he thinks it's the real deal."

Carlos's eyes followed Thom's hand as he closed the wallet and put it away. When he spoke, his voice was flat. "You're taking it to Immigration."

"No," Thom said, "I'm taking it to the lab."

"And then?" Carlos asked.

"And then if it's legit, I'll give it back. And if it isn't, I'll ask José a few questions about where he got it and then help him get one that is legal." At Carlos's grin, Thom frowned and added, "I'm after information that will help us find a corpse or stop a serial killer. I'm not out to cause more trouble for people who suffer too much already."

"St. Jude syndrome," Carlos told me with satisfaction, picking up the fork to spear a piece of cantaloupe. "I can spot it a mile away."

"You'd better start keeping an eye out for something else," Thom said. "Meaning yourself."

"Nobody's interested in a monk." Carlos tapped the cross that lay over his heart. "That vow of poverty tends to turn off the muggers."

"Maybe." Thom motioned out the window with his thumb. "But there's a guy loitering across the street now who was outside the Batistas' apartment complex when we left it. He showed up here about the time you did. He might be following you."

Carlos's eyes moved toward the window, but he didn't turn his head to look. "Short guy who kinda makes you think of one of the flying monkeys of Oz?"

"Yes. You know him?"

"I've seen him around. He's been coming to mass every morning lately."

The dimple appeared in Thom's cheek. "I'd hate to hear what he had to say in confession."

"Judge not that ye be not judged, Detective," Carlos said. His tone was light, but his eyes were worried.

"You want me to go out and talk to him?" Thom asked. "Officially?"

"No," Carlos said. "He's probably a guy with a problem who's working up the nerve to get it off his chest. I'll give him more time and space and hopefully he'll approach me."

I looked out the window at Brother Simon's squat, greasy-haired stalker. Call me judgmental, but he didn't look to me like a guy who had a problem. He looked to me like a guy who *was* a problem.

A very scary problem.

Chapter 7

I've received more than my share of unusual notes from Chaiya over the years, but none were stranger than the one that lay on Uncle Eddie's desk when I returned to it after my "lunch" break the next night. In purple ink on a green pad encircled by puckered-up frog princes my cousin had written:

- a pair of soft felt overshoes (for creeping about in silence)

- a steel measuring tape (for accurately gauging distances)

- screw eyes, lead seals, a sealing tool, white tape (for sealing entrances)

- small electric bells (for construction of motion-detection devices)

- dry batteries and switches (for secret electrical contacts)

- camera, film, and flashbulbs (for capturing images of a non-corporeal nature)

- talcum powder (to detect visitors of a corporeal nature)

- sketching pad and drawing instruments (for maps and diagrams)

- ball of string and a stick of chalk (to mark movements of objects)

- *bandages, iodine, surgical tape, and a flask of brandy (for injuries)*
- *electric torch, matches, and candles (for illumination)*
- *bowl of mercury (to detect tremors in a room or passage)*
- *cinematograph with electrical release (for recording moving pictures*

I'd read through the list twice trying to figure it out when Chaiya appeared in the doorway. "Oh, good, Sammy," she said. "You got it."

I looked at her over the top of the paper. "No, I *don't* get it."

"It's the stuff we need to pick up on our way to the haunted church."

I didn't know what to ask her first: where we'd go to pick up a bowl of mercury, what a cinematograph was, or what she meant by *we* and on *our* way. I started with that last thing.

"I thought you'd want to go ghost hunting with me," she said. When no words escaped my lips, she added, "That's my new procession."

Assuming she meant *profession,* I said, "I thought you were going to be a novelist."

"I dropped the writing class," she said, as if it was "last week" instead of just last night. "My teacher said that a person with my gift for language ought to concentrate on math." The way Chaiya said it told me she was proud of the "compliment." "But I don't like multiplication and derision, so I've decided that since I spend so much time here anyway, I might as well do defective work."

At last! Something she had already mastered. But I said, "*Detective* work, Chaiya. We're private *detectives.*"

"Whatever. At any rate, I'm going to serialize in ghost hunting. That paper in your hand is a list of things I need. I think Nightshade ought to pay for them, don't you? I mean, after all, I'm working on *your* ghost first."

"Where did you get this list?" I said, ignoring the whole ghost ownership thing—and trying to ignore the thought of Chaiya's new career as long as I possibly could.

"Harry Potter wrote it. He's the most famous ghost hunter in the world."

"I thought he was a wizard." I was missing something somewhere, but I didn't think it was in my reading of J. K. Rowling. The thin book Chaiya held in her hand was about half a rain forest short of the latest *Harry Potter and the Whatever of Whosits* novel.

"Huh?" Chaiya's dark, ebony-lined eyes widened. "Sammy, sometimes I don't think you know what you're talking about."

Sometimes I think she's right, but not this time. "The book in your hand," I said. "What is it called?"

"Ghost Hunting for Dummies."

Then at least it was appropriate—for both of us. "And who is it about?" If she said "Harry Potter" again I was going to scream.

"Harry . . . " Chaiya opened the volume and held it up to her nose. "Oh! My mistake. Harry *Price*." She read aloud, "'Harry Price joined the Society of Psychical Research in 1920 where he began his career as one of the world's most famous ghost investigators.'" She shot me an I-told-you-so look and finished the paragraph. "'His investigations of Borley Rectory in England set the standard and established a blueprint for modern-day paranormal investigations.'"

"Modern-day?" I said. "Harry Price compiled that 'up-to-the-minute' list of yours more than seventy-five years ago!"

She closed the book and put her hands on her narrow hips. "How much do you think ghosts have changed since then?"

"Investigative methods must have changed," I said, consulting her list. "Can you imagine us in soft felt overshoes, creeping about in silence and carrying bowls of mercury?"

"Well, maybe not the *silence* part," Chaiya admitted. "You do talk an awful lot, Sammy."

"I'm not taking you on the stakeout tonight," I said to close the subject.

"You know perfectly well that the last time Uncle Eddie called he said you can't go by yourself anymore because of the serial killer," she said. "Knute and Delano are on other cases, and Clueless won't go anywhere with you since you started eating carrot sticks. She was only in it for the powdered-sugar donuts."

Chaiya had a winning argument and she knew it.

"Well, we're not taking any of this silly stuff," I insisted to save face.

Thirty minutes later we were shopping in an all-night Walgreens. (Nobody argues with Chaiya and wins. Nobody.) In the basket we had string, chalk, a sketch pad and pens, baby powder, masking tape, fresh batteries for our "electric torches" (read: flashlights), and big cotton socks to pull over our shoes since felt overshoes had gone out of style sometime in the last half century.

"Where's the iodine?" Chaiya asked, tossing in a package of stick-on bandages in neon colors. When I told her nobody uses iodine anymore she settled for a spray bottle of Bactine. "Brandy?" After a protracted discussion about whether Price had used alcohol internally or externally, we agreed on rubbing alcohol and diet root beer. (Not mixed, of course.)

Since we'd already agreed that neither of us could construct devices to detect motion or "secret electrical contacts" (whatever they were), and since we already had a measuring tape, camera, and digital and video recorders in the hearse, I figured we were good to go. I steered the cart toward the register to check out.

"Wait!" Chaiya said. "We don't have the bowl of mercury."

"No," I agreed over my shoulder, "and we're not going to get it. They don't sell mercury anymore, Chaiya. It's deadly."

"Did Harry Potter know that?"

"Price," I said. "Harry Price. And I don't know if he knew it or not." When I was certain she wasn't following me to the front, I turned back.

My cousin looked down at the list, and her burgundy lips formed a perfect little pout. "How will we 'detect tremors in a room or passage'?"

"There won't be any tremors, Chaiya."

"We won't know that without mercury," she protested, but she took a step forward and my hopes of leaving the store rose. They dropped again when she stopped. "What's a tremor?"

"It's like what happens in an earthquake," I told her. "But it doesn't have to be big. Walking across a floor causes little tremors. I think maybe Price put the bowl of mercury out and watched it in case somebody passed. If he encountered somebody whose footsteps made the mercury jiggle, he'd know it was a real person, but if he saw somebody moving across the floor and the mercury *didn't* jiggle, then maybe it was a ghost. Not that there *are* ghosts," I added hastily.

I needn't have worried about giving Chaiya more ideas about spirits than she already had. She was fixated on jiggling mercury. "I've got it!" she cried out a minute later. "We can get cherry mercury!"

Sure we could. Nevertheless, I followed her to the cold case in back. When she reached for a mini-tub of Jell-O, I smiled despite myself. "Get the sugar free," I advised, thinking that Harry Price should have had it this good. Our tremor detector would not only be as accurate as his, but it would definitely make a better snack. If Mr. Price had tasted *his* tremor detector, he'd soon have been helping haunt the rectory.

* * *

"What kind of haunting is this?" Chaiya asked me about thirty minutes later.

We were parked behind the old mission in Uncle Eddie's hearse (because my car was *still* in the shop), and my cousin was studying her ghost hunter's manual while I watched video footage I'd transferred to my laptop earlier that evening. The footage was from a surveillance camera in the small, private parking lot behind Nightshade, Rest in Peace, and Eat, Drink, & Be Merry. I was pursuing a flash of inspiration that had literally awakened me from deep sleep earlier that afternoon.

Monday night's surveillance video could be the key to The Case of the Kidnapped Corpse. After all, "corpse-nappers" have to park, right? I mean, they can't very well carry a body out the front door and walk down the sidewalk—even on the rather bizarre streets of downtown Phoenix. Ergo, they must have driven into and out of the parking lot. It also stood to reason that they must have driven something long enough to accommodate a body—that or left the feet sticking out a side window. Ergo again, when I saw video of an unfamiliar enclosed truck or van pass Sully's parking booth, I could jot down the license plate for the police, who would then snatch the body snatcher.

It would have been easier if the entire parking lot was covered by the video camera, of course. Then I'd only have had to watch Rest in Peace's back door. But Sully wasn't worried about the buildings' security. He was worried about his new parking booth.

A few months before, in an effort to support the downtown renovation project, Sully had cleaned up his parking-lot-cum-garbage-dump and had it repaved and striped. It looked so nice that he got the idea he ought to start charging non-tenants to park in it, so he built a fancy new booth for the attendant who would collect the parking fees. The problem was that with Sully's buildings situated where they were, the people interested in parking behind them were tenants, customers of his, customers of ours, or customers of one of his two siblings. These people objected to paying for parking—with good reason—so Sully couldn't charge them. Since they were the *only* people who wanted to park there, within a month the beautiful, state-of-the-art booth was obsolete and had to be abandoned. Twenty-four hours later it was vandalized. What with it being the pride of his life and all, Sully had it repainted. Graffiti artists repainted it to suit themselves.

Probably you can see for yourself the pattern that developed. In the third week of the paint war Sully came to Nightshade. Uncle Eddie loaned him a video surveillance camera. The next time the punks showed up, Eddie had their pictures. It took only one visit from Knute and Delano to help the youthful "artists" see the error of their ways and the wisdom of beautifying the cars on the railroad tracks instead. With the problem solved, Eddie wanted to take down the camera, but Sully wouldn't hear of it. He bought the camera, bought new tapes, and turned it on every single night when he left the mortuary.

What I had once considered obsessive may have turned out to be the smartest thing Sully ever did.

"What kind of haunting is this?" Chaiya repeated.

I pressed the pause button. "What are you talking about?"

"There are four types of hauntings," she informed me with as much authority as an Oxford scholar. She held up one chrome-tipped finger. "There is the traditional, intelligent haunting." A second and a third finger rose. "There are the residual haunting and the PK haunting, and . . . " Fourth finger. " . . . there is your classic portal haunting. Which is this?"

"I, uh, have no idea. You're going to have to explain the differences to me—just for the sake of conversation." A conversation, I might add, that I should never have begun in the first place.

Chaiya's face rose from the book with a smile. "Sure!" She flipped a few pages and read aloud: "'PK hauntings are commonly known as poltergeists. Look first for the presence of an adolescent or younger child, as they seem to be the agents of most of the destruction.'"

"It's not that one," I said. There hadn't been an adolescent at San Rafael since 1900.

Chaiya turned to the next page. "'Residual hauntings are the result of unspent energy manifesting itself as if on a theater screen. Although sounds may be heard, no interaction between images and the living can occur because no actual spirits are present.'" She looked up.

"It's that one!" I said with more enthusiasm than I'd felt since taking on the case. I didn't know what "unspent energy" was, but it sounded way better than "ghost of a dead friar." Plus, that "no interaction between images and the living can occur" part had real promise. "Yes, it's that one," I decided.

"Don't be pasty," Chaiya said. While I checked my complexion in the rearview mirror, she turned another page and read, "'Portals are crossover points between mortality and beyond—often graveyards. This is a favorite spot of ghost hunters as the spirits here are much more numerous than in other areas.'"

Fortunately, the old cemetery that had served San Rafael was more than a block away. "I've been in the mission," I told Chaiya. "There are no portals, only rats."

"When are we going in the mission?" she asked excitedly.

This was the quandary. If I told her the truth—that we were never going in there—she'd want to know why we'd stopped to buy ghost-hunting paraphernalia. If I told her the truth about *that*—that we'd bought it because she'd have been impossible to live with if we hadn't—it would only start an argument that would probably end the stakeout if not our friendship.

Unfortunately, I am a very bad liar. Fortunately, I am a very good procrastinator. I said, "Later, Chaiya. When I've looked at all this videotape and you've read more than the first chapter of that book."

I looked down at the laptop and sighed. By the time I'd studied all that footage the sun would have risen. Twice.

My answer seemed to satisfy her. She turned another page and read aloud, "'A traditional haunting is an intelligent spirit's attempt to communicate with the living, often in order to solve a problem. This usually includes noises, lights, and apparitions that can be accounted for in no other way.'"

I looked up with wide eyes.

"*That's* the one!" she said, reading my face like a comic book. She flipped several more pages. "I'll study chapter 5 first."

"You do that," I said, forcing my eyes back down toward the computer screen and trying to concentrate on the image of the Sully Meyers Memorial Parking Booth on Monday, October 24. I'd made it all the way up to about 8:00 P.M. Quite a few cars passed, but that wasn't surprising considering that Sol's deli stayed open until 10:00 P.M.

With my finger on the fast-forward button, I watched Veronica Chavez arrive in her compact car. Now that I thought about it I remembered hearing her in the reception area that night trying to convince Chaiya to stick with beauty school. I glanced at my cousin the ghost hunter and wished Veronica had been more persuasive.

When a van passed the booth, I slowed the viewing speed. It stayed in the parking lot a long time for somebody on a pastrami run. Three more cars came and another two or three left while I waited for the van to reappear. My pulse accelerated. This could be it. I fast forwarded, but only for a second or two lest I miss something. All I saw was Uncle Eddie's hearse leave the lot when Delano took it in to be detailed.

Another car entered. A different car left. I wished I could see the people in the drivers' seats, but the placement of the camera made that impossible. At last I saw what I'd been looking for—the van leaving the lot. I figured it must have been there almost thirty minutes. That was probably twenty-three minutes more than necessary to snatch a body stored in a room adjacent to the back door of a mortuary, but it seemed suspicious all the same.

I had pencil in hand to jot down the license plate number when I caught an unbelievably lucky break. The van stopped right in front of the booth. I watched as a harried-looking woman alighted from the driver's seat and opened the sliding door. A sandwich flew out and hit her in the face. It was followed by a package of chips and a soft drink. About two minutes later, a child was pulled from his car seat for disciplinary reasons.

I hit the fast-forward button. Way wrong van. This lady had too much on her agenda to moonlight as a ghoul.

I fast-forwarded until the surveillance clock read 10:30, telling myself that I shouldn't have wasted my time watching earlier footage. *Come on, Samantha. What do you think the perverts would do while carting out the body, wave casually at the folks who'd stopped by for a ham and Swiss on rye? OF COURSE it had to have happened after the deli closed.* Delano brought back Uncle Eddie's hearse. About ten minutes later Knute drove onto the lot in his clunker. A wino gave the booth a once-over but staggered on. That was it for about an hour of recording time.

On to the next hour. At 11:30 Knute left again. A little after midnight I took out the hearse to stake out the mission. Nothing but parking booth after that—a couple of hours of nothing. My eyes began to ache and my idea seemed less brilliant than it had before. *Even "corpse-nappers" have to park,* I reminded myself. The only other explanation for the theft of Antonio Batista's mortal remains was alien abduction via spacecraft.

From the corner of my eye I saw Chaiya close her book and reach for the Walgreens bag that contained the cherry Jell-O. *Good deal.* I was hungry myself, and sugar-free gelatin beat the carrot sticks I'd brought along. I closed the lid on my laptop the same time Chaiya opened the passenger door of the hearse.

"I finished chapter 5," she said. "I'm going in."

Chapter 8

I'm here to tell you that Chaiya Shade has done some pretty bizarre things in her life.

There was the time when we were Beehives and our Young Women leader took us to Red Lobster to perfect our table manners. Chaiya asked me to go with her to the restroom, and the next thing I knew I was helping her smuggle lobsters from the tank in the lobby to "freedom" in the swimming pool of the motel next door.

Then there was the time when we were Mia Maids and a different Young Women leader (the first had asked to be released or had moved to Alaska, I don't remember which) took us to the Easter pageant at the Mesa Temple. I'll bet there weren't more than a hundred people in the audience who knew Chaiya wasn't supposed to be onstage dancing with the Ten Virgins—or who counted and knew there were now eleven virgins. But our leader knew. And so did our bishop, who was also, as luck would have it, my father. (This time I was guilty only by association.)

And then there was the time when we were Laurels that yet another Young Women leader (the second had asked to be released or had left the Church, I don't remember which) suggested we paint the church's nursery room for our YW Value projects. This was years before I studied psychology at ASU, mind you. I really, truly didn't know that little children could become so jazzed by bright yellow walls with black and orange tiger stripes.

But nothing—absolutely nothing—Chaiya had done was crazier than marching toward a condemned mission in the middle of the night in a city plagued by a serial killer. (Unless it was going into the aforementioned building, armed only with baby powder and cherry Jell-O, to take on the screaming spirit of a deceased friar.)

I was so stunned it took me three tries to open the car door. When I finally mastered the task, I pushed the laptop onto the passenger seat and scrambled out.

"Chaiya!" I called after her. "What do you think you're doing?"

"Ghost hunting," she said calmly. "Bring the last bag, Sammy. It has the first-aid stuff in it."

"Oh, right," I said. "If a decaying wall falls on you or a serial killer cuts your tongue out you're going to need Bactine and a Band-Aid."

"I know it."

I grabbed the bag, slammed the door, and went after my crazy cousin. I didn't take into consideration that Chaiya is quick and fearless—and that she had both the flashlights. By the time I'd stumbled into three dozen ground-squirrel holes in the abandoned lot, she had pulled open a large wooden door—one that I would have sworn was padlocked on my last visit—and stepped inside San Rafael.

"Cool!" I heard her say from within the spooky edifice.

That was true. I had the goose bumps to prove it.

Something that was about the diameter and consistency of a ping-pong ball crunched under my foot as I entered the large, dim room. I shivered, but didn't look down lest the moonlight reveal that it was not a ping-pong ball I had inadvertently exterminated but a large, black beetle.

"What do you think they cooked in there?" Chaiya asked, training her flashlight on the hearth of a fireplace that looked deep and wide enough to roast a rhino.

"Anything they wanted," I said. I chose my next step across the littered stone floor more carefully. "They must have fed dozens of people from this room every day." While Chaiya examined the room by flashlight, I stood where I was and imagined the

Mexican and indigenous women who had baked the bread and stewed the beans, corn, and squash that were the staple crops of that time and place. I could almost feel the heat on my face and the ache in my shoulder muscles from filling and emptying the heavy iron pots. The October breeze that whispered in through the cracks and crevasses sounded like the rustling of baskets of grain, the shucking of corn, and sometimes the hum of conversation as the women worked, talking about—

I shook myself. It is overly imaginative people like me who talk themselves into believing that things like "residual hauntings" actually exist. "Come on, Chaiya," I said. "We're not supposed to be in here. This building's been condemned for a reason." For a second I was distracted by the pink glow of a rat's eyes before it disappeared deeper into the gloom. That second was exactly how long it took Chaiya to slip through an archway into the next room.

If I remembered correctly from the tour with Father Rodriguez, Chaiya was now in a long, narrow dining area. Four halls fanned off from it. Two of the hallways led to catacombs of tiny sleeping cells. One led to the former schoolrooms and work areas. The fourth led toward the front of the building and the sanctuary.

Grateful for the moonlight, but wishing I had a flashlight of my own, I went after my cousin. I was so fast in my pursuit that I practically ran her down inside the doorway. We both jumped.

"Don't do that!" Chaiya said. "I'm using delicate equipment."

What she was using was a snack-sized container of cherry Jell-O. At the moment it was jiggling like crazy.

"That's a tremor," I said sarcastically.

"Write it down in our ghost log."

"Give me a flashlight." I was gratified when she handed me one of her bags. I reached inside, found the flashlight, then looked to see what other helpful items might be there. Besides the blank tablet, I had string, chalk, and socks. *Goody.*

"We should wear those socks," Chaiya said.

"We won't be here long enough to 'creep about,'" I said, turning on the flashlight and then turning back toward the cooking area.

"Well, give me my felt overshoes before you leave." Chaiya looped her bag over her shoulder to give her a free hand to hold out.

"Chaiya—"

"This is my *job,* Sammy." She sounded so much like me that it gave me pause. "May I have my felt overshoes, please?"

I handed her one pair of the cotton socks and watched her balance on one foot and then the other as she tugged them over her platform flip flops. She looked like a funky duck in moon boots.

"I'll meet you back in the car," my ghost-busting cousin said. "But give me the other bags. I might need that Bactine."

"If you were half as brainy as you are brave—" I didn't finish the sentence. Instead, though I still can't believe I did it, I yanked the other pair of socks over my boots.

Chaiya beamed at me. "What room do you think we're in?"

"The dining room," I said. "Father Rodriguez said this room used to be filled with long tables and benches. Everybody sat down at once and, after a hymn and a prayer, ate their one meal of the day in silence."

"I don't think there are any ghosts in here."

Although I agreed with Chaiya, I couldn't help but wonder aloud at her quick conclusion.

She pointed toward a life-sized crucifix that had been carved into one of the thick adobe walls. "Ghosts don't like those kinds of things," she said.

I didn't much like it myself, but since I'm rather argumentative by nature I had to point out, "But this ghost is supposed to be a friar. Wouldn't he like it okay?"

"No," Chaiya said, because she is firm in her convictions regardless of how abstract they are. She led the way across the room toward an area that had once been schoolrooms.

I followed, picking my way carefully through decades' worth of dirt and debris as well as a profanity of beer cans and bottles. I noted, as I had on my daylight tour, that the cans and bottles were covered with a thick layer of dust. Ever since the city had condemned and carefully sealed the building, nobody had been inside it besides the police the other night.

And Father Rodriguez.

And me.

And the ghost.

"How did the . . . uh . . . *who* died here?" Chaiya asked.

"Friar," I said. "It's like a . . . uh . . . " Okay, I knew this. I'd seen Friar Tuck in *Robin Hood.* In the movie he wore a brown robe and a white-rope belt. I thought of Carlos. "A monk!" I said triumphantly. "A friar is a monk."

As it turns out, what I told Chaiya is true, but confusing. You remember that old adage from geometry: a square has to be a rectangle, but a rectangle doesn't have to be a square? Well, a friar has to be a monk, but a monk doesn't have to be a friar—what with friars being Roman Catholic and some monks being Buddhist and all. But the vows Carlos planned to take would make him a Franciscan monk, and thus a friar, like the men who had lived and worked in San Rafael in centuries past.

"What's a monk?" Chaiya asked.

Carlos had said his vows would include celibacy, poverty, obedience, and service, so I told Chaiya that a monk was a guy who did all that.

"What do they celebrate?" she asked.

"Huh?"

"You said—"

"Celibate. It means, uh, they don't get married."

"Monks are like guy nuns," she decided.

They should just say that and save all us non-Catholics a lot of brain cells figuring it out.

"Anyway, how did he die?" she asked, entering a classroom and shining the beam of her flashlight around the walls.

A few desks—none very new judging by the inkwells—remained in the room, as did an empty map holder and two massive chalkboards that were probably worth a fortune for the slate alone.

"The story is that he fell in love with a Papago girl and then hanged himself in the bell tower rather than leave the brother-hood or live without her."

Chaiya's eyes grew wide. "That's soooo romantic. But *sad.*"

"It's a story, Chaiya," I said. "It probably never happened."

"But if it did," she pressed, "isn't suicide, like, against heavenly law?"

"Yes," I said. "I guess that's the thing that supposedly started the curse. Despite a life devoted to God, this guy couldn't be buried in the churchyard because it was hallowed ground and he'd committed a mortal sin according to the tenets of his church."

"And so he cursed San Rafael?"

"There's no such thing as a curse," I said quickly. "I told you a story. But some people believed that it was because of his ignominious burial that things started to go wrong."

"What kinds of things?"

"Well, first there was a drought and the peasants weren't able to raise enough crops to feed themselves and their families. Lots of them left the area to move closer to the river and canals. The mission couldn't have survived without other missionaries bringing them supplies from California."

"And?" Chaiya said.

"And then something contaminated their well." I tried to remember the rest of the story as told to me by Father Rodriguez. "Next were the Apache uprisings in the late 1800s."

"And that's why the mission closed?"

"No, it was open into the early twentieth century. It was probably at its peak in the 1920s and filled with orphaned children when influenza struck. About three-quarters of the children, both the priests, and all but one of the friars died. That's when the mission finally closed its doors for good."

Chaiya considered the unfortunate history. "Sounds like that guy was really ticked off about where they buried him."

I laughed. "It wasn't a curse, Chaiya. You can read about all those things I described in any Arizona history book. Famine, drought, Indian wars, and illness happened to everybody around here, not just to the people at San Rafael."

"But San Rafael got the ghost." Chaiya stuck her nose in one of the sacks and rummaged through it until she came up with one of Nightshade's small digital recorders.

"I'm not telling you the story again," I said, wary of the device in her hand.

"Shh," she said. "I'm capturing EVP."

"What?"

"Electronic voice phenomena." As I wondered how many of those words she actually meant, she continued, "Page 56 in *Ghost Hunting for Dummies.*" Chaiya turned around and wiggled her rear at me while holding up the recorder.

I took the hint and pulled the small paperback from the back pocket of her jeans. I turned to page 56 and frowned. As hard as it was to believe, Chaiya got every word right. Harder to believe, the book said EVP was a "science" that has been around since the advent of voice recorders.

I am not making this up. There are people in this very world with you and me who believe that dead people will come out to chat if you (1) have the right dead person, (2) ask the right questions, and (3) have the right kind of recording device to pick up their answers. Would it surprise you to learn that Thomas Edison (yes *the* Thomas Edison) was one of these people? According to the book, which quoted an article in a 1920 *American Magazine,* Edison began work on an otherworldly recording apparatus that year. Other sources insist he continued the research until his death in 1931. The device has never been found, nor have transcripts of any supernatural conversations he might have made surfaced, but this does not discourage believers like the author of Chaiya's book. Or Chaiya herself, for that matter.

"Hello?" my cousin said into the empty room. "Can you hear me?" She waited patiently for a response.

"I'm the only one who can hear you, Chaiya," I said after several seconds.

"Shh!" she warned. "You can never hear the response when you're still in the room. You hear it later."

I shone the beam of my flashlight on the next few paragraphs in the book. Sure enough, the phenomena don't occur "live" or "in person." You only hear them when you play back the recording. If then. And don't ask me why that is.

"Sorry," I said.

Chaiya nodded her forgiveness and asked the walls, "What's your name?" After pausing long enough for a response that could have included a detailed genealogy, she said, "What do you want to tell us?" Once again she allowed for an essay answer while holding the recorder over her head like the Statue of Ghost Liberation.

"This is silly, Chaiya," I said when I couldn't stand another creepy second.

To my surprise, she agreed. "This room isn't haunted either."

I once again endorsed her pronouncement wholeheartedly, but couldn't keep my mouth shut about it. I had to ask why.

Chaiya shrugged off my question with, "Why haunt a school-room?"

"Why haunt *anywhere?*" I said, following her out of the room and down a hall that led to the sanctuary.

"Unfinished business."

A long, dusty cobweb trailed along the back of my neck and sent shivers down my spine. Of course it was the cobweb. I wasn't spooked by my cousin's theory that a dead friar haunted these halls because of business left undone in mortality. That was silly and I'm not a silly person.

Of course I could never have proven that last statement. I was, after all, once again following my cousin—this time into the dark recesses of San Rafael.

Some people never learn. I wished I weren't one of them.

Chapter 9

"The only person with unfinished business here is me," I told Chaiya as I stumbled over a pile of adobe bricks that had almost returned to the dirt from whence they'd come. It was the middle of the night and we were making our way down a long hall that led to San Rafael's sanctuary. Overhead, a small part of the mission's roof had given way. Moonlight made our flashlights unnecessary, and a cool breeze made the hair on the back of my neck stand on end.

Yes, I'm *sure* it was the breeze, not the delusional thoughts of a dead monk walking the halls with us.

"I should be working," I continued. "Real work. I should be . . . " I didn't finish the sentence. Because I don't like eerie silences, I'd been filling the vast quantities of it found in the old mission with the sound of my own voice. But I was beginning to sound a little whiney even to me. Maybe I should be counting my blessings instead of complaining. There were the "felt overshoes" to be grateful for, for instance. Forget "creeping about in silence." With several decades' worth of bat, rat, and feral cat droppings on the chipped stone floors, the disposable cotton socks were a godsend for my new boots. Plus, ever since I'd slipped the cherry-flavored "tremor sensing device" from Chaiya's bag and eaten the contents behind her back, I was beginning to feel rather pleasantly disposed toward Harry Potter after all.

I mean Price. Harry Price.

"I thought this *was* your business," Chaiya said. "I thought Father Rodriguez hired you to find his ghost."

"There is no ghost!" I said for what seemed like the hundredth time in twenty minutes.

"Father Rodriguez thinks there's a ghost," Chaiya said. "And he's a *priest*. Not a sixteen-year-old-boy priest either. I mean—"

"I know what you mean," I said. "But Father Rodriguez doesn't think there's a ghost."

"Then why is he paying you to invigorate it?"

"Investigate," I said tiredly. "The ghost is vigorous enough without my help."

"Whatever." When movement caught her eye, Chaiya looked up through the crumbling roof. "What was that?"

"A bat, I think. The place is full of them. Especially the bell tower."

"How do we get up there?"

"We don't. We are not hunting bats."

"I know it," Chaiya said. "We're hunting ghosts."

"There is no ghost!" Talk about your residual haunting. If there was something caught in a constantly replaying loop in that mission, it was me and Chaiya.

"Then what's been causing all the spooky lights and sounds and things that people keep telling you about?" she countered.

"Thom says the screaming is from cats fighting," I told her. "Delano says it's local kids playing pranks. Knute says it's mass hysteria—that there are no lights and sounds, but that people like to perpetuate the story for entertainment's sake."

"What do you think?"

"I don't know," I said honestly. "Knute's almost never wrong, but I think there's *something* going on here. I know I heard the scream for myself the other night."

"Did it sound like cats?"

"It sounded like somebody in agony."

"The friar," Chaiya decided.

Or a real somebody in agony, I thought.

I swung my flashlight beam back and forth across the filthy floor. There were signs of people being here—footprints and places where larger bits of debris had been cleared away by somebody's boot—but they neither proved Delano's theory nor disproved Knute's and Thom's. After all, I'd been there with Father Rodriguez. More recently Thom had been there with several police officers. Probably not even Amber the CSI babe could tell me who had walked where and done what.

Okay, she probably could have, but I wasn't going to ask her.

Chaiya started to say something as she stepped through another small arch, but instead she stopped in her tracks and the words died in her throat.

That had also been my reaction upon entering this room with Father Rodriguez.

San Rafael's sanctuary was magnificent at one time—if not by Italy's Sistine standards, then certainly by American Southwestern. Since the only windows were forty feet above the ground, they hadn't been boarded over and most had survived intact. The wavy, handblown glass refracted a milky moonlight that made a row of spectacular granite statues of the saints seem to glow with heavenly light. Even at midnight—or two in the morning or whatever time it was by then—the effect was ethereal and very beautiful.

"Who are those people?" Chaiya whispered.

"You mean the seven stone statues?" I asked, hoping Chaiya didn't see any "people" there that I couldn't. "Father Rodriguez told me they represent saints who were especially significant to this mission."

"They're awesome." Chaiya led the way across the room to the base of the female form in the middle.

For once she had the adjective exactly right. These figures had been hand carved by someone who clearly possessed great talent and a deep love for these people of legend. The work was awesome—and awe inspiring. It amazed me that they'd been abandoned all these years instead of moved to a place where people could visit them. (Sure the Catholic Church owns many of the Michelangelos in the world, but why overlook New World masterpieces?)

"Who is it supposed to be?" Chaiya asked, looking up into the beatific face of the central figure.

It was the only one I knew. "Mary," I said. "The mother of Jesus." I watched Chaiya run her hand over the figure's toes as she gazed up at the cross-topped globe Mary held in her left hand. In her right was a scepter, and on her head a small crown representing the Catholic belief that she is Our Lady, Queen of the Saints. Candles must have once burned at her feet because the evidence of wax was still there, hard and grimy from years of dust and silt.

"Who's this?" Chaiya asked, moving toward the original outside entrance to examine the next figure. This bearded figure held a shield and a palm frond.

"I have no idea," I said, examining the base for a clue. There was none.

Chaiya moved down the line. There was another woman who held a crown of thorns. At the end nearest an outer door, a kind-looking man held a book while a raven perched on his left shoulder. I loved this one best. He reminded me of Uncle Eddie.

Chaiya turned and walked back up toward the altar to examine the three figures to the right of the Virgin. She paused in front of a third female figure. This one held a cross and a remarkably lifelike stone rose around which a serpent was curled. "Who's this?" she asked.

"I don't know," I repeated. Then I had an idea. "Let's take pictures of them and I'll ask Carlos. He'll know."

Chaiya had the camera out of the bag before the name registered with her brain. "Carlos?" (To do the question justice, I would need to put at least three punctuation marks behind it—two exclamation points and a question mark—but I know my editor won't let that pass, so imagine the exclamation points, will you please?) "*The* Carlos? The Carlos who—"

"Dumped me," I said before she could. "Yes, that Carlos." I told her how he'd appeared unexpectedly at the Batistas' and that I'd learned he was now training to become a Franciscan monk.

"Wow," Chaiya said. "*I've* never dated a monk."

I was going to mention the monk-celibacy thing again, but thought better of it.

"So, is Thom jealous now that your boyfriend is back?" she asked.

I mentioned the monk-celibacy thing after all.

"So Thom isn't jealous?"

"No." I didn't mention that Thom probably wouldn't be jealous if Carlos had patterned himself after Don Juan instead of St. Francis, but I did sigh, and that told Chaiya all she needed to know.

"Thom still hasn't asked you out," she observed with more sympathy than I could bear.

"Yes, he did!" I said quickly. "He took me to breakfast this morning." But my voice lacked conviction. Somehow, sixteen hours or so later, pushing fruit around a plate while Thom ate ravenously and waited for Brother Simon no longer seemed like such a romantic rendezvous.

"That's a start," Chaiya said kindly. "And aren't you taking him to the Halloween party on Friday night?"

Ah, the question of the century—at least in my mind. I'd been agonizing over it for two weeks.

My mother's "Harvest Ball" at Shady Acres, held the Friday before Halloween, is legendary. All the residents and their families, the neighbors and their families, and our family turn out. In short, what started as a little get-together in the common room about a decade ago has, over the years, spilled out onto the lawns and now covers most of the block. There is music, dancing, and lots of food. Most people come in costume and stay until well after midnight. A few are still there at sunrise, which is when my family normally gets ready for bed. To truly understand what an important event it is, consider this: Uncle Eddie closes Nightshade only three weeknights a year—for Thanksgiving, Christmas, and my mother's party.

Chaiya noted my hesitation and said, "You're bringing him. Don't you want the family to meet him?"

I did want that. What I wasn't as sure about was whether I wanted Thom to meet my family. My parents are terrific and completely normal, aside from the nocturnal thing, and Thom had already met the only oddball in the immediate family—and the *reason* we're nocturnal—my eleven-year-old brother, Arjay. So it was my aunts and uncles and cousins I worried about. (No, Chaiya is not the strangest of them, as difficult as that may be to believe.)

"My mother wants to meet Thom," she said.

My point exactly.

Just then there was a muffled noise, so faint I wasn't certain I'd heard it. If I had heard it, it would have sounded like somebody dropping a fork in the next room.

"What was that?" I said, taking an instinctual step closer to the altar from which the sound had come, and shining the beam of the flashlight along the floor. No flatware was apparent. Nothing was apparent.

"Don't try to change the subject, Sammy," Chaiya said. "I'll bring LeVar, and you'll bring Thom and . . . "

I listened with one ear and half my brain to Chaiya go on about the young attorney who was her crush du jour, but when she started to give me advice about attracting Thom, I devoted both ears. In the meantime I edged closer to the place from which I thought the sound had come.

(Dear reader, if you think it odd that we would discuss dating in a haunted mission in the middle of the night, then I can safely assume that you are not now nor have you ever been an older-than-twenty, single, LDS female. Those of you who are know that we can, in fact, discuss men in the night despite the fright, in the dark as a lark, on a train in the rain, on a boat with a goat, and/or in a box with a fox. The subject is that engrossing.)

Chaiya had followed me as far as the last two statues in the row. Next to the woman with the rose and snake was a young man with a book who stood eternally in a pond of stone fish. This, of course, caught Chaiya's attention, and she bent down to admire the marine life.

"Look," she said, rising with a metal cross in her hand. "He dropped his cross in the water."

I could tell by the way the silver glinted in the moonlight that the cross was much too new and too clean to have been dropped very long ago, let alone by a carved-stone saint.

"Let me see that," I said, returning to Chaiya's side.

The cross was about four inches long with a hole bored through the top. The little clasp that had once held it to a chain was there but gaped open. I turned it over in my hand, trying to remember where I'd seen it before.

While I was still processing the thought, Chaiya took the cross back from me and tucked it in her pocket. "This is evident."

"It's not evident to me," I began, and then realized what she was saying. "You mean it's *evidence*." And maybe it was, but evidence of what? "Where exactly did you find it?"

When she pointed down at the base of the statue, I knelt and ran my fingers along the ledge of the block upon which the saint stood. Then I moved on to the next—the one of the woman with the rose. It was waxy like the others, but not like them. What was different?

It took me several minutes and a close examination of two more statues to figure it out. The wax at the foot of the rose lady was of a different consistency than what I'd touched at the feet of Mary and the rest. It was softer. Cleaner. Newer. Somebody had burned candles here much more recently than 1920-something. Perhaps as recently as last month. Or last week.

Or last night?

"Hello? Can you hear me?" Chaiya called out to the altar.

The sudden, unexpected voice in the hitherto silent chamber so startled me that I gripped the ledge at the base of the statue, painfully tearing a fingernail in the process.

And Chaiya wasn't even talking to me. She had the recorder out again, trying to capture ESP . . . or SUV . . . or whatever it's called when ghosts talk to delusional people.

"What's your name?" she asked next.

I rose and glanced down at my throbbing finger. There was a fleck of red in the corner under the wax. The nail must have broken to the quick and was now bleeding. I frowned. As filthy as this place was, I'd probably get tetanus and lose the finger. Worst of all, it was my ring finger—the one I dreamed every day of Thom slipping a diamond on.

I unlooped the drugstore bag from my shoulder and rummaged through it for the antiseptic. Meanwhile, Chaiya asked any ghosts present if they had a message for us.

Even after I'd found the bottle and managed to remove three safety seals and a childproof lid while balancing a flashlight under my chin, I didn't have enough hands to apply the stuff. This simple first aid procedure required the hand that was in need of treatment, plus another hand to hold the flashlight to better see the hand in need of treatment, plus one hand to hold the bottle of Bactine, and one more hand to steady the hand that held the bottle of Bactine to keep it from shaking and squirting antiseptic all over my clothes. (Despite my skepticism when it comes to the supernatural, standing about ten feet away from Chaiya's séance was a little unnerving.)

It wasn't going to work. I kept dropping things in turn. Whatever those figures in India with all the hands are called, I'm not one of them. I tried to balance the flashlight under my chin again, but this time my neck must have been sweatier because I lost the grip and the light slid down into my black t-shirt and lodged . . . well, you know where.

At that moment Chaiya turned, saw the strange, glowing apparition in front of her, and dropped both her flashlight and digital recorder. The flashlight bulb shattered, plunging us deeper into the gloom.

At least this night when the neighbors reported hearing shrieks, we'd be able to account for them.

There was a muffled sound that must have come from the sacristy—adjacent to the altar where the priest prepares the sacrament. This time it wasn't a fork falling, it was a human, or maybe an animal, moaning in pain.

Chaiya was at my side before I saw her move. We were both in a panic.

"I'll get it myself!" I said when I realized she was reaching for our only remaining flashlight. It didn't come out as easily as it went in, but at last I got it.

There was another sound then, this one more along the line of a guttural growl.

"Go!" Chaiya cried, pushing me toward the sanctuary door.

She didn't have to push hard, or even twice. We'd been in this creepy building less than an hour, but my nerves were shot. No wonder Harry Price took along brandy for "medicinal" purposes. Diet root beer was not going to do it for me. When we got out of there I'd need powdered-sugar donuts. Probably covered in hot fudge.

But at the archway I came to my senses, stopped, and turned. Here I was, a well-trained, professional private investigator running from a ghost I didn't believe in. Give me a break. If Nancy Drew ever caught some smart-aleck police detective comparing her to me she'd have that lawyer father of hers sue him for slander.

"We're not running away," I told Chaiya.

"We're not?" she said, looking back at the fifty feet we'd covered in under two seconds.

"I mean we're not anymore. We're going back to find out what that was."

As if it had overheard us, the chilling sound came a third time, but this time it cut itself off in the middle like the scream I'd heard a couple of nights before.

"Where is it coming from?" I asked Chaiya. "It sounds like it's in a room behind the sacristy, but there's no room there."

"Maybe there's another *realm* there," Chaiya said with the sincerity of Rod Serling introducing *Twilight Zone.*

I swallowed. "Stop it. You're scaring us both with your ghost stories."

"Ghosts aren't scary. *Ghost Hunting for Dummies* says—"

"If you aren't afraid of ghosts," I interrupted, "why were you running away?"

"Why were you?" she countered. "You don't believe in ghosts."

We glared at each other until we realized that discussing our cowardice had cured it. Whether it was bravery or bravado, with our chosen careers on the line, I led the way back to the area where Chaiya had made her recordings, and she followed.

While I swung the flashlight over every square inch of the walls and floor, Chaiya bent to pick up the recorder she had dropped earlier. Then she began sorting through the contents of her bag. "Where's the Jell-O?"

"I ate it."

"Great, Sam. I hope your stomach can detect tremors."

"It can." It was detecting them right then in fact.

After rejecting several tools of the ghost-hunting trade, Chaiya got out the baby powder and began sprinkling it on the floor at our feet.

I sneezed. "What are you doing?"

"Ghosts don't leave footprints," she said. "This will tell us if anybody walks here."

"The century of dust that's already on the floor isn't enough?"

She ignored me. When she'd emptied the small shaker, she dusted off her hands and held up the recorder to capture one last EVP. "What do you want to tell us?"

I uttered a brief but heartfelt prayer that we'd already heard everything the "ghost" had to say.

At last Chaiya lowered her arm, placed one hand on her hip, and said, "Frankly, Sammy, I think our work here is done."

I looked around one more time but had to admit that she was probably right. There was simply no room besides the sacristy, and the sacristy was empty. Everything had been quiet since the mysterious sound had cut itself off mid-moan. I hoped my partners would believe me when I told them about it. I wished they had been there to hear it themselves. I wished I had proof of—

"Chaiya!" I exclaimed suddenly. "Does that recorder you dropped still work?"

I shone a beam of light on the digital device. She pushed one button then another. There was a rustling sound, and a voice said, "Chaiya! Does that recorder you dropped still work?"

The voice was mine, of course.

"It works," Chaiya said, turning it off again.

I made a fist and punched the air. *Yes!* Recording that mysterious bit of moaning was good detective work if I did say so myself.

The fist I'd made caused the finger with the torn nail to hurt. I shone the light on it. "I tore my fingernail," I complained. "It's bleeding."

Chaiya looked it over. "Not unless you have orange blood." Using the tip of her own nail, Chaiya dug at the wax embedded in my quick. When she removed the small glob, the bright spot of what I'd assumed was blood came with it. She held it into the light. "It's not blood. I don't know what it is. A little piece of flower petal, I think. Maybe it's left over from a funeral."

"Then the funeral was a century ago," I said, taking the wax to see for myself. She was right. It was a tiny bit of flower petal. A fresh flower by the looks of it. An orange flower.

My mind began to compile a quick list of flowers that come in hues of orange: gazanias, chrysanthemums, poppies, zinnias, marigolds—

My heart pounded in my throat. *Marigolds?* Hadn't Thom said that the last body from the string of serial murders had been left in this area? For that matter, hadn't *all* the bodies been left in this area?

We had to get out of this area.

I tightened my grip on the flashlight as I reached for Chaiya's arm to pull her down the stairs from the altar. No arguments or side trips this time. We were leaving as fast as our little legs could carry us. The moans and screams that came from the depths of that mission were not my imagination and they were not a ghost. That left only the unfinished business of a very real, very sinister kind.

Chapter 10

The next night's staff meeting at Nightshade began better than most. After Knute and Delano got over the fact that Chaiya and I had gone alone and unarmed into San Rafael, they were pretty darn impressed by what we'd discovered. On my way home to bed that morning, I'd turned over to the police the silver cross, the wax-encased flower bit, and—after copying them onto a couple of CDs—Chaiya's digital recordings of the strange sounds and moans. Although the guy I'd talked to at the front desk of the police station wasn't nearly as excited about my finds as I was, he'd dutifully put my "evidence" into envelopes, addressed them to Detective Casey, taken my statement, and promised to put it all on Thom's desk.

I felt like a detective of Nancy Drew class—I was still bucking for Sam Spade status, but at least I felt like a detective.

Leaning back in my chair at the midpoint of our meeting, I relayed to Knute and Delano my latest conversation with Uncle Eddie. He and Aunt Elise had decided to take a quick detour to Fontainebleau before coming home, and I was gratified when my two associates had the courtesy not to moan aloud over the fact that I'd been granted a few additional days at Nightshade's helm.

Knute related the details of his latest investigation and got feedback from Delano. With a new angle to consider, he left with alacrity to get to work. Delano hung around. It was almost thirty minutes before I realized why he was stalling. He was waiting for Chaiya. After the vampire hours she'd kept the night before, she was late coming into work. When she finally arrived she was breathless and her eyes were bright with excitement.

"I listened to the CD of the EVP on the way in to work!" she announced by way of greeting. "Wait until you hear it, Sammy!"

Delano looked up from the file cabinet he'd been pretending to search. "Hi, Kodiak," he said with a grin. "Find an exciting new rock group?"

"No, silly," Chaiya said, opening the laptop she'd brought in with her and perching atop her favorite spot in Eddie's office—a wooden unicorn from a nineteenth-century carousel. "EVP stands for electronic voice phenomena."

Delano looked at me, but I nodded. Despite her tendency to mangle the definitions of even two-syllable words used in normal conversation, Chaiya had the arcane ghost-busting vocabulary nailed.

"Some people think it's one way the dead communicate with the living," I explained to Delano. "Chaiya's studying to be a ghost hunter now."

"I thought she was going to be a beautician."

"I was," Chaiya said, "but all the mirrors creeped me out."

Delano's bushy eyebrows rose. "So, mirrors are creepy, but ghosts aren't."

"I know it!" Chaiya said, happy in her belief that Delano understood her. (Believe me, he didn't. Doesn't. Never will.) She looked at me and cocked her head. "Are we working here or what?"

"Some of us are trying," I said. But I set aside the report and waited dutifully for The Chaiya Show to proceed.

Unwilling to miss a minute himself, Delano settled into the electric chair with his long legs draped over one arm. "Electronic voice phenomena, huh? This I've got to hear."

Chaiya pushed a button on the keyboard of her laptop. In a couple of seconds we heard her recorded voice say, "Hello? Can you hear me?" and a rather high, whiney voice reply, "I'm the only one who can hear you, Chaiya."

"Is that the ghost?" Delano asked with a grin. "Sounds more like the Wicked Witch of the West to me."

I made a face at him. (A rather wicked, witchy one, now that I think about it.)

"That's Sam," Chaiya said. "She has a hard time being quiet, you know."

Delano's grin widened, but he didn't dare comment as long as I was signing the paychecks.

"Listen to the rest of it," Chaiya said. Over the next few minutes we heard her questions, long periods of static, and then the witchy voice saying, "This is silly."

Chaiya looked at us expectantly, but neither Delano nor I dared comment until she came right out and asked if we'd heard any ghostly voices. Then we had to admit that we hadn't.

"I didn't hear any either!" she said. "That's what makes this next part so cool." She wriggled forward on the unicorn. "Okay, here we're in the chapel. I'm standing up by the altar and Sammy is hanging around down by the statues. Listen closer. I'll slow it down so you can make out the words better."

Words? Despite myself, I leaned forward.

"Hello? Can you hear me?" Chaiya's words rang out from the laptop speakers. With the speed slowed, it sounded like she was drawling.

Although I listened as closely as I could to what came next, all I heard was the same static I'd heard before. If I let my imagination run absolutely wild it might . . . possibly . . . sound like a giant cat hissing.

Chaiya paused the CD. "Well?"

"I didn't hear anything different," Delano confessed.

She looked so disappointed that I said, "Uh, do you think it was somebody saying 'shh'?"

"You're close, Sammy," she said with a bright smile that I knew Delano would have gladly lied for if he'd thought of it. "But remember the question? I said, 'Can you hear me?' and the ghost said—"

"Yes!" Delano guessed.

Chaiya beamed. "You *did* hear it! Wait until you hear the rest." She pushed a button and we heard her say, "What's your name?"

This time the noise was different from the "shh" we'd just heard. There was more . . . texture . . . to it, for want of a better word. Knowing how sensitive Uncle Eddie's digital recorder is, I tried to remember what I'd been doing at the time since I was standing only a few feet away from the microphone. Of course! I'd broken a nail and was rummaging around in the Walgreens bag looking for antiseptic. That could easily account for the different background noise.

"Did you hear the ghost's name?" Chaiya asked, pausing the machine once again.

This time Delano didn't hazard a guess.

Chaiya's cherry-red lips puckered. "Anybody can tell it's 'Sarah Scott.'" The way Chaiya said it, slowly and with an emphasis on the *s* sounds, made it almost plausible. "Listen again."

This time when she played it over I heard "Sarah Scott" almost clearly.

"Well, that's weird," Delano said, impressed despite himself.

"No, it's not," I replied. "It's human nature. It even says so in Chaiya's book. I read it last night. The author points out that the main problem with EVPs is that most people are so open to the power of suggestion that they can make out anything they want from a bunch of static."

"Why would I want to hear 'Sarah Scott'?" Chaiya challenged.

"I don't know," I said. "But after you suggested it, that's all Delano and I *could* hear."

Delano started to nod, but stopped himself when he saw Chaiya's face.

"Then I won't tell you what this next part says," she pouted. "You'll have to figure it out for yourselves."

The next part gave me gooseflesh. First there was the sound of Chaiya and me shrieking, and then the first unearthly moan.

Delano sat up in the chair. "That's it?" he said. "That's the sound you told us about, Sam?" When I nodded, he said, "Play it again, Kayak."

"We're listening for the voice," Chaiya said, but she replayed the moan anyway.

"It sounds like it's coming from a stone box," Delano said.

"I thought it sounded like it was in another room," I agreed. "But there isn't another room *or* a stone box. Or there isn't one I could find."

"Could it have come from underground?"

I considered. "You know, maybe. The way sound echoes in that empty building, it's almost impossible to say where it came from."

Chaiya's eyes were as wide as I'd ever seen them. "Are you saying you think Sarah Scott is buried under the floor and wants us to dig her up?"

"No!" Delano and I said together.

"We don't know where . . . um . . . Sarah . . . is," I added. "We're speculating. Play the rest of the recording."

The next thing on it was the second moan, then a muffled version of my brief conversation with Chaiya at the doorway, then the third moan—the one that seemed to cut itself off in the middle.

"That's just strange," Delano said after Chaiya had replayed it for him three more times. "I can't decide if it's human or animal."

"It's Sarah," Chaiya said. "She has unfinished business."

If that were true I didn't want to know what business Sarah was in.

"I'll play you the rest," Chaiya said. "Listen carefully because I'm not going to tell you what she says this time." She shot me a meaningful look.

The next sound was Chaiya asking the ghost what it wanted to tell us. There was the static "shh" I'd grown accustomed to, but in the middle was a long "oo" sound that hadn't been caused by a bag rustling—or anything else I could think of.

Delano's bushy red eyebrows knit together. "One more time," he said.

*Shhhhh—a consonant sound?—oooooo—another consonant?—
shhhhh.*

"Well?" Chaiya asked from atop the unicorn.

"It sounds like 'cook' to me," Delano said. "Our ghost must
be hungry."

It sounded like "took" to me, and for a moment my fancy
took flight and I wondered what had been taken from the ghost
of San Rafael.

"Sammy?" Chaiya asked.

"I thought it sounded like 'took,'" I confessed.

"I think you're both wrong." She slid down from the unicorn's
back and patted its painted rump. While I was still rhyming
words in my head—*gook, nook, rook, hook, look*—she closed the
laptop. "I have to study," she said. "I'm only on chapter 6 of
Ghost Hunting for Dummies, you know."

The chapter on EVPs was bad enough, I thought. *Heaven help
us all when Chaiya finishes that book and is back on the case.*

Chapter 11

It was a couple of hours later, a little after eleven o'clock, when the intercom buzzed. "Detective Ca-sey is here," Chaiya said in that singsong voice you don't hear much after middle school. "He wants to seeeeee you."

I sat up straight in Uncle Eddie's chair, pulled the band from my ponytail, and shook out my hair. Then, fearing it would be hopelessly messed up and have one of those awful rubber-band creases in it as well, I reconsidered and started gathering it back up again. I was about three-quarters of the way through the process when Thom appeared in the doorway. As usual, the sight of him caused the immediate dysfunction of the part of my brain that controls rational thought.

"Hello, Sam," he said. "Got a minute?"

I wanted to say no so he'd think I was way too busy to give him a second thought during working hours. (When in fact I probably gave him every second thought every waking moment of my life.) But I nodded instead—which is rather difficult when you're trying to comb hair from your eyes at the same time.

Thom crossed the room carrying a leather attaché case. On his way he used his spare hand to snag the Windsor chair and pull it up to Uncle Eddie's desk. "That was some kind of work you did last night," he said when he was seated.

I felt a flush of pleasure creep up my neck toward my cheekbones and let my hair go. "You got the stuff I left for you?"

"Everything was on my desk when I went in this morning," he said. "I've been working on it ever since. You've drawn a lot of attention downtown." The corner of his lips turned up when I flinched. "Positive attention."

"Does any of it mean something to the investigation?"

"Maybe," he said. Thom balanced the attaché on the edge of Uncle Eddie's desk and opened it. Removing a short stack of papers, he put them in front of me.

The top one looked like a chemistry final and I said so.

His grin widened. "It's a lab report saying that the wax from beneath your fingernail is recent in origin. We've run a complete chemical analysis hoping to be able to trace it back to its manufacturer." He shrugged. "I guess that's a little dicey."

"And you're doing it because . . . ?"

Thom pulled another paper from the stack and placed it on top. "We're doing it because that piece of plant embedded in the wax is from a marigold bloom that was taken from a live plant within twelve hours of ending up in San Rafael."

I let out a long breath. "You mean the Marigold Murderer *was* in San Rafael?"

"No way to know," Thom said. "At least not yet. But the mission is central to the four places we've found the bodies."

Four? "There was another murder?" I asked, knowing the answer by the look on his face.

"They found another victim this morning. Oddly enough, it was a guy who worked day labor with Antonio Batista."

I picked up a pencil from the desk, desperate to gnaw on it to relieve my nervous energy. But since I couldn't very well do my beaver imitation in front of Thom, I settled for fiddling with the pencil instead. "Do you think—?"

"I don't know what to think."

Since I didn't know what to think either, I changed the subject. "Did you listen to the recording I gave you?"

"Several times."

"What did you think about that?"

"I thought that when Chaiya said, 'Go,' you should have gone." His concern made my heart feel like it was growing a little too large for my rib cage. "You know, Sam, sometimes I think you ought to trade in some of that courage of yours for a little common sense."

"That was me shrieking on the recording," I admitted, mostly because I had no control over my brain when he was around, let alone my mouth.

"But it wasn't you moaning."

"No."

Thom pulled his PDA and a stylus from his jacket pocket. Despite the fact that he'd probably put in twelve hours at work already, he was still on duty. "Where did the sound come from?"

"I don't know," I said. "The sacristy was empty. Delano thinks maybe there's a hidden passage under the floor of the sanctuary."

"Maybe," Thom said. "We're researching the history of the mission and consulting with the diocese's building engineer as well as an architect who might be able to give us more insight. If there are more chambers, we hope to find them. It will take time, of course. Probably a week or longer. In the meantime, we had a CSI team there for about ten hours today."

"Did you talk to Father Rodriguez?" I asked. If so, it would have been more than I was able to accomplish. I'd called every hour that evening between six and ten, but neither he nor Carlos had been available.

"I tried to see him," Thom said. "His housekeeper says he's still under the weather." He pulled two empty plastic bags from his attaché. "I need a couple of things from you and Chaiya. First, the shoes you were wearing last night."

I looked down at my boots and then remembered the socks. "We weren't wearing shoes," I said. "I mean, we were, but we had big cotton socks on over them."

"That would explain why we couldn't pick up your treads," the detective said. "I'm sure you had a good reason for wearing socks." He didn't sound sure.

"Yes," I said. "Harry Price—you know, the famous ghost hunter—wore felt overshoes in Borley Rectory for 'creeping about in silence.' We couldn't find any felt overshoes, so we wore men's work socks over our shoes."

Thom said, "Uh-huh," but it meant "please don't tell me any more about your investigative methods." He added, "May I have the socks?"

"I think they're still out in the hearse. Do you need our fingerprints, too?" I was trying to be professional and think ahead.

"I have them," Thom said. "Yours went on file when you applied for your PI license, and I lifted Chaiya's a few weeks ago—the night the mummy disappeared."

I knew that. So much for proving how well I think ahead. "Were there any prints in the mission?"

"Yes," Thom said. "There were several. We're hoping some of them won't match up with yours or those of Father Rodriguez or the police who were there the other night."

"If they don't match, will you have found the killer?"

"We'll have somebody to look at." Thom ran a hand through his hair. "Hopefully somebody besides the guy I'm looking at now."

I watched him reach into the attaché and bring out another plastic bag. This one wasn't empty. Inside it was the silver cross. My breath caught in my throat as I reviewed the words he'd just said: *the guy I'm looking at now.* All at once I knew where I'd seen that cross. I'd seen it on a chain around Carlos's neck. "Surely you don't think . . ." The thought was so distasteful I couldn't finish it.

"For the record," Thom said, "I have to ask if you've seen this cross before."

"Yes. I saw it last night in the mission." I was sorry now that I'd taken it from Chaiya and given it to the police. Who'd have dreamed it could suggest a connection between Brother Simon and the Marigold Murderer?

"And before that?"

"No," I said, tightening my grip on the pencil.

"Sam—"

"I may have seen one *like* it," I hedged. "But there are probably thousands of crosses in the world like that one."

"Have you seen one of those 'thousands' of identical crosses here in Phoenix recently?"

I stared down at the desk and wouldn't reply.

Thom's voice dropped. "Sam, you're the one who gave this to me."

I glanced up long enough to note that while Thom's eyes were apologetic, the dimple that appears only when he frowns cleft his cheek.

"You know I've seen it," I said. "And you know where I saw it."

"I still need you to tell me," Detective Casey said. "Officially."

"Carlos Diego was wearing one like it yesterday." I practically spat the words at him. "Happy?"

If he was he didn't look it. "He's not wearing it anymore."

"How do you know?"

"I saw Brother Simon when I dropped in on Father Rodriguez. He wasn't wearing the chain, so I asked him about it."

"Without telling him about the cross I gave you, no doubt."

"True."

"What did he say?"

"He said he'd lost his cross," Thom said. "He said it was the second one he's lost now due to faulty clasps."

"That sounds innocent enough."

Thom didn't disagree. But he didn't agree either. "My concern is *where* he lost it."

"Did you ask him if he's been in the mission?"

"Yes," Thom said. "He told me he hasn't."

"But you don't believe him."

"I don't disbelieve him." There was more to this; I could tell by the look on Thom's face. At last he told me what it was. "There are marigolds growing all around the rectory."

"This is October," I said when I could speak again. "There are marigolds growing all over the city."

"True enough."

I cleared my throat. "I take it there are no clear fingerprints on the cross or you wouldn't be asking me to say incriminating things about Carlos."

"Chaiya's prints are clear," Thom said. "And yours. There's also a smudged partial that we'll probably never match—certainly not a match that we could use to get a search warrant. Somebody wiped it pretty clean before you and Chaiya handled it."

It wasn't wiped clean before we touched it, I thought. It wasn't "wiped" at all until Chaiya stuck it in the pocket of her skintight jeans and pulled it back out again at my request. This time I didn't confess. "You've reported all this," I said at last, "and named Carlos as a prime suspect?"

Thom extended his hands, palms up. "I'm still investigating, Sam. It's my job."

"Well, I can't believe that Carlos could shoot a person in cold blood, leave his body lying around for a few hours, and then cut his tongue out."

Thom didn't meet my eyes. "I can't believe *anybody* could." After another moment of silence, he added, "Sir Arthur Conan Doyle is famous for the line 'Eliminate the impossible and whatever remains, however improbable, must be the truth.'"

Carlos being a killer wasn't improbable, it was *impossible.* Thom didn't necessarily believe that, however, and he'd pursue it. That was bad enough for Carlos's sake, but poor Father Rodriguez had enough on his hands with the haunted mission— not to mention the Marigold Murderer. Every one of those butchered young men had been in his flock. As had Antonio Batista—he of the missing body. No wonder the priest didn't feel well. He was under enough stress to sicken anybody.

I looked up at the sheepish but determined look on Thom's face and felt a gulf materialize between us. For the first time since I'd fallen in love with him, I wished he wasn't there. I needed time alone to think.

"You said you needed a *couple* more things," I said as a hint he should get at the second thing and then get out.

Thom pinched a strand of my blond hair from Uncle Eddie's desk and held it up with an empty evidence bag. "May I have one from your head?" When I'd complied, he sealed it in the bag and said, "We picked up a couple of hairs in the mission. The lab's running the DNA now."

"And you need samples of Chaiya's and my DNA to continue to eliminate the impossible?"

"Right."

I rose from the chair and circled the desk. "She's in the next room. You can walk down to the hearse with me on your way out and I'll get you those socks you want."

"There's one more thing I wanted to show you first," Thom said. By the time he'd said it I was almost to the door. This left him little recourse but to gather up his bags and follow. "We did find one 'secret' compartment at San Rafael," he said as we reached the doorway. "A very small one carved into the base of one of the statues."

He pulled a parcel wrapped in muslin from his satchel and unwound the cloth. Inside was a book that was scarcely bigger than the palm of his hand. He handed it to me. It was soft and worn and very, very old. "I'd planned to give it to Father Rodriguez this afternoon," Thom said. "Since you're his agent at the mission I think it will be all right to turn it over to you. Pass it on to the priest when you get a chance, would you? It isn't evidence, and I doubt it has much monetary value, but the local diocese will want it. Historically speaking, it could be priceless."

"What is it?" I asked, turning the volume over in my hands and knowing I should be wearing cotton gloves as I did so.

"A journal," Thom said. "It's mostly handwritten prayers and verses of scripture mixed with the day-to-day workings of a San Rafael we can scarcely imagine."

I opened the cover. The paper of the first page was brown with age and cupping at the edges. In the upper corner someone had written *Anno Domini, 1857* in spidery script.

"In the year of our Lord," Thom translated.

"It's written in Spanish?"

"The personal entries," Thom said. "The rest of it is in Latin."

"And you read Latin?"

"Yes."

Of course. Stupid question. But I decided to ask the classicist college-professor-cum-detective another. "Was it written by a priest?"

Thom shrugged. "Probably a friar. Whatever he was besides, he was a gifted sculptor. The name carved into the base of the statues is the same as the name of the man who kept this journal—Manuel Sarasate."

A few feet away, at the reception desk, Chaiya dropped her ghost-hunting manual. It landed on the desk with a thunk, knocked a bottle of water into her lap, then fell and bounced off her foot. She didn't notice the bump on her foot or the sudden soaking of her skirt.

"Did you say Sarah Scott?" she asked with wide eyes.

"Sarasate?" Thom repeated, baffled by her reaction to the name. He hadn't seen anything yet.

"Oh my gosh!" Chaiya cried, jumping up and running to my side. "Omigosh! Omigosh! Omigosh! No *wonder* the ghost sounded like a guy! He *is* a guy! And he's telling us to find his *book.*"

"She thinks she recorded electronic voice phenomena in the mission last night," I explained to Thom, refraining from circling a finger around my ear as I said it.

"I see," he said as if he did. "I've heard of that. What do you think you recorded, Chaiya?"

I didn't know if Thom was humoring my cousin or if he really was interested. What's more, I didn't care. I wanted him to leave so I could decide what to do about Carlos. Probably I'd go over to the rectory to confess that I'd found the cross and given it to the police. (Sure it was after midnight, but Carlos was a night person like me. I couldn't count the number of times in high school that we'd stayed up late playing board games with Arjay—my kid brother who is nocturnal by reason of genetics rather than choice.) He was probably a suspect in a murder investigation at this point. I owed it to him—and Father Rodriguez—to make sure he heard about it from me first.

"Detective Casey is leaving," I told Chaiya before she could respond to his question. "Give him a strand of your hair and then

I'm going to take him down to the hearse to get those socks we wore last night. We threw them in the back, right?"

Chaiya plucked out a glossy thread of raven-colored hair and presented it to Thom without question or comment. "The hearse isn't there," she said. "Delano took it to that all-night car wash to be derailed."

"Detailed?" I shook my head. "He wouldn't have taken it again, Chaiya. He took it in on Monday."

"No, he didn't."

But I knew that he had. I'd asked him to at our meeting Monday night and he'd agreed.

When I told Chaiya as much she said, "He was *going* to take it in, but then Mr. Templeton called with all those questions about his case, and Delano went over to see him instead. He said he'd do it later—and he is. He's doing it now."

At the rate my head was shaking it was likely to come loose from my neck. "But I watched Monday's video surveillance of the parking booth," I told Chaiya. "I saw that hearse leave the lot behind Nightshade and come back later." It was one of few things that had happened lately of which I was certain. "And I smelled the chemicals they used to clean the paneling. My car's been in the shop all week, remember? I had to take the hearse on the stakeout Monday night—not long after Delano brought it back." I turned to Thom. "You smelled the cleaning fluids too, right?"

Thom's face was inscrutable, the way it tends to look when he's thinking something he doesn't want to say out loud. "I smelled something."

There was a simple way to resolve this and shrink the lump that was forming in my throat. I pulled my cell phone out of my pocket and speed-dialed Delano's number. He answered on the third ring.

"Where are you?" I asked, hoping that the sound of gushing water in the background meant that he'd driven cross-country to Niagara Falls.

"Car wash," he said.

"Not with Uncle Eddie's hearse."

"Yes, with the hearse. You think I bring my motorcycle here?"

My head wasn't shaking anymore. It wasn't moving at all. "You didn't take the hearse out on Monday night," I whispered.

"No, Sam," Delano said. "That was you, remember?"

It was me at twelve thirty, but it wasn't me at nine. And it wasn't Knute (I'd seen him come and go in his own car) and it wasn't Chaiya (she'd been talking to Veronica in the front office) and there wasn't anybody else at Nightshade for it *to* be.

I turned to Detective Casey, knowing full well that there was not a spot of color left anywhere on my face except, maybe, for my green eyes. "I think I know how the body snatchers smuggled Antonio Batista's body out of our parking lot." I leaned back against the doorjamb for support. Not only had some pervert stolen a body from next door while I was sitting at my desk, they'd used *my* hearse to steal it.

Chapter 12

There ought to be a law somewhere that says that a night that starts out great cannot degenerate into disaster before one's eyes. I'd gone in to Nightshade that evening with renewed confidence in my abilities as a private investigator. I'd gone in satisfied to know I might have given the police an important lead in one of the toughest cases to ever hit the Phoenix streets. I'd gone in expecting to receive Detective Casey's profuse thanks and then use that moment of goodwill to invite him to my mother's Halloween party for our first real date.

And I'd been wrong, wrong, and . . . let's see . . . yep . . . wrong.

In the first place, competent private investigators do not have their hearses stolen out from under their noses by body snatchers. In the second place, I was very sorry I'd given that cross to Thom without asking Carlos about it first. In the third place, I was sorry that my guilt and frustration had caused me to practically throw Thom out of Uncle Eddie's office.

Being a gentleman as well as a scholar, Thom was still doing everything he could to help me. He'd met Delano at the forensics garage to go over the hearse for any clue that might have survived the night's washing, vacuuming, shampooing, and polishing. I didn't think about who might be on the forensics team—i.e., Amber, the CSI babe. Okay, so maybe I did think about her. Maybe I thought about her so long that when the intercom buzzed I practically jumped out of my seat.

"It's after midnight," Chaiya said. "I'm going home. I finished chapter 8 of *Ghost Hunting for Dummies*."

And that's probably *all* she'd accomplished on Nightshade's time. Ever since Thom had handed me that journal, my cousin had been convinced that she'd recorded the otherworldly mutterings of Manuel Sarasate. Even if there *was* a ghost in San Rafael—which there wasn't—why would he (she, it) instruct Chaiya to look for a book of Spanish trivia and Latin prayers? Still, Chaiya was convinced her EVP was otherworldly, and with such stunning "success" on her first case she had vowed to devote her life to ghost hunting.

"It was a great chapter," Chaiya continued. "'The Ghostly Vigil—Conducting Investigations in a Cemetery Near You.'"

That sounded bad.

"Want to go with me?"

That sounded worse.

"No!" I said with the emphasis on the exclamation point.

"That's okay," she replied. "I have a date with LeVar Zabloudil on Saturday night. He said he'd take me anywhere I want to go."

"And you want to go to a cemetery? That's some first date."

"Second date," Chaiya said. "Our first will be at Aunt Judith's party tomorrow." I heard her gathering up her stuff. "Did you tell Thom to wear a costume?"

I didn't reply.

"Sam?"

I reached for the cord on the intercom, but instead of pulling it out of the wall I let it go with a sigh. I might as well confess. She'd find out soon enough. "I didn't invite Thom."

Either Chaiya sighed or a little of her EVP static had crept into our intercom system. "Samantha Shade, you are hopeless," she said at last.

An accurate observation if ever I'd heard one.

* * *

I pushed the laptop aside after showing Knute and Delano Monday's video footage of Uncle Eddie's hearse leaving the parking lot. It was almost six in the morning and we were finally ending the work night. I hadn't left to see Carlos after all, what with other things—bad things—coming up as they had.

"The best I can figure," I said, "is that whoever wanted Antonio's body was watching the parking lot. They must have seen Sully leave around seven o'clock."

"They didn't waste much time," Delano said. "They heisted the hearse before nine."

"Eight forty-seven," Knute said. He'd been taking notes on a yellow legal pad. He'd seen about an hour and a half's worth of video footage and had scrawled enough notes for a medium-length novel. "They brought it back at 9:32."

"Forty-five minutes," Delano figured. "They couldn't have driven very far before they stashed the body and returned the hearse."

"It took a lot of nerve," I said. "There were people coming in and out of the lot all that time, picking up sandwiches at the deli."

"Not so much nerve," Knute said. "With Eddie's hearse pulled right up to the back of the mortuary, and with both the rear doors open, it would have been almost impossible for a casual observer to see what they were doing."

"And if somebody did see them," Delano added, "they might not have given it a second thought. Putting a body in a hearse isn't exactly unheard of."

"More than nerve," Knute said, "it took *keys*. Sully's place was opened with a key and so was Eddie's hearse."

"We're the only ones who could come up with the keys to both," I said. "You guys . . . me . . . Chaiya. That's it."

"How about our contract workers?" Delano asked.

I shook my head. "Even with business picking up because of Halloween I haven't had to hire any temps since the Graeme case."

"Could have been planned that long ago or longer," Knute said. "Depends on what the snatchers wanted—Batista's body or any corpse they could get their hands on."

"Halloween brings out the sickos," Delano agreed.

"It might not have been Halloween that did it," I said, leaning forward. "Carlos Diego—a monk who's doing social work in the area around San Rafael—knows the Batistas. He doesn't think the drug overdose was an accident. He thinks it has something to do with the body snatching."

Knute, who has known me all my life, knew in a flash that Carlos was the guy who had broken my heart in high school. I could see he remembered by the way one woolly, black-and-gray caterpillar of an eyebrow rose. But all he said was, "What does he think the one has to do with the other?"

"He doesn't know," I admitted. "It's only a hunch, I guess."

"However you look at it, we're gonna get further by exploring opportunity than we are motive," Delano decided.

"No hope for forensics?" I asked.

"Not much," Delano said. "There would have been more, of course, if I hadn't just had it spit polished at the car wash. Lucky break for the loonies." He scratched at his beard. "One thing's for sure. Amber says there *was* a dead body in there. Recently."

Was every man in Phoenix on a first-name basis with that forensics tech or what? Still, there wasn't room in my brain to obsess about Amber because all the cells there were recalling for me in vivid detail how I'd climbed into that hearse not long after Antonio Batista's corpse had been dragged out of it. I shuddered.

"I think Clueless knew," I said. "She went crazy when I tried to shut her up back there."

Delano said, "She probably smelled the whole story. Amber said the body bag must have been opened at some point and the body mutilated." He grimaced. "I smelled the odor myself, and I didn't have the panel open. Even after a thorough cleaning, there were traces of . . . uh . . . body fluids in the carpet fibers."

Antonio's body had been desecrated in our hearse? That was more than I wanted to know. I'd be walking until my car got out of the shop, even if it was ten miles from Nightshade to my apartment.

Knute read my mind, or at least my face. "It's clean now, Sam," he said. "It won't do any good to obsess over it."

I swallowed hard and tried to nod. He was right. I needed to be adult about this. Professional. I could not let my imagination run wild or I'd start screaming like a little girl.

"Bottom line," Delano said, "we can't count on forensics for an answer. All Amber found for certain was evidence of a corpse and we already know who that was. Besides, it will take weeks to get the workup back from the lab."

"Back to opportunity," Knute suggested.

Delano stared into space. Unlike Knute, he rarely writes anything down. He seldom forgets anything either. "Nightshade staff," he began where we'd left off. "If we eliminate ourselves, who else could have snatched the keys?"

"Nobody," I said.

"Think, Sam," Knute advised.

This meant they'd thought of somebody I hadn't. Maybe several somebodies. Maybe a slew of somebodies. For a few seconds I was angry and offended that Knute was still training me instead of working with me to solve the case. (He is big on that "teach a man to fish/teach a girl to detect" thing.) Then my anger was overcome by my gratitude for his wisdom and patience, and I concentrated on concentrating.

"Tucker!" I said when at last there was a bite on my metaphorical fishing line. Ralph Tucker is the custodian for all four businesses in our little cluster. With a master key to all the offices at Nightshade, and all day to spend in our empty portion of the middle building, he had ample time and opportunity to find a key to Uncle Eddie's hearse. For sure he had access to the mortuary next door as well.

"I was thinking of Count Creepazoid myself," Delano said with a grimace.

"Count Creepazoid" is what Delano calls Mr. Tucker's teenage son, Trey. You'd think that none of us would throw stones, what with working in a glass house and all, but Trey Tucker is a little creepy even by our rather liberal standards. Maybe it's because while eccentricity comes naturally (and genetically) to us, Trey works at it. Works *hard* at it. Besides growing his fingernails long and painting them black, he bleaches his face and wears a long, billowing black cape. Strangest of all, he's doing his best to talk his parents into buying him porcelain "fangs" in lieu of the orthodontics sported by most kids his age.

Get the picture? Trey Tucker is a modern-day, middle-class vampire. At least he says he is.

Knute, who doesn't call anybody names even when they've earned them, looked concerned. "You don't think—"

"Who else would want a dead body?" Delano said. "Count Creepazoid heisted his father's keys and—"

"But Trey feeds psychically," I said, staring down at my lap as I worked it out. In another couple of seconds I looked up into the stunned silence and realized what I had said. "I mean, he thinks he does . . . or says he does . . . or something."

Delano leaned forward in amazement. "How do you *know* that?"

"I talk to him," I said. (After all, a girl with delusions of superherohood—that's not a word, is it?—can't stick her nose very high in the air over anybody else's fallacies.) I looked from Delano to Knute. Delano was going to get a headache if he rolled his eyes any higher, but Knute looked pleased. Heartened, I continued, "Really, I think he's a nice kid under all that Goth."

Delano snorted. "Nice for a vampire, you mean."

"He's only trying to be unique, Delano," I said. "Teenagers need outlets."

"Has he considered Junior Achievement instead of Junior Occultism?"

I frowned. "It's all for show. I don't think he's into the occult."

"You don't think?" Delano said. "You said he 'feeds' on people's psyches."

"It's something he heard on one of those reality TV shows," I said. "It doesn't *mean* anything. Well, it means he doesn't drink blood."

"Or doesn't yet," Delano said. "Until he sees somebody do it on TV."

I opened my mouth, but closed it again when Knute held up a hand. "I think we all have to agree he's worth checking out."

"I'm all over him," Delano said, rising from his chair as if he intended to lope across town and drag the kid out of bed before dawn for questioning. Not that I would put it past him. Delano's modus operandi is to act, or overreact, first and let somebody else handle damage control later. I wished Uncle Eddie would come back. He's much better at damage control than I am.

Delano was out the door before it occurred to him that our meeting might not be over. He leaned back in the room. "We're through here, right?"

"Right," I said with a sigh. Besides the fact that we'd reached a dead end, I had something else I had to do before I caught a few hours of sleep. "See you at the party tonight."

Delano grinned. Then, with a quick salute and flick of pony-tail, he was gone.

Knute wasn't in a hurry to go anywhere. After telling me he'd check out Sully's two assistants, Marty Poe and Roderick Harte, two more men with access to the keys to the mortuary, he leaned back in his chair and said, "What were you saying about Carlos Diego?"

"I happened to run into him the day before yesterday."

"I thought the kid was back East going to school."

"He was," I said with a smile, "but he's all grown up and graduated now." Knute has steadfastly refused to notice that Chaiya and I have grown up too. To him we'll always be teenagers. "He's working with Father Rodriguez."

"And he's a monk you say?"

My smile widened. "Going to be. Has a big cross around his neck to prove it."

All of a sudden my smile disappeared. Carlos *had* a cross around his neck—a cross that was now in the possession of a certain suspicious detective who was likely to cause all kinds of trouble for him and my client, Father Rodriguez.

As I've said, my face is only slightly less difficult to read than the funny papers. "Spill," Knute commanded, and I did. As usual, I told him more than I should have. For sure I told him more than I meant to. I could have at least left out the part about how unhappy I was with Thom and how miserable it felt to be unhappy with him.

"*You* gave him the cross," Knute said as if such weren't beside the point.

"That's what Thom said."

"The guy's trying to do his job," Knute continued.

"He said that, too."

"You did the right thing, Sam," Knute assured me. "And so did Thom. Maybe the wax and the flower and the cross will add up to nothing, but maybe they'll be the lead the police need to get a madman off the street."

There was comfort in Knute's words if only because I knew Carlos was not a madman. I wished I knew if he were a liar. He'd told Thom he'd never been in San Rafael. If that was true, how did his cross get there?

I looked up at the grandfather clock. It was a few minutes before seven. How early do monks get up anyway?

Chapter 13

Monks get up plenty early. That is to say, Brother Simon does. He was out in the yard on his knees when I pulled up in front of the rectory not long after dawn. At first I thought he was in the garden saying his morning prayers, so I sat in the hearse intending to wait. But when he saw me there and waved, I opened the door and walked over to meet him. Almost immediately my eyes began to water and I sneezed.

He was gardening, and I'm allergic to marigolds.

"Hey, Sam," Carlos said, rising and brushing the dirt from his pants. He wore jeans and a different NYU sweatshirt. He also wore a chain with a large, silver cross. "Still a Franciscan," he said with a grin when he caught me staring at his chest.

Forget about *How are you today—isn't this nice weather we're having?* I cut to the chase. "I thought you lost your cross."

"Why would you think that?"

"Because Thom . . . I mean Detective Casey . . . told me you did."

Carlos twisted a marigold bloom between his fingers. "Where'd he get that idea?"

"You told him—" I cut myself off, confused. Then I started again. "Detective Casey came to Nightshade last night. He—"

This time Carlos interrupted me. "You work at Nightshade? I never thought you'd—"

"I work there," I said. "I'm a private investigator. I told you that the other day after breakfast, remember?"

"Oh, right."

Some things don't change. Carlos hadn't listened to me when we were dating either. No matter what I talked about—high school trivia, my hopes and dreams, or even my testimony of the gospel of Jesus Christ—he had an uncanny ability to tune me out whenever he wanted to. It wasn't that he was rude or self-centered; he wasn't. It was more that when Carlos focused on his own thoughts, which he often did, nothing could penetrate them. The other day at breakfast he'd been focused on the guy across the street—the parishioner who Thom thought was trailing him. Although I'd chatted about my life as he walked me to my car, I might as well have recited the Gettysburg Address for all the impression I'd made.

"Anyway," I continued, "as I was saying, Thom—Detective Casey—came to Nightshade last night to ask me a few questions about a case he's working. He said he'd talked to you earlier in the day and noticed you weren't wearing your cross. He said you told him you'd lost it."

Carlos tapped the flower to his chest with another smile, but this one failed to make it as far as his eyes. "Here it is, safe and sound."

"Then why did you say you'd lost it?"

"Misunderstanding," Carlos said. "I wasn't wearing it at the time because I *had* misplaced it. Temporarily. Flimsy clasp keeps breaking."

I was relieved. At least I wanted to be relieved, but something about what he said, or the way he said it, didn't ring true. Or maybe it rang true enough, but there was more there that he hadn't said. Or—

I'm trying to say that since the cross was around his neck at that very moment, he clearly hadn't left it at San Rafael. A wave of relief swept over me.

"So, what's the detective's interest in my cross?" Carlos asked, forcing more casualness into his voice than showed on his face.

The wave of relief ebbed away and I hesitated. Then I took a dainty swipe at my nose with the back of my hand. "Could we talk someplace else? I'm allergic to marigolds."

"Sure," Carlos said. He took a couple of steps toward the rectory as if to invite me inside, then apparently reconsidered and led me back toward the sidewalk instead. At the fence that encircled the grassy yard he turned. "Better?"

"Better."

"You were telling me about Detective Casey's interest in my cross."

Actually I wasn't. I was stalling while I decided whether or not to tell him anything.

Get a grip, Samantha, I told myself. *This is Carlos. Besides being an old friend, he's a monk. Besides being a monk he works with your client. His parish is paying you to investigate the mission. You're not speaking out of turn. Anything to do with San Rafael is Brother Simon's business.*

"Chaiya and I were in San Rafael the other night," I said. "We found a cross there that looks exactly like the one on your chain."

Carlos's hand was atop the wrought iron gate. I watched the fingers on his knuckles whiten as his grip tightened. "Where did you find it?"

"In the sanctuary," I said. "There's a row of statues. The cross was at the base of one of them."

Carlos was clearly thinking fast, but he was also listening. In fact, he was listening intently.

"There's more," I said. "We also found fresh wax and a bit of petal from a marigold."

The flower in his hand dropped to the cement. When he spoke it was more to himself than it was to me. "The police have been over the mission, no doubt."

"A forensics team," I said, alarmed that the whitening of his knuckles was spreading to his usually bronze face. Instinctively, I reached for his elbow. "Carlos, what's wrong? *Were* you in San Rafael?"

"No," he said, but his voice sounded flat and regretful. So engrossed was he in his thoughts that it was almost a minute before he felt the press of my fingers in his flesh. When he finally did feel it he looked down at my hand.

"How can I help you?" I asked, thinking that if he'd tell me what was wrong we could work through it together no matter how bad it was.

The words seemed to act as a splash of cool water. Carlos raised his free hand, covered my fingers, and squeezed them. Then he moved away and forced another smile. "Isn't that my line? You're the one investigating that spooky old mission. How can I help *you,* Sam?"

"Tell me everything you know."

"I don't know anything. I've never been in there. I haven't seen the lights or heard the moans." He rolled his eyes. "And when it comes to ghosts, I'm a skeptic at best."

"Me too," I said. "But there was *something* in San Rafael. I heard it, Carlos—three times now, on two different nights. Chaiya made a recording of it."

"Yeah?" I thought I saw dismay flash in his eyes, but it passed so quickly I wasn't certain. "I'd like to hear that."

"I'll play it for you sometime. Now what about the cross?"

"It's a Catholic mission," he said with an exaggerated shrug. "There's nothing unusual about finding a cross there. Who knows how long ago somebody lost it."

"It was identical to yours. It was still shiny."

"It's an alloy," Carlos said. "It doesn't rust and it doesn't tarnish easily. A cross like this will still be shiny in ten years."

Only if the ghost dusted it routinely. "I didn't see it when I was there with Father Rodriguez the week before. Being so shiny, you'd think it would have shown up in the daylight. And even if I missed it, there were police in there after that. They—"

"Back to the police," Carlos said. Despite cutting me off, he was going for a conversational tone and was almost succeeding. "They must have come up with fingerprints . . . or something."

I shook my head. "No prints on the cross. They're still running the ones they found in the mission, but Thom's afraid they'll match those of people we know were in there."

Carlos gazed at the small garden of marigolds. "Like Father Rodriguez."

"Yes. Or me and Chaiya."

"And if all the prints are accounted for?"

"Then it's a dead end, I guess." I studied his face but didn't see any indication that he was worried about his own prints turning up. If anything, he looked relieved. I figured he was glad to have been given a way to clear his name.

Thank goodness for his relief. At that moment I was almost convinced I'd imagined any earlier discomfiture.

Almost.

"I appreciate you coming over to tell me this, Sam," Carlos said. "You're a good friend."

"I work for Father Rodriguez," I said because it was true—and because I suddenly felt disloyal to Thom for running to "tattle" to his prime suspect; I needed to reassure myself that I'd done the right thing. "I'd like to see him."

Carlos glanced toward the rectory. "Sorry. The father's sick this morning."

"Still?"

"Nothing serious. He'll be up and around in another day or two." When he saw me reach for the latch on the gate, he opened it. "Can I give him a message?"

I thought of the old journal in my car. I trusted Carlos with it, but I also welcomed a good excuse to keep it a few more days since I hadn't yet had a chance to look at it. "Tell him what I told you about the mission," I said. "Tell him we're doing our best." I stepped through the gate onto the sidewalk. "And tell him I hope he feels better. He's a good man."

"He is," Carlos said.

I'd reached the hearse before I realized that Carlos had followed me. I paused with my hand on the door handle.

"I meant to ask you something else," he said. "Any news on Antonio Batista?"

None that I wanted to tell him. As a committed social worker, he was probably helping Rosa Batista find a pro bono lawyer to sue Sully for the awful pain and suffering she and Marina must be enduring. When the truth about the involvement of our hearse got out, Nightshade and I would be the next defendants in the suit. "I'm doing my best on that, too," I said, leaving out the part about how abysmal my best was.

I said good-bye, opened the door, and got in the hearse, but Carlos still stood on the sidewalk. There was something else on his mind.

"Got a busy day ahead of you?" he asked.

"Uh, yes."

"No wonder, what with Halloween being on Monday."

I looked at him as though he had delivered the last line in Chinese.

He smiled. "You never could take a hint, Samantha Shade. I'm trying to find out if your mom still throws a great party. What did she call them? Harvest Balls?"

"Oh!" I said. "Yes, she does. It's tonight." My mind raced. Was he also hinting for an invitation? Do monks go to parties? *Halloween* parties? It's not exactly a sacred holiday. What I needed, I thought, was a copy of *Catholicism for Dummies.*

I'd always been taught that common courtesy always holds you in good stead. The polite thing would be to invite him. When I did, it came out like this: "Do you want to . . . I mean . . . you wouldn't want to . . . or, rather, you couldn't . . . I mean, monks don't . . . "

Carlos laughed. It was the old laugh that had caused me to fall for him in the first place. "I want, I could, and monks do. So if that's a lame invitation to the famous Shady Acres Harvest Ball, the answer is yes."

"It's an invitation," I said, smiling broadly. "Seven o'clock until whenever. You know the place."

"Do I! It'll be like the good ol' days."

I blinked. Either Carlos didn't remember "the good ol' days" as well as I did, or he'd overlooked a couple of pretty distinctive changes that had come along in the last five years. For one, he was about to take vows to become a monk. (Not even Chaiya dates monks.) For another, I'd fallen in love (for real this time) with another man. I watched him walk back toward the rectory.

I started the hearse, considering my ungracious invitation to Carlos and wondering how to now graciously invite Thom to the Harvest Ball—what with almost no notice and after brushing him off the night before. As I pulled away from the curb, I glanced toward the other side of the street just in time to see a black garbage dumpster move. Knowing it would take a feline the size of a lion to move a bin that size, I rolled to a stop, curious. Before I could open the car door, a dark, squat figure darted from behind the dumpster and disappeared into a neighboring yard. I didn't get a good look at the departing form, but I knew who it was. Flying Monkey Guy—the man who had trailed Carlos to the restaurant the morning we met for breakfast—was still gooning around.

I looked back at the rectory. Carlos had already gone inside, so I opened my cell phone to call him, or the police, or both.

I reconsidered before finding the rectory's number on the contact list. After all, what would I say to Carlos after, "You know that parishioner you told me not to worry about . . . ?"

And what I could report to the police was lamer yet.

I closed my phone but made a mental note to watch whether the goon followed Carlos to the party that night. I almost hoped he'd show up on my home turf. I'd sic Delano on him.

Maybe I ought to send Delano to the rectory, I thought as I pulled away from the curb. Now there's a guy who's good at getting answers. Much better than me. All I'd ended up with after my visit with the enigmatic Brother Simon was more questions.

Big ones.

Chapter 14

If you want a sneak peak at heaven, step outside on a late-autumn evening in Phoenix, Arizona. The air is soft and cool and smells like citrus. The almost-dark sky is a heart-stopping shade as yet unnamed by crayon manufacturers, and the few trees that shed their leaves do so onto lawns that are soft and green with winter grass. It is no wonder to me, then, that half the senior citizens in northern North America migrate to the Valley of the Sun after Labor Day. Nor is it any wonder that many of them fall in love with our valley and never want to leave it.

The three dozen most fortunate elderly residents live at my mother's assisted care facility, Shady Acres. On this perfect autumn night, they, some of their families, our friends and associates, and virtually everybody else who lives within a half-mile radius were out in force for the annual Harvest Ball.

I walked down the long drive to meet Carlos and smiled at his attire: brown robe, white-rope belt, and sandals. "You didn't come in costume, Brother Simon."

He returned my smile with a grin. "Neither did you."

Is it a sin to slug a monk? Even if you're not Catholic? I forbore just in case. "I'm Sam Spade," I said, fingering the lapel of my trench coat with one hand and tipping my fedora with the other.

"What happened to the Wonder Woman I used to know?"

She'd gained about twenty pounds more than could be decently encased in spandex, but I didn't tell him that. "Come say hello to my parents," I said. "My father is hiding somewhere around back wishing he were in his research lab, and my mother is the smiling blur you see from time to time."

"So they haven't changed," Carlos said.

"Not a bit."

We managed to pass almost fifty whole minutes in pleasantries with my parents, Knute, Chaiya and Kaboodle (or whatever her lawyer/date's name was), and a couple of the Shady Acres residents Carlos remembered who didn't remember him. Then I took the monk-to-be to the long, loaded buffet table and watched him obscure a plate with tamales, crackers with cream cheese and jalapeño jelly, seven-layer bean dip with fresh, hot tortilla chips . . . all my favorite foods. I reminded myself *why* I was wearing a trench coat and reached for the carrot sticks.

At last Carlos ran out of stomach room, and I ran out of people to introduce him to. It was still early and he gave no indication that he was anxious to leave, but I had no idea what to do with my "date" next. (I hadn't had this problem when he was eighteen and wearing something besides sackcloth and crosses.) Assuming he no longer danced, I said hopefully, "Do you play Yahtzee?" Mr. LaMar had a lively game going on under a well-lit pepper tree in the side yard.

When Carlos didn't respond, I looked up at him. He was looking over my head, scanning the crowd. He'd been doing that ever since he'd arrived, come to think of it. "Looking for someone?" I asked.

"Huh?" he said. "No." Lying doesn't come naturally to monks. In the next second he added, "Well, yeah. I thought Detective Casey would be here."

My heart gave a weak little *pulumpump* of disappointment. "No."

I'd lain awake most of the day wishing I had the nerve to invite Thom, but wishing for nerve was as far as I got in the process.

"Where is he?" Carlos asked.

I didn't know, of course, but I was curious why he asked. Before I could pursue it, a five-foot-tall Darth Vader clone strode up and planted himself in front of us.

"Who are you?" Darth asked the monk in a voice made artificially menacing by an amplification device within his black plastic mask. "Friar Tuck?"

"Friar Simon," Friar Simon said.

"Never heard of—"

"Arjay, this is Carlos Diego," I said in an attempt to forestall one of the rude remarks for which my eleven-year-old brother is infamous. "You remember him. Carlos and I dated in high school. He's Brother Simon now."

"I was six years old when you graduated from high school," Arjay pointed out. "I don't remember him."

"I remember you," Carlos said.

No surprise there. It's a rare individual who forgets Arjay—even when they try. Carlos tapped the top of my brother's mask. "Great costume."

"It's not a costume," Arjay said. "It's my regular clothes."

Believe it or not, he was telling the truth. Ever since Halloween costumes had come on the market in August, Arjay had worn the Darth Vader ensemble at least two or three times a week.

I'd better explain briefly for those of you who didn't meet Arjay in the last book. My adopted little brother suffers from a rare genetic disorder called xeroderma pigmentosum—XP for short. It's a condition where the body is unable to strip out nucleotide strands damaged by ultraviolet light and replace them with healthy DNA. In real words, it means that sunlight—any bright light—causes a rapid development of skin cancer that can be fatal. My father's genetic research is what led him to the orphaned toddler. Arjay's adoption into our family nine years before is the reason we became nocturnal. But living nocturnally isn't enough. Even at night Arjay has to cover his skin when in a brightly lit place. Ergo, the Darth Vader costume that swathes every square inch of him in black fabric and vinyl is ideal. Besides, when he wears it into supermarkets, people don't bat an eye, but when he walks in wearing long pants, long sleeves, gloves, special goggles, and a wide-brimmed hat (especially in Phoenix in the summertime) they tend to stare. Go figure.

"I don't remember you," Arjay told Carlos again. (I was secretly happy to hear it since it meant there was one person in my world who didn't recall that Carlos had dumped me.) "Where have you been for the last five years?"

"Back East," Carlos said. "At school."

"How long does it take to learn those monk chants?" Darth didn't wait around for an explanation. Instead he peered around Brother Simon, pumped a fist in the air, and ran toward the street with his long cape flapping behind him.

"Nice kid," Carlos said.

"Not really," I replied fondly. "So . . . weren't you saying that you'd like to play Yahtzee?"

"If you don't mind, I'd rather talk to Detective Casey."

"He's not—" I began, but when I turned to follow Carlos's line of vision, Thom was standing on the sidewalk in front of my parents' house, smiling at the steady stream of words coming from within Darth Vader's black helmet.

Talk about a miracle somewhat near 34th Street!

"I want to talk to him too," I said, practically pulling Carlos across the lawn toward the sidewalk before the welcome apparition disappeared.

Unfortunately, I didn't make it. I was hijacked only a few yards away from where Thom and Arjay stood. Before I realized what was happening, my Aunt Karma grabbed my sleeve and pulled me under a jacaranda tree. Carlos didn't notice my abduction and kept walking. (On the other hand, Carlos also remembers my Aunt Karma, so maybe he only pretended not to notice that I was Sam-napped.)

"Is that him?" Karma hissed.

"Who?" I said, knowing perfectly well who.

"Him."

"Yes," I said, resigned to whatever bizarre conversation would ensue, and grateful that at least we were holding it in private. "That's him."

"Hmm."

There are eight Shades in the generation preceding mine and, believe it or not, Karma is the shadiest. My Uncle Eddie is the oldest at seventy-six and was already married when my father, the baby, came along. Aunt Karma is also in the older half, despite having a daughter (Chaiya) who is my age. Karma was one of the original flower children. She fled Phoenix before graduating high school and eventually drifted to San Francisco. There she attended marches and burned flags and undergarments—and undergarments made from flags and flags made from undergarments. Then, because she's basically a take-charge kind of person, she took charge and began to organize the marches. Eventually she became a professional fundraiser. At sixty-three she's one of the foremost in the nation. If you need to raise money to save just about anything from just about anybody, Karma Shade is probably the woman to call.

But take my advice—don't call her.

"Hmm," she said again. "I'm afraid it's just as I suspected." She had lowered her ruby-rimmed, cat-eyed glasses to stare intently at Thom. (Chaiya gets all her fashion taste from her mother.) "I'm picking up some real strong vibes there, Sammy."

I didn't know what a vibe was. I didn't want to know what a vibe was. But I didn't have to know what a vibe was to know that if Karma's internal meter picked it up, it was likely to shake the world.

When she was almost forty, Karma Shade received a vibe that registered 9.5 or greater on the family disaster scale. An angel—or an angler (she was deep-sea fishing at the time and horribly seasick, thus she has always been a little hazy on the details)—appeared to tell her it was time to "get off her duff and get with the program." In those words. (Well, almost. I reserve the right to edit nouns to maintain my G rating.) She interpreted this to mean she was to "get with" the spiritual program she'd been taught as a child. In other words, if she was going to do her part to replenish the earth, she'd better quit dividing her time between so many causes and get to multiplying.

A woman of action (read: *impetuosity*), Karma went to the first LDS singles dance she could find and married a handsome, three-time train wreck the next week. Within a few months she was Ex Number Four, but she had what she wanted: a baby. Karma gave birth to Chaiya and devoted eight or ten spare minutes to her daughter on the rare occasions the humpback whales and deforested rain forests could spare her services. I don't think there's anybody in the family Chaiya hasn't lived with, but she was with Eddie and Elise the longest. That's probably why she turned out so well. (Relatively speaking.)

Karma continued to peer out at Thom from within the branches of the feathery jacaranda tree. "Hmm," she repeated.

I looked at him too and realized that I did know what vibes are. They're the things that cause your heart to hum and your skin to vibrate for no good reason.

"So what's wrong with him?" Karma asked.

Something was wrong with Thom?

I looked closer. The monk was trying to shoo the kid away, but Darth was holding his ground. (Arjay likes Thom as much as I do.) The cop was trying his best to divide his attention and make everybody happy. I smiled. If there was anything physically, mentally, emotionally, or spiritually wrong with that man, I didn't know what it was. As far as I could tell, Thomas Casey was perfect.

"Nothing's wrong with him," I told Aunt Karma with a sigh. "Absolutely nothing."

She snorted. "Where did he go to school?"

"Oxford," I said with almost as much pride as if I'd gone there myself. "He was a Rhodes Scholar."

"And then?" she pressed. Obviously Chaiya had already filled her in. She probably knew more about Detective Casey than I did.

But I answered anyway. "BYU. He graduated summa cum laude with a master's degree in literature."

"Uh-huh," Karma said as though that told her the whole story. (It wasn't even much of a prologue, was it?) When I didn't say anything else, she continued, "Tell me, Sammy, what are the odds of a bright, healthy Mormon male—especially one who looks like that—staying single for five whole minutes, let alone five whole years, in the marriage mecca of the Church?" Her carefully penciled brows rose. "If nothing else, consider the odds. *Something* must be wrong with him."

I opened my mouth to respond, but no words came out of it.

Well, that's probably not true. More likely, my mouth gaped open of its own volition before my brain had time to form coherent speech. I didn't know if Thom had been at BYU for five whole years, but that wasn't the point. He'd been there five days, and I'd fallen in love with him in less time than that. Judging by Amber the CSI babe, I wasn't the only one.

Why isn't he married? I wondered. I knew he was a little serious and bookish and bossy, but who couldn't overlook that? What, I wondered, could possibly be wrong enough with Thom Casey to counterbalance everything that was right with him?

At last I found my voice and said to Karma, "You didn't marry until you were forty and . . . "

What was the end of that sentence? Certainly not *and there's nothing wrong with you.* I stared at Thom. He must have felt my eyes on him because he looked up.

Very strong vibes there, indeed. Magnetic vibes, in fact. I took a couple of steps in his direction.

"Don't feel too bad," Karma told my back. "You never could pick 'em, Sammy. After all, that last guy who dumped you became a monk."

The *last* guy who dumped me married my visiting teaching partner, but I hesitated to bring it up. I walked toward Thom thinking there was a mystery that mattered. I'd solve it if it was the last thing I ever did.

Karma didn't follow, but she called after me, "Good for you, Sammy! Find out what's wrong with him! Maybe we can fix it."

Maybe Thom overheard my aunt. (It would be my luck.) Or maybe it was too dark there on the sidewalk for him to see how glad I was to see him. He said, "I'm sorry to show up like this."

"No!" I said before the apology was all the way out of his mouth. "I'm glad you're here, Thom! I wanted to invite you to the party. I planned to invite you. I . . . "

What was the end of *that* sentence? . . . *but I'm so in love with you that whenever you're around I can't think straight.*

I couldn't say that—if for no other reason than he didn't give me the chance.

"I went by Nightshade," he said, "but it was closed." He glanced across the yard to where Knute was eating and Chaiya was flirting with her short, sheepherding attorney.

Thom's face was mostly inscrutable, but I knew that if our situations had been reversed and he hadn't invited me to a party that included people I knew plus an old girlfriend of his, I would be hurt . . . devastated . . . fully prepared to die. Thom didn't look devastated, but he did look . . . something. There were little lines around his gorgeous gray eyes and a dimple in his cheek.

I felt horrible. I felt . . . some word that describes worse than horrible.

I reached for Thom's arm. "Please come and eat I want you to meet my parents and Knute will want to see you Delano isn't here yet but will be any minute Chaiya's here with that sheep lawyer she met at the funeral home Sully had to leave before dusk because it's the Jewish Sabbath you know but Carlos wants to talk to you and Arjay couldn't be more excited and me well I'm *so* glad you're here Thom I want—"

With a Herculean effort I dropped my hand from his arm and cut myself off. I was very proud of my self-control. Usually when I start babbling without punctuation somebody has to slap me.

Carlos looked as though he wondered if he should slap me. Arjay laughed. There's a reason Darth Vader doesn't laugh in the movies. It's because the sound that comes out of that mask when he does is reminiscent of a garbage disposal in overdrive. I put my hand over the mouth area of the mask with no effect whatsoever.

Thom must have somehow figured out that within all my words was an invitation to join the party because he declined it with an, "I can't stay. I'm still on duty."

Sure enough, the silver badge was clipped to his belt, and if you looked close enough you could make out a bulge beneath his leather jacket that would be a service pistol. Still, judging by his loosened tie and somewhat rumpled apparel, he'd been on duty a very long time.

Sensing that all the coaxing and babbling in the world wouldn't get him a foot closer to the buffet table, I said, "Policemen have to eat too. Arjay, go get Detective Casey—"

My brother was gone before Thom could protest or I could finish my instructions. I could only hope Thom was fond of chili rellenos and root-beer floats. They are Arjay's favorite foods and he seldom notices anything else when they're on the menu.

"I'm sorry to interrupt the party," Thom said again, this time to Carlos, "but I went to the rectory, too. Your housekeeper told me you were here."

Three cheers for the housekeeper!

"Then you got my message," Carlos said.

"Yes," Thom said. "Finally." He pulled a business card out of an inside breast pocket. "Here's my cell phone number for the future."

"Let's sit down," I interrupted, pointing to a mostly secluded spot nearby that had the added benefit of getting Thom most of the way to the outskirts of the party. If I could get him that far in now, maybe I could get him farther in later on.

Thom hesitated, then nodded and followed me to the small table. I was glad he did. I think he was glad too. Detective Casey looked like he needed to sit down for a few minutes. And who could blame him? Tracking serial killers all day every day would wear anybody down.

Or maybe it isn't a serial killer that has him working all hours, I thought, brightening. *Maybe it's the way Thom's wired.*

I liked that line of reasoning. I loved it, even. Maybe Thom had a compulsive personality disorder. Maybe he had studied eighteen hours a day at BYU. Maybe no girl had seen his face because it was always stuck in a book. Maybe—

Maybe I should quit worrying about Aunt Karma. Why obsess over what she'd said when I knew perfectly well there is nobody in the world screwier than she is?

Or maybe there *is* somebody screwier. I'd temporarily forgotten that the queen of Oddball Island winters at Shady Acres.

And wouldn't it figure she was headed my way?

Chapter 15

"Quick! Hide under the table!" I yelled. "Better yet, let's make a run for it!"

Okay, I didn't say that to Thom and Carlos at the Shady Acres Harvest Ball, but I should have. Millicent Beattie was on a roll. Literally. Her motorized scooter sped down on our formerly secluded table before I had time to raise a cry of warning.

We were seated at three sides of a card table. Millicent screeched to a halt at the fourth, pushing the table into my belly with the handlebars of her scooter. I sucked in, but not enough moved. (How many carrot sticks does a person have to eat to see a measurable difference in waistline, anyway?) Discouraged, I scooted my chair back a couple of inches.

"Why, Samantha!" Millie said, ogling my guests. "I've never known you to have *one* suitor, let alone *two!*"

There must be a gracious and witty reply to a statement like that. (Write to me and tell me what it is, will you?) Feeling neither witty nor gracious, I could only sputter.

"Aren't you going to introduce me?" Millie asked. To Thom and Carlos she said, "Her lovely mother raised her better than this."

Giving me no time to recover enough to retort, Millicent backed up her scooter. For one marvelous minute I thought it would be a drive-by dissing, but she maneuvered around until she was parked sideways. Then she rotated her chair to face the table and leaned forward with her elbows on the tabletop. She had costumed herself as a gypsy, so cheap metal bracelets clattered down her wrinkled arms. Loose, flabby skin puddled on the vinyl. She looked pointedly at me before fluttering long, fake eyelashes from Thom to Carlos and back again.

I suppressed a sigh. Well, I *tried* to suppress it. "Millie, this is Detective Thom Casey and Carlos . . . er . . . Brother Simon." To them I said, "And this is Millicent Beattie. She's a resident at Shady Acres."

"I *reside* there," Millicent said to Thom. "I am *not* a resident."

Webster might have begged to differ, but Thom didn't. It was a good call on his part.

"*Brother* Simon?" Millie said. "Brother *Simon?* As in . . . ?"

As in Simon says go away. I was ashamed of myself for thinking it since it was only slightly witty and not at all gracious.

"I'm a monk," Carlos explained.

"I can see that," Millie responded, plucking at his robe. She released the nappy fabric to straighten her bath-towel turban. "And I'm a gypsy fortune teller. You may call me Madame Zoraster."

"Millie—" I began.

"Madame Zoraster," she reminded me.

"Brother Simon *is* a monk."

"Well, not yet," he admitted. "I mean, technically."

I shot him a that-didn't-help-thanks look while Millie leaned forward to pat his hand.

"Technically I'm not a gypsy," she confessed. "I'm a Presbyterian. Shall I tell your fortune?"

"No," he said.

For a minute I worried that Brother Simon's refusal to participate in her parlor game would offend Millie—and Presbyterian faux fortune tellers everywhere—but she turned to me instead. I knew better than to refuse. I held out my palm for inspection, hoping it wouldn't be too bad. The year before, Millie had predicted my future with a deck of Old Maid cards. You can probably imagine how that turned out.

Her wrinkled face folded into a pucker as she considered the crisscrossing lines on my palm. "This tells me you're conflicted, Samantha," she said. "You worry too much."

Me? Worry? What did I have to worry about, besides haunted missions, missing corpses, and no love life other than an ongoing affair with powdered-sugar donuts?

Millie traced a long, red nail down my palm. "That's your love line." When she got to a place where it intersected with another she looked up in surprise. "Samantha! You've found your true love!"

I pulled my fedora over my eyes so they wouldn't stray to Thom's handsome face. I knew if I blushed any brighter I might glow in the dark.

Millie looked from one "suitor" to the next while she sharpened her tongue. "But which one?" She snatched up Carlos's hand almost before he saw her move and ran a scarlet-tipped finger along his palm. "Ah ha!" she cackled, as if reading from the Apocrypha.

Carlos wasn't amused but Thom was.

"See this line?" Millie said, tilting Carlos's palm my direction. "This man has unfinished business." Where had I heard that before? The same second I'd tied it in with the ghost of San Rafael, Millie intoned, "And you are at the center of that business, Samantha Shade."

Thom no longer looked amused; Carlos less so. He pushed out his chair and rose.

"Don't go," I said quickly. "She doesn't mean . . . " This time my words trailed off. I didn't know what Millie meant, but I did know she was likely to refute my best guess, no matter what it was.

"I only pointed out what is in his palm," Millie said stubbornly, tucking a stray blue curl back up under her turban. "It's not *my* fault his hand is full of secrets . . . and intrigue—*I* certainly didn't design it." She clucked her tongue while turning the seat of her scooter back toward the handlebars. Then she started the motor. "'Yea, though I walk through the shadow of the valley of death, I will fear no evil . . .'"

Millicent Beattie was still reciting the psalm as she scootered off. I was dumfounded—and I'm not a superstitious person. I'm not. I throw spilled salt over my left shoulder and knock on wood because my great-grandmother used to and I think it's a charming way to remember her eccentricities. But I *will* walk under a ladder and cross paths with a black cat. I would live in apartment 13 on the thirteenth floor if my building was more than three stories high. I step on cracks routinely and think nothing of breaking an occasional mirror. I do wish on stars (doesn't everybody?), but I don't carry a rabbit foot (yuck) or set leprechaun traps in my flower garden. Nor do I believe in omens, portends, or signs—or seeking after them. Still, who could hear a "fortune" like that spoken on a late October night and *not* have a chill run down her spine?

"I'm . . . sorry," I said when I could speak again. "Millie does something like this every year. It's harmless. Usually it's funny. Tonight it was . . . " I didn't finish the sentence because I didn't know what it was.

Carlos looked from Thom toward the street and back as if trying to decide whether he most wanted to talk to the detective or flee for his life.

I glanced out toward the street when he did. It was too dark for me to be certain, but I thought I saw a familiar figure hovering just outside the ring of lights. It looked very much like the short, dark figure of Flying Monkey Man. I felt cold all over. That's probably why Thom beat me to the first word.

"You wanted to talk to me, Brother Simon?" he said.

Carlos nodded. "I was, uh, wondering what's new in the Marigold Murderer case." When Thom didn't immediately respond, Carlos swallowed. "What I mean is, with Father Rodriguez being so sick and all, *he* hoped I could find something out for him. There's a lot of concern in the parish. It's our young men being targeted by the serial killer, after all."

I tried to meet Carlos's eyes to see what was in them. His use of the priest's name to validate his interest sounded disingenuous to me, and the end had been tacked on a little too haphazardly. I hoped Thom didn't notice.

He did. "Father Rodriguez *asked* you to speak to me," Thom countered, "or merely *hopes* to hear information from any source?"

There was the hint of a dimple in Thom's cheek, and I didn't like the way he was twisting words. The same pro-Carlos defense mechanism that had caused me to bristle at him the night before kicked in again. "Father Rodriguez is too sick to talk to the police himself, but of course he's concerned!" I said. "Every man who's been murdered has been in his parish!"

"Not exactly," Thom said, the dimple deepening. "The last victim wasn't Catholic."

"But the news said he was found behind St. Cecilia's," I said.

"Yes, but he wasn't killed there." After a beat of silence the detective added, "There's an agenda we don't yet understand with respect to where these bodies keep turning up." He looked toward Carlos. "I don't think it's a coincidence they've all been found in your parish."

Carlos didn't respond. He didn't even blink.

"I went by the parish house this evening," Thom continued, studying Carlos's face for a reaction.

I hoped he didn't see the same fear there that I thought I saw. "Because?" Carlos asked.

"A couple of reasons," Thom said. "One, I wanted to see you. I hoped you could tell me where to find José Gutierrez."

"His apartment is—"

"Empty," Thom interrupted. "Sometime in the last twenty-four hours he and the Batistas disappeared."

"Disappeared?" I repeated.

"Both apartments still have furnishings, but most of the clothes and food are gone," Thom explained. "José, Marina, Rosa—none of them showed up for work today."

This was news to Carlos, and Thom recognized it. "Father Rodriguez agreed that you might know where they've gone," he said to the monk. "He seemed to think that if they were in trouble they would turn to you first."

Clearly Carlos needed to sit down. Since the tabletop was higher than the chair, that's how far he made it. I looked into his stricken face thinking we were both benumbed by the same news, but at the same time that I said, "The Batistas are in trouble?" Carlos said, "You saw Father Rodriguez?"

Thom ignored me to answer Carlos. "I spoke with him about an hour ago. I was fortunate to catch him. He was on his way out."

"Out where?" Carlos said, rising again.

"To visit parishioners, I believe." Thom turned toward me. "Your client seems to have made a speedy recovery, Sam. Despite what the housekeeper and Brother Simon have told us, Father Rodriguez didn't recall being ill. In fact, he says he's merely been busy the last few days tending his flock."

Carlos had already turned and taken a long stride toward the street when Thom said to his back, "*Do* you know where to find Gutierrez and the Batistas, Brother Simon? He could be running for his life."

Carlos turned. "Was José's green card a forgery?"

"Yes," Thom said. "But a very good one."

Carlos smiled grimly. "Now you know *why* they're missing."

"No," Thom said. "I don't. And I don't think you believe that's the reason either."

I pushed back my chair to go with Carlos, but before I could rise, he held up a hand to stop me. "Good night, Sam. Thanks for inviting me." Then he turned and jogged toward the street.

Seeing that he was almost gone, I turned to Thom. "That goon we saw at the restaurant is still following him. I saw him at the parish house this morning and I think he's here tonight, too."

"Don't worry about him."

Easy for him to say. With that pistol he carried and a whole lot of backup just a radio call away, Thom didn't have to worry. Carlos, however, didn't have anyone to protect him but me. I cast the policeman a scathing, thanks-for-nothing look and stood up to follow the defenseless, unsuspecting monk.

Thom rose and grasped my elbow gently. "Really," he said. "Don't worry about that . . . parishioner. He's harmless."

I hesitated. "You checked him out yourself?"

"Yes."

"Why didn't you tell me?" In the next second I withdrew the question to replace it with a statement. "He doesn't look harmless to me."

"He's harmless to Brother Simon. That's who you're worried about, right?"

I nodded.

Thom moved closer. "I wish you'd worry less about him and more about somebody else." He'd said it softly. When I looked up I saw how much he meant the words. For a delusional second I thought he was jealous and wishing I'd think about him instead of Carlos. Then he added, "You need to worry about yourself, Sam."

"Me?" I said, startled. "Don't tell me you believe a Presbyterian fortune teller."

"No, but I can't help but put credence in this." From the pocket of his jacket he removed two see-through evidence bags. Inside one was a single yellow marigold. Inside the other was about a half sheet of ordinary notebook paper upon which was scrawled:

SAMANTHA SHADE
WATCH OUT

You wouldn't have to be superstitious to read a bad omen into that fortune.

Chapter 16

With the Harvest Ball continuing in full swing and only the moon looking on, Thom handed me the evidence bags with the carefully encased note and flower.

samantha shade watch out

The words weren't any friendlier or better punctuated than the first time I'd read them.

I raised the evidence bags both a little closer to my nose to better see the handwriting on the note. It must have been psychologically induced, but even through the plastic the marigold made me sneeze.

Or maybe I'm allergic to threatening messages.

"Where did you get this?" I asked Thom.

"I took it from the door when I stopped by your office." From the same pocket from which he'd removed the bags he took out a small digital camera, which he turned on and extended.

I looked down at the micromini screen and knew I was seeing shots Thom had made of our office door as he'd found it. Although it was like looking at snapshots taken by a mouse, I could make out that the note and flower had been wedged into a crack above the doorknob.

"When did you find it?" I asked.

"Tonight. I tried calling your cell from outside Nightshade, but there was no answer."

I tried to feign a look of surprise. It was either that or admit that I'd forgotten to charge the phone's battery. Again.

"I went from your offices to the rectory," Thom continued. "Then I came here."

For one guilty moment I thought he would apologize again for crashing the party, but instead he said, "I need to take it into the lab, but I wanted you and Knute to look at it first."

It must have been a cue. I looked up to see the giant lumber toward us. Maybe he'd seen the look of dismay on my face, but more likely he'd been waiting for Carlos to leave so he could talk to Thom. They'd become good friends on our last case and, as much as I hated to admit it, Knute regularly saw more of Thom than I did.

Now he shook the detective's hand, cast a toothy grin my direction, and said, "It's about time you got here, Thom. Delano bet me our boss lady would wimp out on issuing an invitation, but I knew better."

I probably sank a couple of inches into the ground while I waited for Thom to squeal on me. I should have known he wouldn't do it.

"Long day," Thom said. "And it's not over yet." He took the bag from me and passed it to Knute. "I found this on the door at Nightshade a couple of hours ago."

Thank goodness the marigold and note were so engrossing. Otherwise Knute would have wondered why Thom had gone by Nightshade when, if I'd invited him to the party, he'd have known we were closed.

"Does the handwriting look familiar to either of you?" Thom asked.

I said "yes" at the same time Knute said "no."

"You can identify it?" Thom asked me.

"No," I admitted slowly, "but it does look a little familiar." I leaned toward Knute to study it more closely. "Or not."

"Maybe we can narrow it down," Thom said. "Who do you know who carries a knife?"

"Huh?" I had no idea what a knife had to do with hand-writing identification, and I said so.

"The marigold was cut, not picked," Thom said.

Knute nodded. "See how the end of the stem is a perfect diagonal? If the marigold had been picked, the edges would be torn."

"Maybe it was cut with scissors rather than a knife," I said to try to appear more observant and/or better trained in forensics than I am. I should have known better than to make an attempt on either count.

"Scissor blades would have pinched the stem," Knute said. "This flower was cut with a knife. A very sharp knife by the looks of it."

Thom was still waiting for an answer to his question, but he'd have to wait longer. Vader had returned and he'd come armed and dangerous.

"Three chili rellenos and a root-beer float!" Arjay announced, holding the plate aloft. Despite the mask's distortion I could hear the satisfaction in my little brother's voice. He considered his mission well executed.

I frowned in dismay at the foamy, congealed mess on the plate. The real Darth Vader wouldn't have served something that unappetizing to a Rebel prisoner.

Arjay saw my displeasure and moved the plate away from me and closer to Thom. "The drink sloshed on the plate a little on the way over," he admitted. "But if the rellenos are cold, you can blame Mom. She kept saying she wanted to get the food for you herself, but every time she picked up a plate somebody interrupted her."

That's my mother. She has more good intentions in an hour than most people have in a week, but she's easily distracted.

"Thanks, Arjay," Thom said, taking the plate.

It was tempting to see if Thom Casey was nice enough to eat the mess to keep from hurting Arjay's feelings. But since I was pretty certain he was, I said quickly, "Arjay, would you do something for me—for Nightshade, I mean? Something very important and top secret." Although I couldn't see his eyes through the dark lens of the mask, I was confident they had lit up. Arjay is much like I was at his age—excited by anything to do with detective work and anxious to grow up and join Uncle Eddie's firm.

"Sure!" he said. "What?"

I took the evidence bags back from Knute. I returned the one with the marigold to Thom, but showed the one with the note to Arjay.

He read the words quickly. "Cool!"

I almost smiled. "This is official police evidence. You have to promise me you won't open the bag."

"I won't!" Arjay said.

Seeing that I was about to entrust an eleven-year-old with a note that could have come from a serial killer, Thom started to object. Knute's beefy hand on his arm was all the reassurance he needed.

"I know you won't open it," I told Arjay. "I know I can trust you." I handed him the bag. "I want you to take this into Shady Acres to Mom's office and make a copy of it. Just lay it on the machine, bag and all, okay? The copier will work right through the plastic."

"Okay!"

I had to grab Darth's cape to slow him down long enough to finish giving instructions. "There's one more thing. You can't let anybody see this. Not anybody. It's top secret, remember? And you can't—"

"I won't tell *anybody* about it!" Arjay said, finishing my sentence. "Not ever, Sam!"

I released his cape and he turned to run. Then, remembering that he was now a duly authorized Nightshade detective on a top-secret mission, he stuck the bag under his cape and sauntered with exaggerated nonchalance toward the main building of the assisted-living facility. He might have whistled, too, if he'd known how.

Thom was still frowning after Arjay when I removed the plate from his hands and left to ditch it in the nearest trash can. I'd scarcely returned from my mission of mercy when the sound of Delano's arrival drowned out the dance music. He pulled his

Harley up to the curb, removed his helmet as he dismounted, then turned to help Catwoman off the back.

I looked at the passenger and my eyes narrowed. She looked exactly how I wanted to look in black. When she removed her helmet and I saw the stylish red hair, I'm afraid I might have hissed. "Why did Delano bring *her?*"

"Amber?" Thom said, following my line of vision. "I guess they must have hit it off when Delano brought your hearse into the forensics garage the other night."

Delano was headed toward the dance area when Amber caught sight of Thom and steered Delano our direction instead. The introduction of Amber to Knute was scarcely complete before Knute told Delano he owed him ten dollars.

Delano grinned at Thom and then turned back to Knute with a shrug. "I'd have bet you a hundred bucks she wouldn't have the nerve to ask him," he said. "Good thing for me you're cheap."

I watched Delano reach for his wallet, and I tried to let him pay up, promising myself I'd slip an extra ten dollars of my own money into his next paycheck, but integrity got the best of me. (I was in Young Women for six years. At fifty-two weeks a year that's three hundred and twelve recitations of the values in the YW theme, not counting all the times we said it at girls' camp, conferences, etc. I guess you could say it sunk in.)

"I was *going* to invite Thom," I told Knute miserably. I turned to the detective. "Honest! I was going to call you. I was—"

"Waiting for a hard freeze in the nether regions?" Delano asked with the wolfish grin I'd come to hate at times like this. He put the bill back in his wallet and held out a hand for the one Knute now owed him.

"You didn't invite Thom?" Knute asked in the tone of voice he'd used when I was six and had done something naughty enough to warrant a time-out atop Uncle Eddie's unicorn.

Of all the people to come to my rescue, it was Amber. But I don't think she spoke up with any intention of saving me embarrassment. I think she was taking advantage of an opportunity to flirt with Thom. For sure she had taken hold of his hand—the one with the marigold still in it. "Taking your work home now, Detective?" she purred.

"You've done some work on the Marigold case," Thom said, turning his hand over so the bag fell into Amber's soft palm. "What can you tell me about this?"

Amber looked down reluctantly. I knew how she felt. It's the way I always feel tearing my eyes away from Thom's face.

Delano didn't miss what was going on. He put his wallet away and slipped his arm possessively around Amber's shoulder. Or maybe he did miss it. Maybe he had another agenda altogether because he was looking toward Chaiya to see if she had noted his arrival.

She hadn't. She was dancing with Zoodaboogle.

"It was cut," Amber said, examining the marigold's stem. "By a razor blade, a scalpel, or an exceptionally sharp knife." She looked up at Thom. "Just like—"

The CSI tech caught herself in time, but I suspected she was going to say, "Just like the ones found on the bodies." If that were true, it was a detail the police hadn't shared with the public. Probably one of many details.

Amber continued to examine the flower, turning the bag over in her hand. "But it's not the same flower, Detective. The others were *Tagetes temurfolia,* and this is a *Tagetes erectus,* I think." Dumbing it down for us amateurs she explained, "That's two different types of plant. The first is commonly known as a Mexican marigold. The second is American in origin. She returned the flower to Thom with a small, self-congratulatory smile on her full lips. "Is there a reason you ask?"

"Yes," he said.

By the time Thom had briefed Amber and Delano on what he'd found on Nightshade's door, Arjay had completed his second assignment.

"Thanks," I said, taking the newly minted copy from my brother and sticking it in the pocket of my trench coat. I gave the bag with the original back to Thom. "You did good, Arjay."

"Do you have another job for me?" the Darth clone asked hopefully.

I thought of the plate he'd brought Thom and turned to Amber. "Are you hungry? Arjay would be happy to bring you something from the buffet."

This wasn't as wicked as it sounds. One look at that woman's prominent hip bones was enough to assure me that she would refuse. (I have a theory that people who look like her exist solely on kelp and bottled water.)

"I'd love any food you want to bring me!" Amber exclaimed.

Okay then, maybe it *was* a little wicked. "He'll bring chili rellenos," I warned her. "With extra cheese."

"Wonderful!" she said. "Sour cream?"

I swallowed. "Uh, yes. Do you want a root-beer float?"

Amber laughed. "Bring it on. I haven't eaten since six."

Six yesterday? The day before yesterday? The Tuesday before that? I was still wondering about the dietary habits of the thin and fabulous when Amber explained breezily that she had a "very fast metabolism."

Right. I'd read about women who can eat like hippopotami and never gain an ounce. But only in fiction. Fiction written by men, come to think about it.

"I'll get it for you!" Arjay said. In a swirl of cape he was off again.

"So this is the note, I take it," Amber said, moving nearer to Thom to take a look.

"Yes!" I said, taking the bag from his fingers and thrusting it at her so she wouldn't have an excuse to stand so close. Despite myself, I hated Amber. Or perhaps I only loved Thom.

"We can lift prints from the paper," Amber told him, retaking her ground at Thom's elbow. "If there are any." She fluttered her long, thick lashes up at him. "It would have been better if you'd called me to the scene to see how this was placed on the door. I could have taken prints."

Better for who? I wondered.

Thom didn't respond but reached into his pocket and showed her the camera. Then he showed her an evidence bag that contained prints he had lifted from the door himself.

"Why, Tennyson!" she purred. "You might be as good as everyone says you are."

I couldn't very well scratch Amber, but maybe I could kick Delano. Twice. I wanted to kick him once for bringing her, and then I wanted to kick him again for mooning over Chaiya instead of being attentive enough to notice that his date was flirting with my date.

(Dear reader, I know what you're thinking. You're thinking that Thom wasn't exactly my date. But he was *there,* wasn't he? How many times have you read that motive and opportunity add up to murder? Well, I'm here to tell you that romantic motive and miraculous opportunity can also add up to a night to kill. This could still turn into a date if I could keep Thom at the party long enough. And get rid of Amber.)

"Do you know anyone who carries a knife?" Amber asked me.

I started, thinking she had read my mind. (Not that I'd meant "get rid of her" in the classic sense usually favored by mystery writers.) Then I realized it was the same question Thom had asked me earlier.

"Delano carries a knife," I said. "He's the only one I know who does. But his handwriting is way different from what's in the note. Whoever wrote that writes much . . . loopier . . . than Delano."

How was that for a scientific definition? Now I wanted to kick myself.

Amber smiled. It was clearly no secret to her that I was no competition professionally . . . personally . . . period.

"Not that I think Delano *did* write it," I added lamely.

"Thanks loads for the vote of confidence," he said.

"But you said it looks familiar," Thom reminded me.

"And then I said, 'Or not,'" I reminded him.

"Maybe it's handwriting that you see rarely," Knute suggested. "There must be some reason it rang a bell. Think, Sam."

Think? I'm not overly adept at that under the best of circumstances, and he wanted me to do it while standing next to the perfect Amber with Thom looking at us both? Not likely.

"It doesn't look familiar to me," Delano said, leaning over Amber's shoulder to examine the evidence bag. "All I can say for sure is that it was written with a felt-tip pen."

"A roller ball, I think," Amber said. "See the indentation there—and the little splotch at the beginning of the *s?* Classic roller ball."

Next she'd tell us the person who had used the pen was a left-handed, arthritic dwarf.

"Probably written by somebody who is right-handed," she said. "And most likely long-fingered and dexterous."

I'm not even a good guesser.

"That's pretty good," Delano told her admiringly, but his eyes were on the other side of the lawn. The dance had ended and Chaiya was on her way to the punch bowl. "Hey, what say we check out that buffet table for ourselves? Arjay's a good enough kid, but I bet he makes a lousy waiter."

"Um, all right," Amber agreed with thinly veiled reluctance.

"Take your time!" I urged them. "Eat. Dance. Talk to people. Play a game or two of Yahtzee."

"You'll be with Sam, right?" Delano asked Thom. Then the grin returned as he remembered why he'd won ten bucks. He looked up at Knute. "You better keep an eye on her."

"Yeah," Knute said. "And I'll make a strong suggestion that she sleep here this weekend. We can reevaluate the situation come Monday."

"I don't need a babysitter!" I said, wishing I had a dollar for every time I'd said that since joining the staff at Nightshade. I'd surely have a fortune to spend on liposuction—or whatever else it took to look enough like Catwoman to captivate a certain tall, fair detective we both knew and salivated over.

"I'll be here a while longer," Thom said.

I changed my mind in half a flash. I will gladly be babysat every night for the rest of my life—and then some—if Thom Casey will only volunteer to do it.

My heart swelled in surprise and joy. It might have burst if he'd been looking deep into my eyes when he said he'd stay. Instead, Thom was looking down at the evidence bags.

Chapter 17

"The peculiar thing is the marigold," Thom said.

He had not only remained at the Harvest Ball, he'd sat back down—a miracle I can only attribute to the last fourteen wishes on my favorite wishing star.

But I'm not superstitious.

A few minutes later my mother turned up with Arjay and the platter of food she'd wanted to bring Thom since he'd arrived. After chatting for a few minutes, she left, taking Arjay with her. She looked as if she'd like to take Knute as well.

I love my mother.

"The marigold is meant to make the note more threatening," Knute said.

"I don't know," Thom replied. "I agree that the flower is punctuation, but I'm not sure it's a threat. I wonder if it might be meant as warning from somebody who cares for Sam and wants her to be careful."

"Like who?" Knute asked.

I knew who Thom suspected—or thought I did—but waited to see if he would admit it himself.

"Who knew you were in San Rafael?" Thom asked me instead of answering Knute's question. "And who knew they could leave you the note tonight without being seen because they also knew Nightshade would be closed?"

If he could ignore questions, so could I. I was not going to name Carlos no matter how broad his hint. "The note writer could have gone up sometime during the day," I said. "Everybody knows we're closed days."

"The flower shop downstairs is open," Thom pointed out. "Leaving the note after five when there's nobody around to run into on the stairs would have been smarter."

Knute had been looking back and forth as if we were playing verbal table tennis. At last he said to Thom, "You think it was Carlos Diego."

The detective didn't respond.

"Just because I told Carlos that Chaiya and I had been to the mission and then invited him to the party doesn't mean he's the one who left the note!" My voice was a little louder than what is natural in conversation. This was happening a lot when Thom and I discussed Brother Simon.

"No," Thom agreed. "That's circumstantial. As are the marigolds—*Tagetes patula and erecta*—that grow outside the rectory where he lives."

I bristled. "Why do you think Carlos is lying?"

"I don't necessarily think Brother Simon is lying," Thom said evenly. "But I do think he's careful to tell only half of what he knows—if that."

"You think he's protecting someone?" Knute asked.

"Probably," Thom said. "Possibly himself."

"How can you say that?" I protested. It was remarkably easy all of a sudden to ignore the fact that I'd thought the same thing myself that morning. "He's a *monk!*"

"I wasn't sure you'd noticed."

What did that mean? I blinked twice but the meaning wasn't any clearer.

"The cross is pretty hard to miss," I said sarcastically.

"When he knows where it is," Thom said.

"Carlos didn't lose his cross in the mission," I pointed out. "He had it on tonight."

"He didn't lose that one," Thom agreed. "But here's an interesting piece of trivia I picked up recently: those crosses are made by a group of Franciscans in Italy and worn throughout the order. I'd hazard a guess that every brother has a spare or two."

"Then they're common," I said. "Anybody could have lost it in San Rafael."

"Right," Thom said. "Anybody who's a Franciscan monk working in downtown Phoenix, Arizona. There must be . . . how many would you say, Sam?"

I hadn't cornered the market on sarcasm. I looked down at the table. "It doesn't make sense. You'll never convince me that Carlos Diego is the Marigold Murderer."

"No," Thom said. "I'd never try to. I've never thought it."

Knute leaned forward onto the card table. It didn't break under his considerable weight, but it caved a little. "But you think he knows something about the serial killer."

"Not necessarily," Thom said. "But he knows something about something—the victims, the mission—something he doesn't want to share. He's very interested in gathering all the information he can, but he never volunteers anything himself."

As much as I hated to admit it, Thom was right. Whereas Carlos had practically pumped me for information, he had been evasive about my questions in return. And the things he had told me— about Father Rodriguez being too sick to talk to me that morning— might not have been true. They weren't true, according to Thom.

"You talked to Father Rodriguez?" I said.

Thom nodded. "Briefly. He seemed in a hurry."

"And he told you he hasn't been sick?"

"Not in so many words," Thom said. "I said I'd been trying to reach him, and he apologized and said he'd been out caring for the needs of his parishioners. On the other hand, he didn't look well at all."

"Maybe he got up out of his sickbed. I'm sure he's worried about the Batistas and José."

"He has reason to be."

My next breath caught in my throat. "You don't think José will be the next victim of the Marigold Murderer, do you, Thom?"

"This isn't public knowledge," the detective replied, "and Lasovik doesn't put much credence in my theory, but I've been able to link most of the victims to Antonio Batista—at least tenuously." My eyes widened as he continued. "The first man killed was from the same Mexican village. The fourth did some day work with him digging ditches. I can't determine for sure that Batista knew the second victim, but they were both recently in Mexico and returned to Phoenix on the same day and at the same border crossing."

"And the third victim?" Knute asked.

"Nothing yet," Thom admitted. "There were no personal effects on the body besides clothing. We couldn't even make an ID until the family came forward after the report hit the news."

"The link could be his green card," I guessed. "Maybe it was a forgery. Maybe Antonio's was a forgery too—like José's."

"There is no green card," Thom said, but he nodded, so I knew I was thinking along the right lines. "The victim and his family were undocumented."

Knute let out a long breath, and distaste swept over his gentle face. "Then you're dealing with a coyote."

"Or a vigilante," Thom said. "The execution style of murder could go either way, but the mutilation is probably too time-consuming for a coyote. A vigilante might do it thinking he's making a point."

Knute nodded.

(A note to readers who don't live in a border state and may think a coyote is a wolflike scavenger of the desert: you're right. But there's another kind of coyote: a two-legged variety that preys on people too uneducated to have any idea how to immigrate legally into the U.S. They bring naïve Mexican nationals across the desert illegally, charging exorbitant fees and often abandoning them to death at the first sign of trouble. There's nothing worse than a coyote. Unless it's a self-appointed vigilante with a warped sense of justice.)

I was terrified for José and for the two women who relied on him now that Antonio was dead. And I was terrified for Carlos as well. He was, after all, doing all he could to help the people the killer hated. Would that make him a target as well? "Does Carlos know where José and the Batistas are?" I asked Thom.

He frowned. "Before I talked to him tonight I'd have said yes, but judging by the way he reacted, I might have been wrong."

"Maybe he went to find them," I worried aloud. "We should have gone with him, Thom. If Carlos does know something, he's in danger too."

"Brother Simon is okay," Thom said. In the next breath he added, "I wouldn't tell you that if I didn't believe it."

I believed him. Or maybe I only wanted to believe him.

I sat in silence, thinking. Worrying. Obsessing. Antonio Batista might be a link to the serial killer, and I was a link to Antonio Batista. How many people had I unwittingly put in danger? I'd taken Thom, a Phoenix police officer, to the Batistas' home because I was too big a coward to go by myself. Had that caught the attention of the wrong people and added to the bereaved family's peril? Or had Thom's taking José's green card caused them all to disappear because they feared deportation more than anything else? And what about Carlos? I was also responsible for making Thom suspect him of . . . whatever he suspected.

I wanted to kick myself. I should have handled my own problems instead of relying on Thom for help. At the very least I should have thought it through a little better before dropping the cross from San Rafael off at the police station. If something terrible happened to José, the Batistas, or Brother Simon, it would be my fault.

My horror never reached full bloom because another thought—a random one—kept niggling for attention at the edge of my consciousness. I stopped obsessing long enough to try to pinpoint it. It didn't have to do with the disappearance of Antonio Batista's body. It wasn't anything to do with José Gutierrez's phony green card either. It was . . . what? In the next second I had it. It was the cross! I switched on my internal DVD player to call up the two interviews I'd had with Father Rodriguez. Then I asked Thom, "Was the priest wearing a silver cross tonight?"

"Brother Simon?" Thom said. He looked unhappy that we were back to that topic. "Yes, but—"

"No," I interrupted. "Father Rodriguez. When you saw him tonight, was he wearing a silver cross like Brother Simon's?"

"No," Thom said. "The cross he wore was wooden and on a gold chain. It looked handmade—probably Mexican."

"But I think he *did* have a silver cross," I said. "I think he was wearing it when he first came to Nightshade for help. He may have been wearing it when he took me on the tour of San Rafael." I looked down at my lap, unable to say the rest out loud. The priest may have lost the cross then—the cross Chaiya later found. If that was the case, my abysmal powers of observation and/or memory might have caused Thom to start bulldozing mountains out of molehills.

"*Now* you think Father Rodriguez had a cross like Brother Simon's," Thom said. He looked as though he expected me to next remember that I'd seen little green men wearing them too.

When I nodded, Knute frowned along with Thom. "Then why didn't you mention it when Thom asked you about it last night?"

"Because . . . I'm stupid."

I didn't actually say that because it wasn't entirely true. I didn't tell the truth either. The truth is that I'm scatterbrained around Detective Casey. There is something about that man that immediately transports part of me back to those excruciatingly awkward days of junior high. (I don't remember Ned Nickerson affecting Nancy Drew this way, do you?) That, added to the surprise of seeing what I thought was Carlos's cross and fearing the worst, had made me duller than usual.

"Why, Sam?" Knute asked again when I didn't respond.

"Because I'm stupid!" I said after all.

"No," Thom said. "I caught you off guard and made you defensive of your friend. You're a good detective, Sam."

I looked up at him in amazement and gratitude and wished Knute weren't there so I could have kissed him. Not that I would have. (I wasn't brave enough to invite him to the party, remember?)

Knute saw through me as usual. He pushed out his chair and said he wanted to get some guacamole to go with his taquitos, but I knew I wouldn't see him again until Thom left.

That wouldn't happen anytime soon. Not if my name was Sam Spade.

I mean Samantha Shade.

Whatever.

Chapter 18

I overslept the next evening, but when I finally woke I didn't get out of bed. Why get up and do anything else when I could lie there daydreaming about Thom Casey? No, all my secret hopes and dreams hadn't come true overnight, but they were close.

All right—closer.

Thom hadn't been in a hurry to leave even after Knute excused himself. When he had eaten, I managed to drag him up from the table and off for a round of introductions. He talked for quite some time to my father (who usually disappears into the shadows at the first threat of conversation with a nonscientist) and played a couple of games of glow-in-the-dark table tennis with Arjay. Then—and this is the part you've been waiting for—when I walked him down the driveway to finally say good night, he kissed me.

Yes, ma'am (or sir)! Dreamboat Detective Thomas Casey kissed me smack dab on the . . . cheek.

But it was incredible. For about ten seconds from the time his lips left my skin I had no heartbeat, no pulse, and no brain activity whatsoever. Fortunately, Thom carries within him a unique form of resuscitation. Before he walked away he raised his hand to the spot he had kissed. It was as if a bolt of electricity flowed through my temple into every cell in my body. My heart beat again—wildly. If Dr. Frankenstein had had Thom's touch, he wouldn't have had to wait for lightning storms.

Obviously, I hadn't been able to fall asleep, even after eight more hours of party and another eight hours of helping my mother clean up from the party. When I finally did sleep I dreamed about . . . I probably don't have to finish that sentence.

And this brings us back to where this chapter began—me lying on the bed going over every one of Thom's sentences . . . words . . . nuances. Well, that and fantasizing about what could have happened if I'd had the presence of mind to turn my lips toward him just before that kiss.

I knew I should get up. I always get up super early on Saturdays—say four in the afternoon or so—so I will be able to take a nap the next time a four rolls around on the digital clock. I need to nap at 4:00 A.M. because my singles ward meets at noon. Most people think a later meeting time is great, but most people aren't nocturnal. Imagine if *you* had to go to church from midnight to 3:00 A.M. That's what time church feels like to me. I consider it a good Sabbath when I don't fall asleep in Gospel Doctrine class. I consider it an even better one when the class doesn't fall asleep. (I'm the teacher.)

I stretched, thought about Thom, and closed my eyes again with a happy sigh.

"Hey!" Arjay shouted, banging on the door. "Mom wants to know if you're alive in there. It's seven o'clock."

Despite what I'd told Knute about not needing a babysitter, I'd spent the night at my parents' house, after all. This wasn't because I was afraid of somebody lurking in the shadows to menace me with marigolds and roller-ball pens. It was because Chaiya had invited her mother to stay at our apartment on one of the rare weekends Karma was in town, and I wanted to give the two of them time alone.

Sure I did. I'd have spent the night in San Rafael with the ghost if that's what it took to avoid listening to Aunt Karma wonder aloud what was wrong with Thom.

"Sammy!" Arjay said.

"I'm up!" I said, rolling sideways and putting my feet on the floor so it would look like I'd told the truth when my suspicious little brother opened the door to check.

He didn't open the door. He was in too big of a hurry to get next door. "Consuela's here!" he called on his way downstairs. "She's making sopapillas."

My mother's right-hand woman at Shady Acres, Consuela Ramon, is internationally famous for her sopapillas. A Mexican delight that is in the same food family as scones, this fried bread is a miracle unto itself. Consuela mixes the dough with Mexican vanilla and then drenches the fried pillows in honey, cinnamon, and a couple of other spices she won't divulge. Believe me, they are to die for—not only delicious, but light enough to float right off your plate.

"I'm on my way!" I called back, already salivating. I knew I'd better get next door before Arjay, my dad, and the Shady Acres residents left me nothing more than a heavenly aroma.

Within ten minutes I was dressed and seated in the spacious, industrial-style (but dimly lit on account of Arjay) kitchen at Shady Acres. My parents' house has a perfectly good kitchen, of course, and we usually eat at home, but never when Consuela makes sopapillas.

By the time I'd grabbed my first piece of puffy perfection, honey dripped from Arjay's chin onto his shirt. My father wasn't faring much better. I was clearly several sopapillas behind and falling back fast. (In case you're wondering, sopapillas *were* on my new diet. Why not? Anything light enough to float off a plate couldn't possibly be fattening. Right?)

"I liked Thom," my mother said from the far side of the room where the light was bright enough for her to work. "He seems very nice."

"And," Consuela added from the stove, "he wasn't half bad to look at."

I grinned back at her.

My father looked up from the newspaper. "I liked him too. What's wrong with him?"

I rolled my eyes. "Nothing's wrong with Thom, Dad. Since when do you listen to Karma?"

One eyebrow rose and he went back to scanning the article. It was his way of saying, "Good point."

"Detective Casey's great!" Arjay declared. He loves to have the definitive word on a subject. "He plays a mean game of table tennis. But did you know he *reads* books instead of waiting for them to be made into movies?"

This was directed at me and, yes, I knew it. It was one of the idiosyncrasies I tried to overlook. Another was Thom's tendency to quote dead authors in lieu of carrying on conversation like normal people.

Hey! I thought suddenly. *Maybe that's what was wrong enough with Thom to keep him from being married.*

No, I told myself in the next second. *There are bound to be women out there who read as many classics as he does.*

But . . . the little voice in my head continued . . . *maybe they never hooked up because of that no-talking-in-libraries rule. Maybe—*

"I'm gonna be a detective when I grow up," Arjay said, breaking into my thoughts. "Like Detective Casey."

"You mean you're going to be a private detective at Nightshade," I said with a smile. How many times had he told me that? At least as often as I'd told my Uncle Eddie the same thing when I was a girl.

"Nah," Arjay said. "I'm gonna be a cop like Thom." Seeing that I was hurt, he added, "Have you seen his gun?"

My father glanced up in concern. "Have you, Arjay?"

"No," my brother admitted. "But I bet it's way cool! Sam doesn't carry a gun."

"Let's hope not!" my mother exclaimed.

Let's change the subject, I thought. My parents love me and want me to be happy, but they make no secret of the fact they think I'm in the wrong line of work. I once overheard my father tell Eddie that he hoped he'd close Nightshade when he retires instead of turning it over to me. My parents want me to work at and eventually take over the other family business—Shady Acres.

"When is Eddie due back?" my father asked before I had thought of another subject to introduce.

"Wednesday."

"Good."

I didn't know whether it was or not. On one hand I adore my Uncle Eddie and have missed him like crazy. On the other hand I've loved being interim head of Nightshade. And what if he *did* close the office? What would I do then?

Now that I'd been so rudely reminded that my day of reckoning was about ninety-six hours away, I wondered how my performance would look in my uncle's estimation. Setting down the sopapilla, I used my sticky fingers to mark the plus and minus columns that were forming in my head.

On the plus side, Nightshade was still operating and we had about the same number of clients as usual—maybe a few more because of the time of year. In other words, I hadn't dragged the business under quite as fast as Delano had predicted and I had feared. Moreover, I had busted that sleazy city councilman and thereby received great publicity for the firm.

I stared at the plate for a minute, then picked up my sopapilla again. There were probably more triumphs to add to my list, but my innate modesty prevented me from thinking of them right off the top of my head.

Yeah, that was it.

On to the negative column. A certain priceless Egyptian mummy had gone missing on my watch, but that wasn't all my fault. Besides, I think I could have found it if I'd really wanted to. But there was a "ghost" on the loose in San Rafael that I couldn't find no matter how hard I tried. Plus, the establishment next door was still missing one dearly departed, and I winced every time I remembered that Antonio Batista had departed (the second time) in Uncle Eddie's hearse. I had to get his body back before Uncle Eddie came home and was met on the front stoop by his lifelong friend Sully Meyers.

I had to.

I looked up at the clock, dismayed to see that it was almost nine already. I wanted to call Knute and Delano and get a little work done before Saturday night turned into Sunday morning.

Uncle Eddie is very strict about not conducting business on the Sabbath. He won't even work a case at midnight Monday morning, but waits to reopen Nightshade at eight Monday evening. He doesn't work Saturday nights either, unless it is in the interest of keeping the ox out of the mire.

I figured the mire around my ox was deep and wide enough to require a little pre-midnight action on my part. My two colleagues had been investigating the Tuckers and the staff at Rest in Peace. Hopefully one or both of them would have something to report.

By the time I'd returned to my room for my cell phone, it was ringing. Since it was playing a melody from *Looney Tunes*, I knew the caller was Chaiya.

"Can I borrow some of your clothes?" she asked as soon as I'd flipped up the top of the phone and before I'd said hello. "I have a date with LeVar tonight."

"And you want to wear something of *mine?*" Something was wrong there. "Chaiya, do you have a concussion?" As you know, I wear black, basically. (Or if you prefer, basic black.) My cousin despises black. If a garment is of a hue not appearing in a rainbow, Chaiya won't touch it.

"Yes, I want to wear something of yours," she said. "And no, I don't have a condition. Really, Sammy. If anybody should be worried about sharing our clothes it's me. Remember that rash you—"

"Never mind," I said.

"Some of the stuff at the back of your closet almost fits me," she said as if that would be a selling point. Presumably she meant that she'd already tried on my "skinny clothes" and they were only a size too big. "I'm a desperate woman, Sammy."

"Flattery" would get her everywhere. "Take anything you want, I guess." Then I asked, "Where are you going, anyway?"

"You don't remember?"

"You told me already?" Then I remembered that she *had* told me and I did remember. I sat down on the bed. "Chaiya, you're not really going to the cemetery to ghost hunt, are you?"

"Where else would I wear your clothes?"

"That's creepy," I said, ignoring yet another slam on my wardrobe.

"I know it!" she said happily. "But I'll be home by eleven forty-five. The Spirit goes to bed at midnight."

I wondered if the Spirit went to cemeteries. I supposed it did—when dragged there by insane innocents like my cousin. Next I wondered how to end our conversation so I could call Delano. My customary "have fun" wouldn't cut it tonight.

"Aren't you going to wish me luck?" Chaiya said.

"No." Who knew what kind of luck Chaiya was hoping for in a graveyard? I sighed. "Why don't you go see a movie tonight like eighty percent of the dating couples in America?"

"In *your* clothes?" Chaiya said. "Please!"

I hung up on her. But after I did I said a quick prayer that she'd be safe and LeVar Zabloudil would be sane. I couldn't pray for sanity for Chaiya—some things are too much to ask for.

I pressed the speed dial for Delano's cell. He answered on the second ring. "Did you get a chance to talk to the Tuckers?" I asked, knowing that Delano isn't much on hi-how-are-yous, or phone conversation of any kind.

"Yeah," he said. "I saw Ralph and Count Creepazoid yesterday. I didn't get a chance to tell you at the party." I waited for him to go on. "That kid creeps me out, you know?"

I couldn't help but smile. I'd learned in a psychology class in college about the mirror effect. It's a theory that says traits we find the most off-putting in others are often characteristics we possess ourselves. In this case Delano's statement was a little like Lon Chaney criticizing Bela Lugosi for making a different kind of horror movie.

When I didn't respond, Delano said, "Get this, Sam—the kid was wearing gloves. Black leather gloves."

I knew what he was aiming at. CSI hadn't found any prints in Sully's morgue or on our hearse that didn't belong there.

"There are a hundred cop shows on TV," I responded. "There couldn't possibly be anybody in America stupid enough to commit a crime these days without wearing gloves."

"He wears them all the time," Delano argued. "That's weird."

And so were Trey Tucker's red lips, white face, and long, flowing cape. But people who go around looking and acting weird don't necessarily go around doing wrong. I knew that better than most people. I asked, "Where was he on Monday night when the body disappeared?"

"He says he was partying with friends," Delano told me. "I haven't had a chance to check it out yet." After a pause he added, "But Ralph insists there's no way the kid could have come up with a key to Rest in Peace. He says he keeps all the keys to all the buildings he works at locked up with his cleaning supplies. They're in a metal box in the back of his truck."

"But where does he keep the key to that box?"

"Combination lock," Delano said. "I checked. Ralph swears he's the only one who knows the combination." His voice lowered. "He seemed real upset about me asking so many questions about Count Creepazoid."

Who could blame him? It couldn't be easy raising a teenage vampire when you were a hard-working conservative with a tendency toward narrow-mindedness. I didn't know who I pitied most—Ralph or Trey. As hard as it might be to have a Goth son, I doubted it was much easier for Trey to have a father like his. Of the two of them, I liked the soft-spoken Trey better than his oftentimes bigoted parent. I didn't know Trey all that well, but I'd read some of his poetry and it had led me to believe that the "vampirism" was for show. He didn't have a truly twisted bone in his body.

"I guess we'll have to check his alibi," I said.

"All over it," Delano responded. "And I'm heading over to the mission in a little while. I thought I'd hang out there for a couple of hours since we didn't stake it out at all last night."

I let out a sigh of gratitude. "Thanks, Delano. I hated to ask, but I'm sure glad you're doing it." Speaking of things I hated to ask, I wondered about the wisdom of the request I was about to make. Before he could hang up I took the plunge. "You know that old cemetery near the mission?"

"Around the corner, behind the tenement?"

"Yes. Could you . . . uh . . . could you swing past it a couple of times while you're in the area?"

"Something going down?"

"Chaiya is going to be there. She's ghost hunting again tonight. But, Delano," I hastened to add, "she's with a guy."

There was a brief pause. "Isn't she always?"

"You'll go by? But you'll be discreet."

"Discreet is my middle name."

"Don't forget that," I cautioned before hanging up to call Knute.

Delano *would* forget it, and asking that little favor would turn out to be one of the biggest mistakes I could have made. But I didn't know that then. I didn't know a lot of things. It would be another forty-eight hours before the pendulum swung the other direction and I tumbled into a pit of circumstances too ghastly to foretell.

Chapter 19

I hung up the phone and glanced at the clock in my room. There was still an hour or so before I needed to join my family for our midnight "lunch" and Sabbath family time after that. Good deal since I had more work to do.

I'd just finished talking to Knute. Like Delano, he didn't have much to report. He thought Roderick Harte was above suspicion, but had checked his alibi just in case. His "gut" told him that if either of Sully's two assistants had lent the ghouls a key or helped with the heist of Antonio Batista's body, it was Marty Poe. Normally I would say that a gut isn't much to go on, but since it's Knute's entrails we're talking about, I listened to what he had to say.

Besides being more nervous at being questioned than Knute thought was common or called for, Poe couldn't recall where he'd been on Monday night, though he promised to call us when he "remembered." He also had a new bicycle chained outside his more-than-modest apartment.

That was about as incriminating as Trey's party and black gloves in my opinion, but when Knute suggested we put a tail on Marty to see if he picked up any more expensive toys, I agreed. Knute's a little too large to shadow someone himself, so I called in one of our part-timers—a college guy newly home from a mission—and asked him to start Monday night when Marty got off work.

Since that was as far as I could get on the Batista case in the middle of the night, I next pulled out the copy of the note Thom had found at Nightshade. I wanted to study the handwriting again after a good day's sleep to see if something new jumped out at me.

Nothing did.

I sat down at the desk, opened my laptop, and logged on. I knew researching marigolds would be a long shot, but a long shot was better than no shot at all. Besides, if nothing else, maybe I could learn something interesting and intelligent to drop casually into conversation with Thom the next time the Marigold Murders came up.

The search engine gave me almost fifty hits. There was more to know about marigolds than I'd imagined. When I finished marveling over the millions of people who go to the time and effort to make all sorts of arcane information available online, I opened the first site that wasn't trying to sell me marigolds.

Botanical: Calendula officinalis (LINN) Family: N.O. Compositae

Too scientific. I couldn't remember any of that, no matter how hard I tried.

The next site was better.

"The common marigold is familiar to everyone," it began, "with its pale-green leaves and golden-orange flowers. It is said to be in bloom on the calends of every month, hence its Latin name." Okay, so it wasn't *much* better. I wondered what a *calend* was. Or at least when a calend was. Reading on, I learned that Old English authors called the flowers Mary Gowles or Oculus Christi. Old English authors? That might come in handy. Thom was familiar with a lot of authors. I'd remember those names for marigolds for sure.

The next site told me that marigolds were once used to give cheese a yellow color. Interesting, maybe, but useless.

The site after that caught my eye. According to the herbalist who wrote it, people once believed marigolds could endow a person with supernatural powers.

"It must be taken only when the moon is in the Sign of the Virgin and not when Jupiter is in the ascendant, for then the herb loses its virtue. And the gatherer, who must be out of deadly sin, must say three Paternosters and three Aves. It will then give the wearer a vision of anyone who has robbed him."

Wow. With vision like that I'd know who had stolen our hearse to heist Sully's client! Whimsically, I read the instructions again. I was almost sure I was "out of deadly sin" but the rest lost me. *Paternosters* and *Aves* sounded Catholic. I might be able to convince Brother Simon to help me out. But there was still the astrology stuff to consider. Neither of us would know *when* to gather marigolds and recite Aves.

I sighed, resigned to continuing detective work the hard way.

I skimmed several additional sites and learned that the marigold has long been associated with the Virgin Mary.

That's all I learned. I had nearly decided my time could be better spent lying on the bed daydreaming about Thom when a final site, way down at the bottom of the screen, caught my eyes and practically yanked them out of my head.

"*Cempazuchiles:* Yellow marigolds; symbols of death."

What do you want to bet I'd received one of *those?*

It took me two tries to get my finger to press the key that would take me to the site. When I did I was in Mexico. Specifically I was looking at an index of words associated with the Dia de los Muertos, or Day of the Dead.

I'd heard of that. It's an occasion when people—mostly Latin Americans—get together around Halloween to have something that looks from a distance like my mother's block party.

Turns out it's more than a block party.

I read the two pages quickly and learned that the Dia de los Muertos involves rituals that the indigenous people of Mexico have practiced for more than three thousand years. Even the arrival of conquistadors—and Spanish priests—couldn't eradicate the spirits of the old Aztecs. The best the Catholic Church could manage was to move the festival back a few months to make it coincide with All Saints' Day and All Souls Day (November 1 and 2), thus turning it into a Christian holy day. It is still celebrated, according to the writer, in Mexico, parts of Central America, and a few southwestern states in the U.S.

States like Arizona. There had to be more localized information on the Net. I hit more buttons, looking for customs that fell closer to home. I was amazed at how many sites I found, and the quality of them. There was even a place where I could print out a children's packet featuring leering skull masks and the skeletal remains of house pets to color at my leisure.

Maybe later.

I read on and learned that Dia de los Muertos celebrations are alive and well in modern-day Arizona. People still fashion altars in their homes to honor the dead and offer them gifts of things the deceased loved in life. They decorate with elaborate tissue paper cut-outs (papel picado), bake sweet rolls topped with bits of dough shaped like bones (pan de muerto), and give their children candies in the shape of skulls—often with the kids' names carved into the foreheads. Then they gather together at cemeteries where there is la llorada—the weeping—but also at picnics and celebrations with dancers donning wooden skull masks (calacas) in honor of their deceased relatives.

Does that sound creepy to you? It did to me. But according to experts ranging from priests to anthropologists, Dia de los Muertos isn't macabre or scary. It's a "healthy, reassuring, and sometimes humorous" way to honor the dead and treat death itself as an "inevitable and welcome" part of life.

I wasn't convinced. Marigolds tied into this somehow, and despite the anthropologists' reassurances, death wasn't welcome in *my* life. Receiving a symbol of it anonymously a couple of days before Halloween, All Saints' Day, All Souls Day, and/or Dia de los Muertos *was* creepy.

I found a reference to marigolds farther down the page. The writer said that cempazuchiles have long been used on the Dia de los Muertos because of their pungent fragrance. People in the oldest villages in Mexico scatter marigold blossoms from the graves to the altars in their homes to help the dead find their way back to their families.

Excuse me for being culturally insensitive, but . . . *ick*.

I lowered the lid on my laptop, lost in thought. Did what I'd just learned cast any light on why someone had left *me* a marigold? Was it deeply symbolic in a way I didn't understand, or was it meant to make me think of the Marigold Murderer and thus be hyper-creeped out? In short, was it a threat, a taunt, or a caution?

There was no way to know.

Wondering about marigolds led me to wonder about the Marigold Murderer. What did he know about marigolds and the Day of the Dead? Was there a connection—or was it a coincidence? I mean, it might have been a coincidence. Maybe he used marigolds because that's what grew in his front yard. Or maybe he bought them at Home Depot because they're cheaper than roses from a florist.

I didn't want to think about it anymore. I couldn't think about it anymore. I set the laptop aside and went downstairs to help my mother prepare lunch.

* * *

By 6:00 A.M. Sunday morning my father had left for an early high council meeting and my mother and brother were napping before church. Arjay was probably only trying to nap. Sunday meetings are about the only time he goes out in the daylight, and then he goes so thoroughly swathed that he looks like the Invisible Man trying to stay visible. Arjay loves Sundays.

I wasn't sleepy either. Not even the knowledge that I'd probably be zonked by noon could slow my mind long enough for sleep to come. After almost an hour, I gave up and sat up. My cell phone was on the dresser, charging. (Miracles happen every day.) The fact that it hadn't rung all night was reassuring. It meant my prayers had been answered and Chaiya's cemetery date was uneventful.

At least that's what I believed at the time. Whoever said "ignorance is bliss" really knew what he was talking about.

Next to the phone was a small bundle wrapped in muslin: Manuel Sarasate's journal. I reached for it and sat back down on the bed. I'd never taken advantage of the rare opportunity to look at it, and this might be my last chance. Now that Father Rodriguez was well (if ever he'd been sick), I'd have to turn it over to him.

Once freed from its protective cloth, the old, handwritten book fell open in my lap. The pages were soft and brown, and the once-black ink had faded to sterling. Most remarkable was the calligraphy—handwriting so beautiful I couldn't help but run my finger over it. Every six or eight pages was a passage that Sarasate had bordered with vines, flowers, birds, and other intricate and exquisite designs. I paused for quite some time over a passage adorned with calla lilies: *Coeleste pulset ostium; Vitale tollat praemium: Vitemus omne noxium: Purgemus omne pessimum.*

Latin. I wished I could read it. Most likely it was a prayer or a psalm that had been particularly meaningful to the friar. Isn't that what Thom had said most of the book contained? But then hadn't he added that Sarasate recorded some of the day-to-day happenings at San Rafael? It was the latter I yearned most to read.

Not that my Spanish was much better than my Latin.

I turned a few pages and caught my breath at another drawing. This wasn't an illustrated verse. It was a sketch of a robed man holding a book while a raven perched on his shoulder. I'd seen it somewhere before.

San Rafael. It was a drawing of one of the saints who Sarasate would later bring to life in stone.

I flipped a few more pages and found more sketches of the saints. Most interesting to me were the woman with the rose and the man among the fishes at whose feet Chaiya had found the cross. I wanted to know more about them and I wanted to know it right then. Fortunately, I knew someone to ask.

Wrapping the book carefully, I took it next door to Shady Acres. Mr. Chavez was where I thought he'd be—in front of the large picture window in the common room watching the sun rise over the hump of majestic Camelback Mountain.

"Each new day is a thing of joy and beauty," he said as I pulled up a chair next to his wheelchair.

I nodded. The sunrise *was* beautiful, but I had come to him (and come to Earth, for that matter) with a one-track mind. Right now it was focused exclusively on the journal.

"Did you see Veronica on Friday night?" Mr. Chavez asked.

I shook my head, then changed it into a nod with the result that my face moved in circles. I couldn't remember if I'd seen her or not. Come to think of it, I had. When Thom and I stopped to say hello to Chaiya we'd heard Veronica still trying to convince her to give up ghost busting and return to beauty school. How could I have forgotten? At the time I'd wanted to kiss Veronica almost as much as I wanted to kiss Thom—but for different reasons, of course.

"She was beautiful," I told the proud grandfather.

He nodded. "And that new dress! Wasn't it lovely?"

"Gorgeous," I said honestly.

"She is doing very well," he confided. "She worries that I will outlive my ability to pay for my stay here, so she gives me money whenever she can."

Hard-earned money at that. I wondered if Mr. Chavez knew that his granddaughter moonlighted doing hair and makeup for corpses. Veronica Chavez was a braver woman than I'd ever be.

"Do you have a minute to give me?" I asked, hoping to distract him from his favorite subject, worthy as she was.

"For you, Samantha, I have all the remaining minutes the good Lord allots me."

I smiled. Mr. Chavez was well into his eighties, but still one of the most charming men on the planet. "Would you read something to me?" I asked. "Translate it, I mean."

Juan Chavez had been born in Mexico and raised in Phoenix, and he had spent his adult life teaching high school Spanish. For sure he could read Manuel Sarasate's personal entries. I passed him the cloth-covered bundle and explained briefly what it was.

He held it carefully, reverently. At last he opened to the frontispiece. It was a drawing of the mission as it must have looked when Sarasate arrived in 1858. "San Rafael," Mr. Chavez said as if it were a prayer.

I sat in silence as a minute or more passed. The old man gazed down at the picture in his lap but saw something more distant. His rheumy brown eyes sparkled.

"You know the mission," I said.

"I took First Communion there," he said. "Just before it was closed."

"I didn't know you're Catholic."

"It was a lifetime ago," Mr. Chavez said regretfully. "But the best of my lifetime, I think now."

I thought of what it must have been like to have seen San Rafael in its years of glory. I could scarcely imagine how grand the statues must have looked when clean, polished, and glowing in the light of day. "Do you remember the sanctuary? The saints?"

"Ah, yes!" He closed his eyes and a single tear navigated the canals on his face toward his chin. "Benedict, Rita, Jude, Luke, Dymphna, Anthony, and Mary, Our Blessed Mother." His fingers trembled as he used them to cross himself. The action was tentative, made by one long-accustomed to it, but longer out of practice.

"They're beautiful still," I assured him. "There are drawings of them in this journal. The artist sketched his ideas before sculpting them in granite."

"This book was penned by the friar who carved the statues?" Mr. Chavez's voice was low, as if it was too much to believe.

"Yes," I said. "He hid it inside the base of one of the statues. It was only recently discovered." I knew by his face that I'd better give some explanation for what I was doing with such a priceless treasure. "It belongs to Father Rodriguez—a local priest. He . . . lent . . . it to me. I need to give it right back, but I'd like to know more about it first."

I apparently wasn't the only one. Mr. Chavez turned pages and murmured to himself in Spanish. I watched him pore over the book for almost twenty minutes. I was dying to know what he read, but reluctant to interrupt when he was so clearly enraptured.

Finally, when he came to the illustrated verse I'd admired earlier, I pointed. "I wish I knew what that says."

The old man raised it closer and studied it in earnest. After a few moments his frown of concentration turned to a smile. "'So may we knock at Heaven's door, And strive the immortal prize to win, Continually and evermore, Guarded without and pure within.'"

I was too engrossed in words as beautiful as the artwork that surrounded them to realize he'd read Latin. When it finally sunk in, I remarked on it with admiration.

"I didn't read it so much as remember it," he admitted. "My mother took me to Vespers every Sunday and holy day. Vespers were sung in Latin. She taught them to me in our native language on the way home. When I started school, she insisted I memorize them in English as well."

"I understand that some of the entries are in Spanish," I said. "Have you read them? What did Sarasate write about?"

Much to my dismay, Mr. Chavez shrugged. "Day-to-day trivialities, Samantha. There is little more than a line or two here and there."

I felt vaguely let down. Then I wondered what I had expected in the first place. I guess I thought that since Manuel Sarasate had come from about the same time period as the "ghost," perhaps he'd known the friar who had committed suicide—the one some people believed still haunted San Rafael.

"Does he mention *any* people?" I asked.

"Only the padre," Mr. Chavez said. Seeing the look of disappointment on my face, he turned back a few pages. "No, I am wrong. He refers to a young Papago woman as a student of great promise. And there is another friar mentioned—an older man who Brother Vincent believes does not approve of him."

I assumed that Brother Vincent and Manuel Sarasate were one and the same—like Carlos Diego had become Brother Simon. "What did he write about them?" I pressed.

"He wrote very little besides quotations from the book of prayer," Mr. Chavez reminded me. But he was still a schoolteacher at heart, and finding me a rapt pupil, he added, "This is what I know from the little I've read: Brother Vincent thought Father Sebastian a good priest, very strict but devout. He knew that the other friar, a Brother Clemente, thought his artistry frivolous and his manner prideful. Brother Vincent was fond of a particularly bright student." He raised his hands. "That is all, Samantha. The only other person mentioned thus far is a sister—probably a nun—about whom he says only that she died tending the sick."

I nodded gratefully. "Will you look through the rest—to the end?"

"With great pleasure."

I watched as he did so. At first it was all I could do not to reach forward and turn the page when he lingered overlong at a picture or slipped into a reverie of childhood memories when a Latin word or phrase lit up a synapse. After a time, however, the book fell closed under his hand, and I realized that he'd only looked at two or three more pages before falling asleep.

I slipped the book from beneath the knotted fingers, patted Mr. Chavez's hand, and tucked his lap robe more securely around his withered legs. "Thank you," I whispered. On my way across the empty room, I turned to the last page, curious to see if there was a date there that would tell me how long Sarasate had kept this particular book. The last page was blank. The page before that was blank, and the page before that was blank as well. I flipped more pages. Why hadn't I noticed that the last dozen or more pages of precious paper had gone unused? Something had happened to Manuel Sarasate before he finished his journal.

But what?

I turned to the final entry and my hands began to shake. *Suplica para un Muerte Bien.*

I know a little Spanish. *Muerte* is Spanish for death. *Bien* is good. *Suplica* I didn't know, but assumed it came from the same root as *supplication.*

"Supplication for a good death?"

Had Manuel Sarasate fallen ill with the same malady that killed the nun?

What is "sick" in Spanish? I asked myself. *Enferma?* I looked at the pages preceding the last entry very carefully, but the word didn't appear. If he hadn't been sick enough to expect to die, why had he so carefully transcribed and illustrated the prayer for a good death?

And why was it the last thing he ever wrote?

I had to know.

Chapter 20

"Did I wake you?" I asked Thom when he mumbled something that might pass for "hello" into the phone. I knew it was still early Sunday morning, but I'd wanted to catch him before he left for church. Obviously I had.

"Sorry to call so early," I said. "This is Sam. Samantha Shade. From Nightshade. You know?"

Stupid. Stupid. Stupid. I was tempted to bang the phone against my forehead. *Why* couldn't I talk to that man like a grown-up?

"Yeah," he said. "I know." His voice was deep and still thick with sleep. "What's up?"

I'd already awakened him; I might as well press forward. I said, "Can I ask you something?"

"Sure. Ask me anything. Do you want the major themes of Shakespearean drama, or a brief but scintillating overview of the writings of William Butler Yeats?"

"Uh . . . no."

"No," he repeated. "Lasovik either. Alas, they remain the things I know best."

So he'd had a bad day—night?—at the office. Probably a string of them. "I'm sorry, Thom."

He let out a breath. Maybe it was a sigh. "What can I do for you, Samantha Shade from Nightshade?"

"Remember that journal you gave me to give to Father Rodriguez? The one found in San Rafael?"

"Uh-huh."

"Did you read it?"

"I glanced through it. When we determined it wasn't evidence, I turned it over to you."

"*Would* you read it?" I asked. "I . . . I need to know what it says."

"May I ask why?"

"I, uh, think it might shed some light on my case."

It was a beat or two before Thom responded. "So now *you* believe Sarasate is the ghost Chaiya recorded the other night?"

"No!" I said. "Of course not. Chaiya didn't record a ghost—just some static and a weird moaning sound. There isn't a ghost, Thom. I know that. But there *is* something."

Which, of course, couldn't possibly have anything to do with a 150-year-old journal. I knew Thom was thinking the same thing. "I want to know what Brother Vincent wrote in the book," I confessed. "I know you're busy, but there isn't much you'd have to read. Most of it, as you said, is psalms and stuff. I don't care about that—only his personal entries. I could drop it off at your apartment this morning, and you could look at it whenever you get a chance."

The silence that ensued was probably only a few seconds in duration, but it was long enough for me to die three times as I realized Thom Casey probably thought this was a ploy. I knew perfectly well there was nothing wrong with that man. I also knew that with so much being right with him I wasn't the first girl to call him up with a lame excuse to drop by. Let's face it—I was probably more like the 101st.

"Sorry to put you on hold," he said just before I sank into the floorboards. "I got another call and needed to check the ID. But, sure—bring the journal over."

* * *

Even if Thom would never read the journal, it was worth the trip to deliver it. It was even worth the mortification of having him think I'd taken it over as a lame excuse to see him. And it wasn't an excuse—lame or otherwise—I swear.

Thom lives in the historic Arcadia district, a neighborhood most of us in the Valley only drive through and then dream about for the rest of our lives. I found his charming bungalow at the end of a long drive that curved around a turn-of-the-century mansion.

Okay, maybe the main house wasn't big enough to be called a mansion, but it was big. Thom's bungalow was shaded by stately cypress trees and was only steps away from a sparkling swimming pool.

My eyes must have been round and my mouth agape when he answered the door. He looked from me to the pool and said, "No, the Phoenix PD doesn't pay more than you imagined. I lucked into this. My landlady says it makes her feel secure to have a cop living in her backyard."

Either that or she liked the view from her picture window. The scenery was indeed amazing.

Thom followed my eyes down his rather tight-fitting T-shirt and rumpled chinos and ran a hand through his tousled hair. "I went back to sleep after you called," he said by way of apology. And got up looking like that? I'd spent more than an hour dressing and doing my hair and makeup and didn't look half as good as he did. "You look nice," Thom added.

Maybe he wore contacts and didn't have them in yet. Still, I reached for the doorjamb in case my feet floated up off the porch. That settled it. I would continue to borrow my mother's clothes until I could replace at least part of my black "vampire" wardrobe with pastels. But I wouldn't shop until all those carrot sticks finally paid off.

After I'd peeled my tongue from the roof of my mouth I said, "You had to work last night?"

"Everybody worked last night. Profiling led us to expect another Marigold corpse to turn up."

"Did one?"

"No."

"Then maybe you've stopped him."

Thom didn't look like he believed my wishful thinking. He did look like he needed to go back to bed. I extended the small, fabric-wrapped leather book. Before he could take it we were interrupted by a sound that fell somewhere between fingernails on a chalkboard and the cry of a banshee.

While I cringed in terror, Thom looked up at the eaves and said, "Here, kitty, kitty." Out of nowhere dropped the roundest, blackest, wickedest-looking cat I had ever seen. Thom grinned. "'You ought to know Mr. Mistoffelees! The Original Conjuring Cat.'" Either he was quoting poetry or he was more sleep deprived than I'd thought. "'His manner is vague and aloof, you would think there was nobody shyer—but his voice has been heard on the roof.'"

Uh-huh. Now that the not-very-shy Mr. Mistoffelees was on the ground and leaning against Thom's ankles, I could take a better look at *his* roundness. "Thom, I think—"

But he hadn't finished the poem. "'At prestidigitation and at legerdemain he'll defy examination and deceive you again.'"

I wouldn't know what *that* meant without consulting a dictionary. But as smart and observant as he was, one small detail had eluded the remarkable, literate Detective Casey. "Thom, I think your cat is pregnant."

"I think so too." His grin widened at the look on my face. "Didn't you tell me just the other night that T. S. Eliot was the next author on your reading list?"

I probably had. Then I'd promptly forgotten the fib. (I shouldn't lie. My memory is too bad for it.) Still, I attempted another just the same. "I, uh, misplaced the book."

"I can fix that." Trailed by his pudgy cat, Thom walked across a neat living room to one of several overflowing bookshelves. He returned with a slim volume of *Old Possum's Book of Practical Cats.* "It's a classic," he said, showing me the cover. "Famous enough to attract the attention of Sir Andrew Lloyd Webber."

"*Cats?*" I said, trying to hide my amazement and failing. "T. S. Eliot wrote *Cats?*"

"Not on purpose," Thom said. "But he did receive a post-humous Tony Award for an unwitting contribution to the lyrics."

"I have the CD!"

"Remarkable what literature contributes to the world—even inadvertently."

I knew Thom was teasing me, but I didn't care. I exchanged the book in my hand for the one he offered and checked the contents. Reading through *Mr. Mistoffelees* as quickly as I could, I found the punch line:

"And not long ago this phenomenal Cat produced seven kittens right out of a hat! And we all said: OH! Well I never! Did you ever know a Cat so clever as Magical Mr. Mistoffelees!"

Okay then.

Thom looked down at the muslin-covered journal in his hand. "Is there anything specific you want me to look for?"

"I want to know about Manuel Sarasate's life," I said. "I want to know if the journal has all those blank pages at the end because he died before he could finish it. I want to know everything about the people he worked with." I told Thom what Mr. Chavez had told me—and what I had seen written on the final page—a prayer for a good death. "I want to know *him*, Thom. It's impor-tant to me."

Thom smiled. "Then you do think Sarasate is your ghost."

"No! I just feel like there's something important in his journal. I don't know what, or even why I feel that way."

"I'm glad to have a chance to read it," Thom said. "Thank you."

"Really?"

"Really. I'll read it now and give you a call. Maybe we can get together tonight—if you're free."

Was I free? If I wasn't, there were no bands on Earth I wouldn't break to become that way. Forget marigolds, missing corpses, haunted missions, and threatening notes. I did. At that moment my life felt as close to perfect as it ever had. Thom had loaned me a book I'd have to come back to return, he'd agreed to read the journal, and he'd suggested we "get together" that night. I was so happy I could have left the hearse on his driveway and floated to church.

"I hope nothing comes up," he said.

Suddenly, gravity came back into effect. He meant "nothing" like another dead body—a body that was missing a tongue and had a marigold placed between its lips.

Chapter 21

A Halloween party was in full swing next door at the deli when Arjay and I opened the Nightshade offices on Monday night. My little brother had seen the crowd and wanted to drop in for pastrami, but I'd been insistent about getting to work. Not that I knew why. Come ten o'clock, I was still the only one of the staff who'd shown up.

"What do ghosts drink on Halloween?" Arjay asked from the electric chair across the room.

I rested my forehead on Eddie's desk. "I don't know."

What's more, I didn't want to know. My brother had been telling me ghost jokes for the last two hours. (Everyone with a preadolescent in the family knows this is the equivalent of ten days.) I wanted him to stop. The only thing I wanted more was to know where Delano and Chaiya were. Knute had called in from his stakeout at San Rafael, but I hadn't heard from the others. Because I'd stayed at my parents' house, I hadn't seen my cousin since the Harvest Ball, or spoken to her since her Saturday-night date. But she didn't need me to remind her to show up at work, did she? And where was Delano? He'd never missed a night of work that I'd heard of.

"Ghoul-ade!" Arjay delivered the punch line with gusto. "What do ghosts put on top of their strawberry shortcake?"

I raised my head from the desk enough to shake it. It was a caution for him to stop telling riddles before my head exploded.

"Whipped scream! What's a haunted chicken?"

"No more jokes!" I opened a side drawer of Uncle Eddie's desk in search of a pain reliever—or a gag for my brother's mouth. Either one would have worked for me.

"A poultry-geist!" Arjay exclaimed. "Where do baby ghosts go while their parents are out haunting?"

"I mean it, Arjay!" I couldn't find a gag *or* an aspirin. "I'll—"

"A day-scare center!" He rolled over onto his back in the big chair and hung his head over the edge. "Who's the most famous ghost detective?" My brother was on some kind of manic joker-coaster and throwing my cautions to the wind. "Sherlock Moans. Why did the ghost cross the road? To get to the Other Side." He made himself laugh so hard with that last one that he had to grab hold of the chair's legs to keep from falling on his head. (Too bad about his quick reflexes.) "Get it?" he chortled. "The *Other Side*."

I rolled my eyes. It must have been almost as good as a chuckle because he beamed. "One more, Sam."

"*One* more? Do you swear?"

"Cross my heart. One more—but only if you laugh."

"Great. It's funny already."

"Okay. This isn't a ghost one, but it's close." Arjay sat up again. "Why do demons and ghouls hang out together?"

"I don't know," I said, picking up the desk phone to call Delano.

"Because demons are a ghoul's best friend!"

Trust me, you'd have thought it was the funniest thing I'd ever heard in my life.

Gratified at last, Arjay slid off the high seat. "There's a *Grave Guardian* marathon on." I knew that the cheesy *Grave Guardian Presents Tales of Mirth and Mayhem* was one of his favorite shows. "Want to watch it in the break room with me?"

"As tempting as that is," I said sarcastically, "I came here to work."

But I was the only one. Even Arjay had noticed. "Where is everybody?" he asked from the door.

"That, my dear Sherlock Moans, is the first mystery I plan to solve tonight."

Within moments I heard eerie music emanating from the next room. Thank goodness. If I was lucky, the marathon would last all night. I reached for the phone on Uncle Eddie's desk and dialed Delano's cell.

"Didn't get me," his recorded voice announced smugly. "Don't leave a message. I won't listen to it."

That was helpful. Not. I hung up and called Chaiya.

"Hi!" her recorded voice said breathlessly. "This is Chaiya, but you know that or you wouldn't have called!" Giggles. "Leave me a message and I'll call you back. My all-time world record for returning a call is fifteen seconds, but who knows, maybe I'll break it for *you*."

I sincerely doubted she'd break a record for me, but I left a message anyway. Then I returned the receiver to its cradle and stared at it. I was sorely tempted to call Thom, but he'd said he'd call me when he had a chance. Something must have come up because our Sunday night date had never materialized, nor had I heard from him. I wouldn't call. I'd wait him out. The last thing I wanted to do at this stage of our relationship was seem pushy—or needy.

I moved a few papers needlessly around the desk while I considered what I should do next. My mother had given Arjay a Halloween vacation from home school, but maybe I should take him back home anyway and join Knute at the mission. Maybe we'd get lucky and catch the ghost. After all, it *was* All Hallows' Eve. Name a better night to haunt a run-down old building.

On the other hand, I thought, since it was a run-down old *Catholic* building, maybe the ghost would wait until the next night: All Saints' Day. Or, since it was a run-down old Catholic building built by *Mexican* peasants, maybe the night after that— Dia de los Muertos—would hold the most appeal. I was still pondering the plethora of spooky nights ahead when the intercom buzzed.

A call to Judgment Day would have surprised me less. When my heart resumed beating I reached for the button.

"Good news!" Arjay said through the speaker. "I thought of another one. What did the mother ghost say to the baby ghost?"

"Arjay!" Seven different ways to make my brother become a ghost flashed through my mind.

"Okay, okay," he said. "I'll tell Veronica instead of you." But he didn't turn off the intercom. "The mother ghost said, 'Don't spook until you're spoken to!'"

Veronica didn't laugh. Her voice sounded strained when she said, "Can I talk to Sam?"

"One moment please," he said importantly. "I'll see if she's in." The intercom clicked off then buzzed again a couple of seconds later. "Miss Shade? There's a Miss Chavez here to see you."

"Will you *please* go watch *The Grave Guardian?*"

"Does that mean 'send her in'?"

"Yes, Arjay. Send her in." *Then send yourself—*

My thoughts were interrupted when Veronica appeared in the doorway. She looked terrible. There were dark circles of mascara under her eyes from crying, and her right cheek was purplish and puffy. I jumped up and hurried around Uncle Eddie's desk. As I did, another figure appeared behind her. It was the tall, thin young man she'd been with at the Shady Acres Harvest Ball.

He laid a hand on her shoulder. "I'll wait out here in front, Ronnie. Okay?"

She nodded but didn't turn to look up at him. She stared only at me and looked scared to death.

I crossed the room and took hold of her hands. "Veronica! What is it? How can I help you?"

She withdrew her icy fingers. "Don't be nice to me, Samantha! I don't deserve it. I can't stand it."

Nonplussed, I motioned toward a brocade chair adjacent to Uncle Eddie's desk and was gratified when she nodded and went to it to sit down. I followed but didn't reclaim my chair. Instead, I leaned against the desk and waited.

It was a few moments before she spoke. When she did, I could scarcely hear what she said.

"I—I've done something terrible."

In the silence that came next I wondered what terrible thing this very nice young woman could have done. While I wondered I exchanged looks with Quoth, the stuffed raven, and counted the ticks of the old grandfather clock upon which he perched. *One. Two. Three. Four. Five . . .*

"I have to say it and get it over with," Veronica decided aloud about the time I reached seventeen. But instead of blurting anything out, she looked down at her lap and twisted her fingers together as if trying to wring a confession out of them.

I started over. *One. Two. Three. Four. Five. Six. Seven.*

"I took the keys to your uncle's hearse!" Once the first words were out, the next gushed by so fast my brain couldn't keep up. "Last Monday," she said when I had finally recovered enough to tune in. "I didn't plan it, Sam. It just happened. I came over to Nightshade to talk to Chaiya about coming back to beauty school. I was going in the back entrance when a guy stopped me and asked if I worked here. I said no but I had friends who did and he offered me a thousand dollars if I could get him the key to your hearse."

The story of the big, bad wolf stopping Little Red Riding Hood in the woods and asking for Grandma's picnic basket was a little less believable, but not much.

"I thought it was a joke," Veronica continued. "I told him it would be easy to get the hearse. All I had to do was tell Chaiya I had a new eye shadow. I knew I could go through her desk while she was in the bathroom trying it on."

And I knew without being told that when the guy convinced Veronica he wasn't kidding it had happened exactly that way. Although Veronica Chavez was probably the last person in the world I would have suspected of anything underhanded, I must have looked at her like I thought she was a body snatcher because she burst into tears.

"I didn't know what he wanted the key for!" she said between sobs. "I swear I didn't, Sam. He *said* he just wanted to win a bet with his friends. He said it was a prank and he'd bring the hearse back in perfect condition and nobody would ever know what we did." By the end, her voice was almost inaudible. "And I really need the money." She covered her face with her hands. "Or at least I thought I did."

Sometime in the last thirty seconds I'd gone from leaning to sitting. Thankfully, my rear had made contact with the desk instead of hitting the floor. There were so many questions in my head I didn't know which one to ask first. In fact, I wasn't certain I could articulate any of them. At last I managed, "Him who?" Veronica looked up with tears running down her swollen cheek. "I mean, who did you give the key to?"

"Some guy," she said. "I'd never seen him before."

I wanted to tell her how stupid that sounded, but clearly she already knew. I sighed. "And you also gave him your key to Rest in Peace."

"Of course not!" Veronica cried. "I don't have a key! I only go in when Sully or Marty are there with me." More tears. "And if I'd had *any* idea what he was going to do with your hearse, I'd have told you or Sully or called the police or *something.*"

I was gratified to hear that a girl who had no problem with grand theft auto would draw the line somewhere.

"Do you still have the cash?" I asked, assuming the thief hadn't paid with American Express and hoping I could lift fingerprints from the bills.

She shook her head. "I bought a new dress and gave the rest to my grandpa."

Who had probably stowed it under his mattress instead of putting it in Shady Acres's safe. But if it was anywhere on the premises, Veronica's involvement could turn out to be a godsend since prints or other forensic evidence on the money might eventually link it to the body nappers.

"I hope they put me in prison forever," Veronica murmured.

That was a little much. If they lock people up for being stupid, Veronica and I might end up sharing a cell.

I reached forward to brush the hair off her soggy face. "You're not going to prison—or even to jail. I won't press charges. The hearse is back and I believe you. You never could have guessed what that guy would use it for. Nobody would have guessed that." I withdrew my hand. "You will have to talk to the police, though, and describe the man as best you can."

Veronica reached into her handbag and retrieved a folded sheet of paper. "I drew his picture on the way over," she said, handing it to me. "All I had was an eyeliner pencil."

The picture was electric blue, but incredibly good. I looked from it to Veronica. Whatever words of admiration I might have said about her artistic talent died on my lips. She wasn't crying as she had been, but the look she'd had in the doorway—the one of dread—was back.

"I haven't told you *why* I confessed," she whispered.

There was more? It was *worse?* I sat back down.

"I saw the guy again today," she said. "This afternoon. I was coming out of Rest in Peace after doing a client for Sully. The guy was in the parking lot."

My heart beat a little faster. "Waiting for you?"

"I don't think so," Veronica said. "He seemed surprised to see me come out the back door of the mortuary. I think he was watching Nightshade."

"Did you talk to him?"

"I didn't want to," she said. "But before I could get to my car he stood in front of it." Her face had paled so much that the bruise on her cheek looked like a plum. "I tried to get back in the mortuary but he grabbed my arm."

I couldn't take my eyes off her cheek. "He hurt you."

"He hit me," she said, lowering her eyes. "I lied. I told him I didn't know where you lived or anything about you. That's why he hit me."

"He wanted to know about *me?*"

"He kept asking me about the 'babe in black.'"

I'd always wanted to be called a babe. Wouldn't you know when it finally happened the circumstances would take all the joy out of it? "But why—?"

"I don't know, Samantha! That's all there was to it. He asked me a few questions, then he hit me and then he said that if I told anybody anything I'd be sorry."

And yet, though hurt and terrified, she'd come back to Nightshade anyway. She'd done it for me.

"Thank you, Veronica," I said. "That was very brave."

"My boyfriend wants to take me out of town for a few days," she said. "His mother lives in Flagstaff. But I couldn't leave before I warned you." She took my hand. "I'm so sorry, Sam! I'm so very, very sorry!"

She rose and threw her arms around my neck. I hugged her back while my brain raced a million miles a minute. Why was the violent hearse-heister interested in me? Why now? Until Veronica Chavez walked through the door ten minutes ago I hadn't been an inch closer to solving the mystery of Antonio Batista's disappearance. Surely nobody was worried about being busted by *me*.

"Do we call the police now?" Veronica asked. She took a shaky step back.

"Yes," I said. Then I looked from her battered face to the picture of the blue-tinged thug. "No."

I walked over to the window and peered out into the darkness. Judging by the number of people still on the street, the party at Eat, Drink, & Be Merry was still going on. Thank goodness. The Halloween party next door had probably saved us both. With so many people coming and going, the thug must have been afraid to approach Arjay and me when we came into Nightshade. The same commotion probably protected Veronica and her boyfriend a little later.

But, obviously, none of us should push our luck any longer. That party wouldn't last forever.

"Go with your boyfriend," I told Veronica. "But take the front stairs. There are more people that way."

"You think he's still out there?" she asked with a nervous glance toward the window. "You think he's still watching?"

"I don't know," I said. "But if he is, he saw you come up." I reached for her hand to try to stop it from shaking. "Don't worry. There are too many people around for him to try anything. Go to Flagstaff for a few days. Chaiya has your cell number. We'll call you when we want you to talk to the police."

"You'll be okay?"

"I'll be fine."

Veronica squeezed my fingers, then darted for the door. There she turned. "You're the best, Sam. And I *am* sorry. I'm really, really sorry."

I followed her and her boyfriend through the reception room and locked the door behind them. Then I went to find Arjay. He was too engrossed in the Grave Guardian's tales of mirth and mayhem to do more than glance up from the couch.

"Get your stuff," I said. "We're going—" I cut myself off before saying "home." If there *was* somebody watching for me, and if he followed us away from Nightshade, the last place I'd lead him to was my parents' house and Shady Acres. "We're going to go see Knute at the stakeout," I decided. The big man could take Arjay home while I—

Frankly, my dear, I didn't know what I'd do.

Chapter 22

As usual, Knute's thought process was better than mine.

I like to think he's more logical because his head—and therefore his brain—is so much bigger than mine, but besides that he's more than rational, he's clairvoyant. (Remember how I told you that in the second chapter and it didn't quite pan out? Well this is a better example.) Before I could cross the room to turn off Arjay's TV show, my cell phone rang. It was Knute.

See there?

I slipped into the next room to talk. After telling him I'd been unable to reach Delano and Chaiya, I filled him in about Veronica's confession and how I thought I should get Arjay away from Nightshade in case the hearse thief was still hanging around.

This is where logic comes in. Knute wanted me to stay put until he could get there. Even if we made it out of the offices safely, he was worried about me and Arjay being waylaid between Nightshade and San Rafael, and he was also concerned Chaiya might show up to an empty office and a bad dude.

He was right, of course. He's always right.

"Sam," Knute said as I was about to close my phone, "you know where Eddie's gun is, right?"

"Yes." It was under the false panel in the desk.

"It's loaded."

I knew that, too. I tried not to think about it, but I knew it.

"Get it out," Knute continued. "Put it someplace Arjay won't see it, but in a place you can get it fast if you need it." Knute knows me too well. "Get it now, Sam," he said as if he could see me rooted to the spot.

I took a step toward Uncle Eddie's office.

"Move."

I took a couple more steps. Having built up momentum, I was on my way.

"I'm on the way," Knute said. He hung up because he doesn't talk and speed at the same time.

On. The. Way. Those were the best three words I'd heard all night—right up until the next minute when my cell rang again and a different male voice said, "Sam, it's Thom."

Those three words were even better.

"Thom! I'm so glad to talk to you. I—"

"I only have a minute."

The way he said it gave me pause. Or maybe reaching Uncle Eddie's desk is what did it. I sat down in the chair and hesitated before pulling the top drawer toward my chest. "Another body?"

"Yeah."

"The serial killer?"

"Ballistics would indicate, but this one was found by a canal with the tongue still intact."

I sprung the latch to open the false panel, but I didn't reach for the revolver. "What does that mean, Thom?"

"We're not sure," he said. "But I think—"

I heard a gruff voice in the background bark, "Tennyson! When you're through chatting could you get your smart (word deleted) over here?"

"I'll let you go," I said. I recognized Lasovik's bark and knew that his bite was worse.

"Wait, Sam," Thom said. "I can't explain now, but I need you to promise me—"

From the background: "Casey, *now!*"

Thom again: "Promise me you won't go back inside San Rafael."

He'd said the words quickly—what with his job on the line and all—but I knew he was waiting for an answer.

He got a question instead. "Why?"

"Sam—"

More background barking. Lasovik must be rabid.

"Okay," I said quickly. "I promise." Thom could ask me for the moon and I'd try to get it for him. "But you have to promise to call me back when you have time to explain."

"As soon as I can."

The line went dead.

I stared at the phone until the grandfather clock bonged once for the half hour and brought me back to the present. Fortunately, since Uncle Eddie was the only one who knew how to wind it properly, it was running almost five minutes fast. I still had a few minutes to hide the gun before Arjay's program ended.

I pulled the revolver from its hiding place and looked around the room for another, more easily accessible place to stash it. Then I realized that with only one entrance to Nightshade, I should put it in the reception room and make my stand there if I had to while Arjay was safely—or at least semisafely—in the back.

A minute later I stood next to the antique fortune-telling booth and looked around Chaiya's cramped office.

"Sam?" Arjay said from the next room. I could tell by his voice he was headed my way. "Is it time to go?"

With no other hiding place in sight, I slipped the revolver under the fortune teller's wide, waxy hands. Her green glass eyes seemed to register her surprise, but she remained mum and expressionless otherwise.

I was just in time because in the next second Arjay stood in the doorway. "What do you call a little ghost's parents?" Fearing a sharp word (or gut punch), he ducked back into the hall before calling out, "Mummy and Deady!"

"You're going to be dead-y in a minute!" I told him, reaching around the door frame to nab him for a thorough tickling. "Where did you get all those awful jokes?"

"One of my e-mail pals sent them to me," he said, breathless with laughter.

"Send them back!"

When I had tortured my little brother long enough, I pulled him back into the break room and turned the TV back on.

"Hey!" he objected. "I thought we were going to go hang with Knute."

"Change of plans."

"How come?"

"Because."

"Because why?"

Knowing that my little brother can stretch a game of twenty questions into two hundred and beyond, I said sharply, "Because I'm the boss." I held up a hand to keep him from saying anything else. When he was obediently, if rebelliously, quiet, I pointed to the television screen. "Watch the show." Then I turned to leave.

Arjay plopped onto the couch in a sulk but said loud enough for me to hear through the doorway, "Chaiya's right. Being in charge at Nightshade *did* make your head big. You *do* think you're the boss of the whole world."

I froze. Then I turned and stuck my big head back in the door. "Excuse me?"

Arjay stared silently at the TV, but the "you heard me" came through loud and clear.

"When did Chaiya say that?" I couldn't decide if I was hurt, offended, or enlightened. Maybe I was all three.

"Tonight."

I went back into the room and sat on the arm of the couch. "You talked to Chaiya tonight? When?"

"She called while you were with Veronica," he said. "I started watching *The Grave Guardian* and forgot to tell you. Sorry." Clearly he wasn't.

"What did she say? Aside from me thinking I was the boss of the world and all."

"She said to tell you she wasn't going to call in, but she's too processional to sink to your bevel." Arjay grinned at his ability to remember our cousin's exact, nonsensical words. "Oh, and she's not coming back to Nightshade until Uncle Eddie gets back."

"Why?"

Now I was the one asking twenty questions, but I couldn't stop myself.

Fortunately, Arjay was nicer to me than I'd been to him. "She's mad at you for what you did Saturday night."

What had I done? I wracked my brain but could only remember talking to Chaiya on the phone, lending her my clothes, holding my tongue at her thoughtless remarks, and praying for her when we hung up. What was wrong with that?

In the next second I knew what else I'd done. I'd sent Delano to the cemetery to check up on her and LeVar Zabloudil.

What do you want to bet Delano's middle name *isn't* Discreet?

"And she isn't speaking to me," I said, "so it doesn't matter how many times I call her cell phone because she isn't going to answer."

"That's right," Arjay confirmed.

"Has she changed the lock on our apartment yet?"

"She didn't say. Probably."

I sighed. "Did Delano call? Is he 'out sick' tonight because he's mad at me too?"

"I didn't talk to Delano," Arjay said. But he was interested enough in the turn the conversation had taken to ignore the opening scene of the next episode of *Grave Guardian*. "What did you do, Sam?"

"Grown-up stuff."

Arjay made a face before turning his back on me. I regretted my words. Not only is my brother now eleven years old, his IQ is about ten points higher than mine. (Arjay is a genius, by the way. I only point this out in case you wonder just how dumb a blond I am. Only dumb enough to treat Arjay like a little kid.)

"Chaiya had a date on Saturday night," I said. "But she was going someplace I thought might be dangerous, so I asked Delano to go by to check on them."

"That was dumb," Arjay said, delighted.

"He *said* he'd be discreet!"

"Delano?"

I massaged my right temple. "Yeah, I know. That was dumb."

Arjay's response was forestalled by a sharp rapping on the outer door. He jumped up to answer it.

"Sit down!" I said louder than I should have. "I'll get it."

"Why is the door locked?"

"It . . . we must have forgotten to unlock it when we came in." I moved to the doorway. "Stay here, Arjay. I mean it." Since there was no other phone in the room, I pulled the cell from my pocket and tossed it next to him on the couch. The gesture was meant to look casual and offhand, but it made his eyes widen.

"I'll go with you," he said.

"No." I forced a smile. "I'm the boss of the world, remember? And I say you'll stay in here and be quiet."

I locked and closed the door behind me and walked down the short hall past the research rooms and Uncle Eddie's office. In the reception area I paused in front of the fortune teller. Glancing her direction, I'd have sworn she met my eye and tightened her grip on the revolver.

As I tried to peer through the thickly frosted glass panel to see who stood on the other side, all I could think about was how flimsy a protection it afforded. Why lock the door in the first place when someone could break the glass and unlock it in two seconds?

"Who is it?" I asked, modulating my voice to sound confident and unafraid. (Too bad it came out more on the uncertain and apprehensive side.)

The mystery caller didn't answer. He knocked louder.

It was apparent that whoever was on the other side of that door had no intention of going away. I knew the longer I hesitated, the better the chance Arjay would come out to see what was going on.

With a quick *here we go* look at the fortune teller, I grasped my weapon in one hand. With the other hand I reached for the doorknob.

Chapter 23

Aside from losing an occasional client, Sully Meyers is a lucky man.

He was particularly lucky this All Hallows' Eve. Despite his banging on the door loud enough to raise the dearly departed next door, and despite his being too deaf to respond when I asked him to identify himself, I didn't use my weapon on him.

One blow from that '40s-style telephone could have killed him.

(Come on. You didn't think I'd pick up the gun, did you?)

"Samantha," Sully said as I lowered the phone, "your door was locked."

"Oh?" While Sully stepped past me, I set aside the heaviest blunt instrument I'd been able to lay my hands on and tried to look innocent. "I wonder how that happened." Then I leaned up against the closed door, slipped a hand behind my back, and locked it again.

"Trick or treat!" Sully said, extending a bulging, grease-spotted bag from his brother's deli. "It's pastrami—your favorite." He raised a gnarled finger and shook it at me fondly. "I couldn't help but notice you've been losing weight, Samantha."

Thank goodness I hadn't killed him!

I hugged Sully, took the bag, and swooned over the delicious aroma. "Thank you!"

"If you could not come to the party, the party should come to you!" Sully exclaimed. "It does not rival your mother's gala, of course, but for Sol's first Halloween bash, it was a good one."

"It's not over, is it?" I didn't want the party to end, especially before Knute got there. The more people on the street, the better.

Sully shook his head, but it meant yes. "We are old men, Samantha. We can't party all night like we used to."

From the corner of my eye I caught sight of a slight shadow creeping down the hall from the break room. It held aloft a rectangle that resembled a disconnected computer keyboard.

(We are remarkably short on defensive weapons at Nightshade.)

"It's okay, Arjay!" I called out. "Mr. Meyers is here. He brought pastrami."

The keyboard clattered to the floor and my brother arrived seconds later to claim the bag. When Sully politely refused an invitation to the *Grave*-fest, Arjay was on his way back to the break room, probably to rummage through the fridge for a cream soda. At least I wouldn't have to worry about there being anything left but a dill pickle to tempt me into abandoning my diet.

"Thanks so much," I told the kindly mortician again. "You're wonderful."

Sully walked to the door but didn't try to open it. Good thing because I hadn't unlocked it yet. "I was wondering . . . " he began. I tried not to cringe because I knew exactly what he wondered. "Any leads on Mr. Batista? Anything at all?"

"Yes!" I said because I couldn't look into his sweet, hopeful face and say anything else. (Besides, it was finally true.) "We got a huge break tonight." I pulled Veronica's drawing out of my pocket. "Do you know this man?"

Sully looked down at the blue face. "No," he said at last. "Who is he?"

"We think he's the one who took the—" I caught myself before I said "hearse." I hadn't "gotten around" to telling Sully that the body snatchers had used our hearse to make their getaway. I was saving that information for another day—a day when I had a whole lot of good news to couch it in—say, the day I solved the case. "The dearly departed," I concluded. "We think this man . . . kidnapped . . . the corpse."

"And you got this information from . . . ?"

"Ver—" I bit my tongue. I'd share that tidbit in the confessional about the hearse. "Ver-y reliable sources," I stammered.

Sully nodded and handed back the picture. "Your source is a gifted artist," he said. "I have long admired her skill with a makeup pencil."

I looked down at my shoes and wondered if he knew about the hearse as well.

"Thank you for your efforts in my behalf." Sully jiggled the doorknob. I couldn't make myself look up, but I heard him turn the lock. "You might want to get Mr. Tucker to take a look at this door, Samantha," he said on the way out. "It seems to have developed a knack for locking itself."

* * *

I stood at the window to watch the last of the revelers leave Eat, Drink, & Be Merry. Just before I panicked, Knute's old clunker turned the corner. My imminent despair became instant delight.

It's true that I sometimes—mostly at singles conferences—act like I believe women need men as badly as fish need bicycles. But the truth is we *do* need men. I was particularly grateful at the moment for the one who had just pulled up behind my office. Still, I ran to Uncle Eddie's desk so I would look busy and unconcerned when Knute came in. I knew my act wouldn't fool him any more than it had Sully, but a girl has to try to keep up appearances.

I looked up when the big man entered the office, and affixed a nonchalant smile to my face. It faded rapidly at the sight of his severe expression.

Knute held Uncle Eddie's revolver in his open palm. He crossed the room in three long strides and laid the gun on the desk. "You're better off keeping this in the drawer, I think."

"You saw it?"

"You thought you *concealed* it?" He shook his graying head. "That was careless, Sam. Worse, it was dangerous. What were you thinking? You knew you had a punk around and a child in the office."

I considered his implication and felt my face go from white to pink to scarlet. Talk about incompetent. Knute would never say it, but I bet that's what he thought.

I opened the drawer, slid the gun into it, and flicked the panel back into place. "I'm sorry, Knute. I only had a second to hide it. Arjay was coming." I forced myself to stop making excuses and to blink back the tears. He looked so disappointed in me I wished I'd never told him about Veronica or called him back to the office. I'd have rather faced anything the punk could have done to me than Knute's disapproval. "I'll be smarter next time."

"You won't have any 'next times' if you don't think the 'this times' through better."

I nodded and swiped at the single tear that made it through my defenses.

Knute turned away. He wouldn't look at me. Couldn't look at me. I knew my carelessness put him in a hard place. He'd rather walk through a cactus patch than make me cry, but he'd invested the last six months trying his darnedest to make a good detective out of me.

Had he failed? As much as I willed it away, the old expression "you can't make a silk purse from a sow's ear" kept coming to mind.

Another tear escaped. What kind of detective was I? I must have read a hundred books about schoolgirls, old ladies, house-wives, journalists, gardeners, nurses, Egyptologists, cooks, and novelists who were brilliant amateur sleuths. They seldom doubted themselves, rarely messed up their hair, and *never* flubbed a case. (They were probably all skinny, too.) And then there was me—a professional detective who was better suited for . . . anything else. My parents were right. I *should* be working at Shady Acres instead of Nightshade.

"Thanks for coming to my rescue," I told Knute, meaning so much more than what he'd done that night. "I'm ready to go home now." I didn't mention that I was ready to stay there, but I was.

"I came to take *Arjay* home," he said gruffly. "Nightshade closes at five." He was trying to remain stern. For the most part he'd succeeded. "I ran into a couple of people down in the parking lot," he continued. "One is the beat policeman who replaced Thom when he was promoted to detective. He'd been checking out the crowd at Sol's party. I told him we had reason to suspect the body snatcher might return to the scene of the crime, so he's going to hang out in the lot for an hour or so while he catches up on paperwork. Delano or I will be here before he leaves."

I didn't ask Knute how he'd managed to reach Delano when I couldn't. I knew it had everything to do with that modern marvel—caller ID.

"You said you met a couple of people," I said as Knute turned to go.

"Yes, I did. You're a good detective, Sam." Though delivered in an offhand manner, I knew that despite everything, Knute meant it. Once again my eyes watered. "Chaiya's here. She claims she stopped by to get something from her desk, but I think she wants to yell at you." His dark eyes twinkled. "Don't let her go out alone. Let her keep yelling at you until Delano comes or I get back."

"That shouldn't be a problem," I said ruefully.

"Back before you know it." Knute lumbered out the door and down the hall to retrieve my little brother.

I wondered what I would do without Knute, but I didn't wonder long. The outer door had no sooner closed and locked behind him and Arjay than Chaiya marched into Uncle Eddie's office, the picture of righteous indignation. She threw one purple-clad leg over the unicorn and hoisted herself into the saddle. I sat behind Uncle Eddie's desk and eyed the sharp golden horn upon her trusty steed, thinking this must be how the Black Knight felt when facing Sir Lancelot.

"I am *furious* at you!" Chaiya began. "I am *inferiorated!*" She leaned forward. "That means I am very, very mad."

I'd gathered that.

I nodded contritely. "I'm sorry, Chaiya."

Sometimes the best defense is a total lack of offense. The quick apology caught my cousin off guard. Her kohl-lined eyes narrowed suspiciously. "What are you sorry for?"

"I'm sorry that I sometimes act like I'm boss of the world." I looked down at the desk in contrition, saw Veronica's drawing, and folded it up to return it to my pants pocket. Then I looked up. "And I'm *very* sorry I sent Delano to the cemetery Saturday night. I shouldn't have, I guess, but I was worried about you. Chaiya, he *said* he'd be discreet."

"Detached from others?" Chaiya huffed. "As if! He came right over where we were and attached himself."

"Discreet," I repeated. "It means careful about what one says or does."

"No, it doesn't," she insisted. "It means detached from others. *Discrete* was in *Reader's Digest* this month. It's my word-power word for the day."

I frowned and reached for the dictionary. "Spell it."

"D-I-S-C-R-E-T-E."

What do you know? For once she was right. I might have to start listening to her.

"Okay," I said. "So Delano is neither discreet *nor* discrete."

"I know it!" Fortunately for me, Chaiya is as quick to forgive as she is to anger. Probably quicker. She tossed back her hair. In honor of Halloween, she'd done it up in spirals that made it look like glossy Ramen noodles. "In case you're interested, LeVar was about to *kiss* me when Delano showed up. It would have been our first kiss—and we've had *two* dates."

It might have occurred to me how creepy that was—kissing a *lawyer,* and in a cemetery at that—but I was thinking about poor Delano instead. I hoped he hadn't seen the almost-kiss and thought I'd set him up to get even for all the times he'd razzed me about Thom. I hoped—

"And I'd *already* been distracted by the grave guardian."

Did she say what I thought she said? I didn't think so. I thought I'd been watching too much TV with Arjay.

"You wouldn't believe how busy that cemetery is on Saturday night," Chaiya continued. "LeVar and I parked at the apartments and walked over—so we could sneak up on the ghosts, you know? But people came from everywhere. Partiers. A grave guardian. And this was all before—"

"Whoa!" I interrupted. "Do you keep saying *grave guardian?*"

"Yes," she said, curls bobbing. "Didn't you ever see that show? Arjay loves it. It's hosted by a guy with wild hair who wears a black robe and—"

"In the cemetery?"

"Don't be silly. It looks like a cemetery, but it's only a film set with—"

"I'm talking about the *real* grave guardian, Chaiya!"

Please tell me I didn't say *REAL* grave guardian.

I pulled a hand through my hair, but resisted the urge to pull my hair out. "Tell me about the man you saw on Saturday night."

"LeVar?"

"No—"

"Delano?"

"No! That other guy. The grave guardian."

"What about him?"

"What did he look like?" She raised an eyebrow. I took a deep breath and tried again. "You saw him . . . ?"

Her cherry-red lips puckered into a pout, and she crossed her arms over her chest. "You don't listen to me, Sammy. I don't know why I bother converting with you."

"I'm *trying* to listen to you."

"I saw him in the *cemetery!* Where *else* would I have seen a grave guardian?"

"Where in the cemetery?"

"Everywhere." She shrugged. "He was wandering around looking for something. I think he was trying to decide which grave to guard."

Chaiya doesn't make things up; she must have seen something unusual. I suspected it was a kid in costume—maybe even Trey

Tucker, who doesn't live far from San Rafael—out looking for kicks or trying to freak people out. But I couldn't dismiss it entirely. Not with all the strange things going on in the nearby mission. "LeVar saw him too?"

"Not a chance." Chaiya giggled. "LeVar couldn't keep his eyes off me—even in *your* clothes—long enough to see anybody else. He would have kissed me, too, if Delano hadn't shown up."

Timing, they say, is everything. "I hope Delano didn't make a scene." I knew he had.

"As if the noise from his motorcycle wasn't enough," Chaiya said, "he yelled my name from the street. LeVar had to go over there to talk to him."

"And left you there alone with a weirdo prowling around?"

I could probably forgive Delano because he didn't know what was going on, but what had that supposedly sane, conservative attorney been using for brains? Really! I sometimes think my father ought to abandon his current genetic research long enough to determine the direct correlation between a rise of testosterone and a sudden drop in IQ.

"So," I concluded, "while the men fought over you, you sat there and watched the grave guardian?"

Chaiya shook her head. "He disappeared."

"You mean he left?"

"It was more like he disappeared. But I watched the partiers leave. They came just before Delano, so they didn't know anybody else was in the graveyard until he pulled up and yelled."

"Partiers?"

She nodded. "Four guys. One of them was already drunk. I could tell because his two buddies had to drag him out of the backseat and hold him up. The other guy had something shiny in his hand. A bottle of booze, I think."

I knew she was trying to impress me with her powers of observation and deduction, so I nodded. But I wasn't nearly as interested in the partiers as I was the disappearing grave guardian. Although separated by a housing project, that ancient, long-abandoned cemetery was close enough to San Rafael to make me think there might be a link between my ghost and whoever was hanging around there trying to scare people.

I wanted to change the subject back to the weirdo, but Chaiya hadn't finished her partier story. "The drunk was underage," she said. "I know because when they saw Delano get there and LeVar stand up and me sitting there watching them, the guy with the bottle stuck it under his coat real fast." I paid a little more attention now, but she'd reached the end. "Then LeVar went over to fight with Delano, and the guys got back in their car and sped off to party someplace else."

"And then?"

"And then Delano had already ruined the whole night and I was mad at him—and mad at you. And he was mad at me—and mad at you. And LeVar was mad at *everybody*—especially you— and sulked all the way back to the apartment and didn't kiss me good night! Are you happy, Sam?"

"Well, I did do you a favor by getting rid of LeVar."

She looked around for something to throw at me, but came up empty-handed. (I'd long before cleared Uncle Eddie's valuables from within unicorn-reach for exactly such occasions.)

"Seriously," I said. "I'm sorry. Okay?"

Her lips twitched a little. "Okay. I didn't like LeVar Zabloudil that much as a person, but, man, what a name!"

"What a name," I agreed.

A few seconds passed. Then, from beneath lowered lashes, Chaiya asked, "Do you think Delano is hot?"

"Tempered? Yes."

"You know what I mean, Sammy! Do you think he's good-looking?"

"Well . . . in a scruffy, hairy, angular, red-headed werewolf sort of way . . . no." But I didn't say it. In fact, I hoped Chaiya *did* think he was attractive. I said, "Absolutely. Don't you?"

"Maybe if he cut his hair and trimmed his beard a little. He has nice eyes, don't you think? And great teeth."

"He's never going to cut off his ponytail, Chaiya," I warned. "No way. Not even for you."

"Samson cut his hair," she said with a smile for which Delilah would have sold her soul. (If she'd had one.)

I nodded. "Look at how that turned out."

Chaiya's brow wrinkled. She'd only listened to the part of my Sunday School lesson that interested her. Once it veered past romantic toward moralistic, she'd tuned me out. "It ended badly?"

"Yes."

"Oh. Well—"

"But Delano's got gorgeous eyes," I reminded her. "And great teeth." Straight. White. Pointy. "Looking good." Gratified by her smile, I was about to return once again to the subject of the grave guardian when the phone on the desk rang. I picked it up instead. "Nightshade Investigation."

The woman caller might have sounded vaguely familiar if she hadn't been almost hysterical.

"The police won't listen to me!" was the first completely coherent sentence I heard. It was followed by, "*Nobody* will listen to me! Nobody will believe me, but he's in trouble, I know he is! I found your number on the father's desk. If you can't help me, I don't know—"

"Who's in trouble?" I asked. "Who is this?" The name she gave meant nothing to me, but when the woman added, "Father Rodriguez's housekeeper," I gripped the receiver. "Father Rodriguez is in danger?"

There was a long silence punctuated by sniffles. "No. Brother Simon."

Carlos? I drew in a breath that I forgot to release as I thought of Flying Monkey Man and the missing Batista family. I'd listened to Thom when he told me Carlos wasn't in danger. I'd believed him. He'd been wrong.

"It's almost midnight and he hasn't come back," the woman continued. "Brother Simon is always in by nine. It's a rule of his order. I called the police, but they don't care. They say he has to be gone more than twenty-four hours before they'll talk to me. They say—"

"Do you know where he went?"

There was another silence. Longer this time.

"Please!" I said. "I want to help."

"I think he might have gone to the graveyard," she said. "The old one. The one that used to be by San Rafael before they put up that awful slum."

"Did Carlos—Brother Simon—go there to meet someone?"

A long, broken sigh and then an almost inaudible, "Yes."

"Who?"

I might as well not have asked. The line was dead.

Chapter 24

"I have to go," I told Chaiya as she followed me from Eddie's office into the research room across the hall. The window there overlooked the back parking lot.

I said a prayer as I pulled up the blinds. It was answered even before I'd finished asking. The squad car was still there; the thug wasn't.

Chaiya's eyes were large and round. She had no idea what was going on, but she knew Knute had practically dragged Arjay home. She'd seen the mysterious call terrify me, and now she knew I was also afraid of something outside.

I tried to appear calm and matter-of-fact as I said, "Lock the front door as soon as I leave. Then go back into the break room and lock that door, too." According to Veronica, the hearse-heister was only after me, but I wasn't willing to bet my cousin's life on it. "Push the couch up against the door and don't move it until Delano gets here or Knute comes back."

"I'm not speaking to Delano," she reminded me.

"You don't have to speak to him. Just stay close to him."

"I'm going with you."

"No, you're not!"

"Yes, I am." Chaiya balled her hands into fists and put them over her narrow hips. It's something she'd done since we were kids. If I hadn't been so worried about Carlos—and about who might be waiting for me to leave Nightshade—I would have smiled when she said, "You're not the boss of me!"

"Yes, I am. Until Uncle Eddie comes back, I *am* the boss."

"What are you going to do, boss?" she said. "Sit here with me instead of looking for Carlos? I don't need a babysitter."

I hate it when she sounds like me. It's like she's holding up that mirror thing I told you about. Besides, I didn't have time to argue. Every second I spent debating was a second in which Carlos might be in trouble. Might be—

"You can't lock me in the back room," Chaiya continued, following me down the hall to the front office. "And you can't keep me from following if you leave without me."

It was a convincing argument and she knew it.

"It's too dangerous." I was already out the front door. I hoped she'd lock it behind me.

She didn't. Or, if she did, she locked it with herself on the wrong side. "It'll be safer if we stay together," Chaiya said. "They taught us that in Brownies, right?"

"We're not Brownies anymore."

"I know it! Now I wear pretty colors and you wear black."

I smiled despite myself. I know I often complain about Chaiya being flighty, nonsensical, and occasionally infuriating. I hope I also remember to mention she's the most loyal and courageous person I know—and my best friend in the whole world.

"It's a bad idea to come with me," I repeated as we ran down the stairs toward the parking lot.

"I have lots of bad ideas," Chaiya said. "Remember that time we sneaked onstage to dance at the Easter tangent?"

"*You* danced."

She grabbed my jacket from behind. "You didn't go onstage with me?"

"Not even."

"Oh my heck! Samantha Shade, you are so dead."

I paused with my hand on the door that led to the parking lot, but I didn't push the long, metal bar. I wasn't sure I could.

"Not really," Chaiya said, her voice breaking. "That's a figment of speech, you know."

"I know." I pushed open the door and was greeted by a gust of cool night air. Either I was giving myself the chills or it was nippy. I thought it was the latter. It was almost the first day of November, after all. Summer must at last be releasing its grip on the Valley of the Sun to make way for autumn.

The uniformed police officer looked up when we entered the parking lot. When I waved, he nodded a greeting and went back to his paperwork. Otherwise the lot was empty.

At least I hoped it was empty.

"Let's take my car," Chaiya said, frowning at the hearse.

"Good idea." If someone was staking out Nightshade, there was little wisdom in eluding him here just to advertise ourselves farther down the block. Besides, arriving at a cemetery in a hearse seemed a little, well, not uncreepy—even to me.

"I'll drive," she said. When we rolled to a stop beside Sully's parking booth, Chaiya looked up and down the street. "Which way?"

"Left," I told her. "We're going to the same graveyard you were at on Saturday night." I watched the muscles in her long, slender neck constrict as she swallowed. Nevertheless, she pulled forward. "Father Rodriguez's housekeeper told me Carlos went there tonight to meet somebody."

"The grave guardian?"

"No! A parishioner probably. Somebody in his church."

"At an old cemetery?" Chaiya rolled her eyes. "Those Catholic monks ought to get offices like LDS bishops."

Rather than speculate what Brother Simon had been thinking, I agreed he should have an office.

"He couldn't have gone to their *house?*" Chaiya pressed.

"The apartments next door to the graveyard are part of his parish. You saw them, Chaiya. They're tenements. You have to go outdoors if you want any privacy at all." I didn't add that outdoors was probably safer, too, but I bet it was.

I scanned the street behind Nightshade as Chaiya drove. There were the usual vagrants, night crawlers, and somnambulists—plus a handful more prowlers out and about because it was Halloween—but nobody looked anything like the Little Boy Blue Veronica had sketched. I relaxed into the seat.

Well, I *would* have relaxed if every muscle in my body hadn't had other ideas.

I couldn't stop thinking about the cemetery. "The grave guardian," I said to Chaiya. "You know he had to be some kid dressed up for Halloween."

"Then he needs a calendar. He was two days early."

"Okay, maybe he dresses that way all the time. Maybe it was Trey or one of his friends. The Tuckers live in an old neighborhood not far from there."

Chaiya nodded. She even managed to relax the death grip she had on the steering wheel. Like me, she'd looked beyond the vampire trappings to the potential Trey. He didn't scare her. "Is it okay if I turn on some music?"

"Please."

Wouldn't you know the CD currently in her player featured the greatest hits of Andrew Lloyd Webber? When "Music of the Night" filled the car, I gasped involuntarily.

Chaiya hit the button to advance to the next selection. Madonna crooned "Don't Cry for Me, Argentina." "Better?"

"Much."

We listened to a couple of songs from *Evita*, then one from *Joseph and the Amazing Technicolor Dreamcoat*, without exchanging a word. When Sarah Brightman began to sing about "everything being all right," I wondered what Chaiya was thinking. I didn't ask. Everything *wasn't* all right. She probably regretted her hasty decision to come with me. I knew I should regret it too, but I didn't. The closer we got to the graveyard, the more pleased and grateful I was to have her along.

"I brought the Bactine," Chaiya said out of the blue. "I have all my ghost hunting paranormal in the backseat."

I turned to see. Right on top of the pile of paranormal-seeking paraphernalia were two flashlights. I turned back around and closed my eyes. Thank goodness Knute couldn't see me now. How stupid does one detective have to be to run out to a grave-yard in the middle of the night without a flashlight?

In case you're trying to stick up for me in your mind (you'd do that for me, wouldn't you?), I'll point out that both the hearse and my VW are fully stocked with everything I need for surveillance—and almost anything else. But I'd agreed in a heartbeat to take Chaiya's car, remember? What I hadn't remembered was to grab the bag of stuff from the hearse before we left. I'd been too apprehensive about the thug—and too worried about Carlos. How many times had Delano told me I had to learn to keep my emotions in check? However many times it was, it hadn't been enough. Once again I had reacted first and thought it through later.

Knute was right. If I stayed in this line of work much longer without getting smarter, one of my poorly executed "this times" would cost me a whole lifetime of "next times." I could only hope this night wouldn't be the "this time" that did it.

"You are wonderful," I told Chaiya sincerely. "You are beyond doubt the smartest person in this car."

"Really?" she said, pleased. "Most people say I'm the pretty one."

* * *

San Rafael seemed to glow in the moonlight as we passed by it a few minutes later. I craned my neck to look back and wished I could solve the mystery of its ghost. A place so stately and beautiful deserved to rest in peace.

Barbra Streisand's voice on the CD was as haunting as the thought of the mission. Without consciously thinking about it, I'd started to sing along. The song was from *Cats*—the one about turning your face to the moonlight and finding the meaning of happiness on your way to a new life. (I'm paraphrasing.) Of course it made me think of Thom.

Where is he? I wondered. *Home sleeping after another eighteen-hour workday?* It was probably too much to wish he would dream about me, but I located a star through the windshield (or maybe it was a jet approaching Sky Harbor International Airport; we can't be too picky here under the bright lights of the big city) and wished it anyway.

"You should call Delano," Chaiya said, proving once again that she got all the brains *and* beauty allotted to this generation of our family.

I should have done it before we left Nightshade. I should have at least left a note. *Truly,* I thought, *tomorrow I will turn in my detective license and go to work at Shady Acres.*

I nodded and reached around the paper in my pocket for my cell phone. Then, removing the drawing, I unfolded it in case the slim phone had ended up between the creases. It hadn't. I tossed the picture on the dash and dug deeper. I checked my jacket pockets. At last I undid my seat belt so I could straighten out my legs to check the front pockets of my pants.

I *always* carry my cell phone—even when I don't remember to recharge the battery. Where in the world . . . ?

Just like that I knew. I'd tossed it on the couch in the break room so Arjay would have it to call 911 if he had to. One thing had led to another and I'd never picked it up again. It had probably slid between the cushions when my little brother got up to come to my rescue, so neither of us had noticed it there.

"I don't have my phone," I confessed. "You call Delano."

Enough time passed for me to wonder how far she was going to carry this "not speaking to Delano" thing. But finally she said, "I didn't bring my phone. We left so fast. I—I left my purse on the desk back at Nightshade."

Chaiya slowed the car to look for a break in the concrete divider that would allow her to make a U-turn. It was probably too good an idea for me to argue with, so I kept my mouth shut for once. But there was no break in the divider. Chaiya had to go all the way up to the next street. Just before she turned around I caught her arm. "Wait! Go on up the street. I think that's Carlos's car."

She glanced at me disapprovingly but obeyed.

It *was* his car. "Park behind it," I said.

We were on the far northern corner of a derelict graveyard that covered a city block and did nothing to detract from the area's urban blight. Because there are laws against relocating graves without permission—even if you want to erect a perfectly good slum on the spot they occupy—and because the Catholic Church had never granted permission, most of the graves had been unmoved and untouched since the eighteenth and nineteenth centuries. I doubted they would ever be moved—or cared for. The remains of the friars, converted Papagos, and Mexican peasants who had built and maintained the old mission would rest beneath mounds of trash, weeds, and crumbling tombstones until the trumpet sounded to herald their resurrection.

"It's sad," Chaiya said softly.

It was. The cemetery stood very much alone. There were no supermarkets in this pocket of poverty—and no mom-and-pop stores, either—so two city streets simply ended their runs in the tenement lots. Since most of the residents were too poor to own cars, the streets were usually deserted. Adding to its solitary nature, one side of the graveyard was flanked by an empty lot that had become an unofficial dumping ground. On the other side, the Arizona Department of Transportation had constructed a high wall to spare freeway motorists even a distant view of the area that progress had forgotten. Even the apartment buildings on each of the remaining sides, ruins themselves, turned their backs. The only windows facing the cemetery were the tiny bits of frosted glass required to vent bathrooms. Thus, although San Rafael's cemetery wasn't far from the downtown area of one of the larger cities in America, it was so forgotten and dismal it might as well have been on the edge of Death Valley.

"We should go back for Knute and Delano," Chaiya said as I snatched a flashlight from the backseat before reaching for the door handle of her car. "When they get to Nightshade and see we're not there and didn't leave a note or call them or anything, they're gonna freak."

She didn't know the half of it. She hadn't seen the "samantha shade watch out" note, or been told about Blue Boy and his assault on her friend Veronica. But we were already there and Carlos's car was there and there was no way I could make myself leave before I checked it out.

"A couple of minutes," I promised, swinging open the door. "Give me two minutes to look at the car. Then we'll go for help."

"Knute is going to kill you."

"I know."

"Uncle Eddie is going to fire you."

She added that because she thought in my mind it would be worse. I didn't take the time to tell her I'd probably resign first and save him the trouble. "Two minutes," I said and climbed out onto the sidewalk.

Since Chaiya left her car running and the headlights on, I didn't need the flashlight. I could see into every corner of the small, locked car. A religious medal hung from the rearview mirror, and there was a Bible on the front seat with rosary beads draped over it. On the backseat was a robe, neatly rolled and tied with a white-rope belt. A few papers lay next to it. There was nothing unusual for a car that belonged to a novice monk. I walked to the front of the car and laid my hand on the hood. It ·was as cold as I'd expected it to be.

I circled to the back and knocked on the trunk. I shone the beam from my flashlight on the pavement underneath the car. At last I straightened and gazed out over the cemetery. Nothing moved but the dry, dying branches of the few trees not already claimed by Phoenix's long drought. I watched for a full minute, but every movement I noted could be attributed to the wind.

Grave guardians must get Halloweens off.

I looked up and down the street. Even the homeless had taken shelter elsewhere. That or the street was too much of a wasteland to attract them in the first place.

Chaiya rapped on the windshield and held up two fingers. My time was up. I turned and walked reluctantly back to her car and opened the door on the passenger side.

"Anything?" she asked as the dome light flicked on.

"No."

"Why would Carlos just leave his car here like that?"

"I don't think he would." I looked back and forth between the buildings. There were maybe two dozen dim lights glowing in the bathroom windows, but I couldn't knock on the doors of each of those apartments looking for a monk.

Webber's CD still played in Chaiya's car. Now a couple sang "The First Man You Remember." I thought about Carlos, the carefree, kinda-dense Catholic kid I had loved in high school. And I thought about Brother Simon, the caring, dedicated man of God he had become.

I couldn't walk away before at least *trying* to find out what had happened to him tonight. Not with the frantic voice of the housekeeper still ringing in my ears. No matter if I had to stay on that street by myself on the eeriest night of the year, I couldn't leave until I knew if Carlos needed me.

Chapter 25

I tried not to look at the graveyard as I leaned in the car and told Chaiya to go back to Nightshade without me. (Deciding to stay there alone doesn't sound like a particularly bright thing to do as I write it either. Nevertheless, that's what I did.)

With the dome light on, my cousin noticed Veronica's drawing on the dashboard and picked it up. "I know him," she said conversationally. She motioned for me to get in the car at the same time as she tossed the picture back where it had been.

Even if I'd planned to get in, I couldn't have moved after that statement. "You *know* that guy?"

"Well, I don't know him, know him," she said with a shrug. "We never dated or anything. We only flirted in the parking lot."

"You *what?*"

"Are you going to get in?"

"No." But I sat on the seat with the door open because I wasn't sure my legs would continue to hold me up. I dropped my flashlight on the seat and picked up the picture. "You met *this* man."

"I know it!" Chaiya said. "Close the door."

"*This* man," I repeated, holding the picture up to her face.

"You keep saying that." She frowned. "Frankly, I'm a little worried about you, Sammy. First the grave guardian had you going, and now it's this blue guy. Maybe you're working too hard. I'm glad Uncle Eddie's finally coming home." The furrows in her forehead deepened as her eyebrows rose. "Or is it *Thom* who has you so discombobulated?" She tapped the stereo console to call my attention to the Andrew Lloyd Webber hit that had just begun. "Love changes everything, you know."

I took a deep breath and returned the picture to the dash. "Chaiya, this is important. Where did you meet the guy in the picture? Was it in the parking lot outside Nightshade?"

"Of course," she said. "How many parking lots do you think I hang out in?"

"*When* did you meet him?"

"A long time ago."

"Last Monday?"

"Yes! I remember because it was when I was studying to become a novelist." She tapped me on the knee. "Being able to observe and remember details is crucible if you want to be a good writer."

I nodded. "Tell me all the details you remember."

"Your blue guy was looking at the hearse when I got to work," Chaiya said. "He was cute, so I bragged about the hearse belonging to my Uncle Eddie." She considered. "Well, he was *sort of* cute. On a scale of one to ten he was—"

"Did he ask if he could borrow the hearse?" I interrupted. On a scale of one to ten, I had zero interest in how cute Chaiya found the criminal.

"How did you know?" she asked, amazed. "You're a good detective, Sam. You know that?"

I wished people would quit saying that. No wonder I had delusions of grandeur.

"Anyway," Chaiya continued, "he wanted to borrow the hearse long enough to drive it past some guys he knew. It was like a dare—or maybe a bet—because he said if I gave him the key and didn't tell anybody about it he'd split the thousand dollars he won with me."

I wondered what she'd say when she found out that the guy gave her friend the full thousand an hour later.

"I didn't do it, though," she said quickly. "You can't trust anybody these days." I was glad to hear her say it—but surprised. Chaiya is the most trusting person I know. "I didn't know if he was a good driver," she continued. "If he put so much as one little scratch on that hearse, Uncle Eddie would kill me."

I rolled my eyes. "Speaking of which, why didn't you say something about that guy when we found out the hearse was stolen?"

Chaiya gasped. "The hearse was *stolen?*" In the next second she frowned and felt my forehead. "You really *are* working too hard, Sammy. I saw the hearse in the parking lot tonight. It wasn't stolen."

I pushed her hand away. "You honestly don't know that somebody stole it last week then brought it back?" Chaiya shook her head. It was probably true. How *could* she know if nobody told her? Probably nobody had. We all have a bad habit of treating her more like an occasionally functional piece of office equipment than a colleague. "But you heard about a body being stolen from Sully's mortuary."

"I've heard and heard and *heard* about that," she said with a sigh. "It's all LeVar wants to talk about."

"Whoever took the body used our hearse to take it."

I expected shock and surprise, but Chaiya's face registered revulsion. "I will *never* ride in that thing after somebody hauled a dead guy around in it!" I didn't have the heart to tell her she already had. If Chaiya had been a comic book character, a little light bulb would have appeared over her head. "You think that's why Blue Guy wanted me to loan it to him? You think *he* took it to steal the body?"

"I know he did," I said. As gently as I could I told her about Veronica's most recent visit to Nightshade.

Most of the non-cosmetically applied color had left my cousin's face by the time I finished. "There's one part I don't understand," she said.

That put her way ahead of me. There were several parts I didn't understand. I didn't understand how Veronica could have been so stupid. I didn't understand how the snatchers knew we wouldn't miss the hearse for an hour. I especially didn't understand why the thug had risked coming back. Veronica claimed he'd come for me, but none of this could have anything to do with me.

Could it?

"Why is that guy after you?" Chaiya asked.

"I have no idea."

"Close the door!" she said, putting the car in reverse. "We're getting out of here right now!"

I swung my legs out so my feet hit the sidewalk. Over my shoulder I said, "I can't, Chaiya. I have to look for Carlos. But I want you to go back to Nightshade and tell Delano where I am."

"I can't," she said. "I'm not speaking to Delano." She put the car in park and turned off the engine. In another minute she stood next to me on the curb. "What do we want from the backseat? Just the flashlights and Bactine?" She opened the rear door and reached in. "I think I'll leave the rest. I don't feel much like ghost hunting tonight, do you?"

I shook my head as I accepted a flashlight. Not only did I not feel like ghost hunting, I didn't feel like jeopardizing my cousin and terrifying my coworkers either. "Chaiya, you—"

"You're still not the boss of me." She closed the door and pressed down on her keychain remote to lock the car. The little *whoop* made me jump. "Yeah," she said, rubbing her arm to relieve the gooseflesh. "Me too. This place is a lot creepier when you're not on a date."

"I know you don't want to leave me alone, Chaiya," I said. "And I appreciate it, I really do. But it would help me more if you went back to Nightshade. Nobody knows we're here. Nobody knows *where* we are. If something happens—"

"Not the boss of me," she sang. Then she sobered. "But please let's hurry. Where do you want to look for Carlos?"

I *wanted* to look under my bed back in our apartment, but I said, "In the mausoleum. I hope he's in there."

Chaiya scanned the graveyard and her eyes narrowed. "If he isn't, shouldn't we be able to see him? I mean there's nobody standing arou—" She cut herself off midword with a gulp. "Oh."

Oh.

I couldn't have said it better myself. If Carlos was anywhere in that graveyard except the mausoleum, it was a safe bet he wasn't standing.

Chapter 26

As explained earlier, I'd met Carlos Diego while working on a Habitat for Humanity project. Now, six years later, I thought that if I lived through the night and found him alive and well, we should organize a splinter group—Habitat for Deceased Humanity—and dedicate our first efforts to San Rafael's forsaken burial ground.

And, yes, it *is* funny the things one thinks about while picking one's way through a graveyard in the middle of the night. Mostly, though, my thoughts focused on remaining upright. It wasn't an easy task. In some places the weeds had grown waist high. Not only did they make walking hard, they obscured the beer bottles, ground squirrel holes, and broken pieces of tombstone to the point that Chaiya and I stumbled along like a couple of zombies newly accustomed to mobility.

Carlos wasn't in the mausoleum or behind it, so we began a search of the surrounding grounds. I don't know how long it took us to get about halfway through because I didn't have a watch. Or a cell phone. Or Father Abraham's ability to tell time by the positions of the stars in the heavens. All I knew for sure was that it was very late at night—or early in the morning, depending on how you looked at it.

"This is All Saints' Day," I told Chaiya when the realization dawned on me. It was reassuring to know that All Hallows' Eve had been replaced at midnight by a kinder, gentler holy day.

"Saints preserve us," she said, pausing before a grave that had its marble sentry of an angel still in place, albeit with only one wing still attached. "Do you believe in guardian angels?"

"I don't know. I guess so."

"I do," she said. "I hope mine is with me right now."

I hoped that too. And I hoped Brother Simon's guardian angel was by his side—wherever that was.

After walking a few minutes more, I wrinkled my nose at a faint but unmistakably foul smell. "What is that?"

"I don't know," Chaiya said. "But I smelled it Saturday night too."

We were on the other side of the cemetery from the garbage dump, but I pointed that direction. "The wind must be carrying it over."

"I don't think so," Chaiya said, hanging back. "I think it's coming from up ahead." She pointed toward a granite sepulchre that stood atop a wide stone platform. The above-ground tomb was surrounded by a thickly weeded area, but it looked as though the weeds had been cut, or at least flattened, in a few areas.

That explained the smell. "Some cretin's been dumping his trash there," I told her.

Although I'd continued to walk forward, Chaiya hadn't moved. She was looking toward the street that lay between us and the high wall. "That's about where the partiers stopped on Saturday night," she said, pointing. "Maybe one of them was sick."

Whatever was up ahead didn't smell like sickness—or liquor. It smelled like . . . I couldn't put my finger on what it smelled like, but it was rank.

"Sammy . . . " Chaiya began and I took a step back toward her in concern. "Oh. My. Gosh." She continued to stare toward the street as if seeing an apparition in full technicolor. But there was nothing there to see. At least there was nothing there I could see.

"Chaiya! What is it?"

"Blue Boy."

"Huh?"

She rushed forward and grasped my arm. "Blue Boy. The guy in Veronica's drawing. The horrible, hearse-borrowing body stealer who's after you!"

Okay, now that I knew *who* she was talking about, I could wait patiently for her to tell me *what* she was talking about.

"He was at the party," she continued.

"You mean here? You saw him *here* on Saturday night?"

Chaiya's head bobbed up and down. "At the time I *thought* I knew one of those guys who was holding up the drunk. But then I thought, 'How could I know him?' I mean, it's not like I associate with partiers."

My thoughts began to churn at an alarming rate.

Or maybe it was my stomach.

"Was that a coincidence?" Chaiya asked, so rattled she got the four-syllable word right.

It was my mind churning for sure. Some people's brains function like sophisticated computers, but mine works more like an older-model washing machine. Snatches of things I'd seen and learned in the last couple of weeks tossed and turned in my mind—colliding, separating, going around in circles. I had bits and pieces of information everywhere—too much to sort out. Then, for no reason I could determine, a timer went off and the spin cycle stopped. I tingled all over.

Dizzy, I looked around for a place to sit that wasn't littered with glass and cast-off syringes. There was a large headstone nearby that was mostly intact. I made my way toward it, hoping its owner wouldn't object to my use of it.

"Sammy?" Chaiya said. "Tell me it was a coincidence."

I didn't answer. I sat down. I thought I knew now what had happened—or at least part of it—but I didn't *know* I knew. To know I knew, I needed to know three more things.

You don't know what I'm talking about, do you? It's like this: as much as I didn't want to be on the right track in the extraordinarily awful thing I suspected, three things would tell me if I was.

"Chaiya," I said, "the men you saw here on Saturday night—were they Latino?"

"The drunk was," she said, "and maybe one of the others. But two were blond."

That was one.

"Did you see a bottle?" I asked. "Or did you see a glint of something shiny and assume it was glass?"

"I didn't see it very well," Chaiya admitted. "I thought I saw the neck of a bottle, but the guy holding it hid it in his coat as soon as he saw me."

That was two.

I turned my head. Three was up ahead in the weeds. Three was the cloying odor that *wasn't* rotting trash. I knew now why it was familiar and where I'd smelled it last, but I still had to walk over there to confirm it. "Wait here," I told Chaiya.

"No way."

"I'm going to go see what smells so bad."

She wrinkled her nose. "Yes way."

I grasped the flashlight tightly in my palm and was surprised that perspiration didn't cause it to slip between my fingers like a greased baton. I rubbed my other palm on my pants and switched the flashlight to the drier hand, just in case.

I was still fifteen feet away from the sepulchre when I saw a spot where weeds lay crushed and broken on the ground. Knowing—or at least fearing—what I would see, I moved closer and trained a beam of light in the center of the spot. Then I arced it slowly back and forth.

As I had suspected, the weeds were stained and the dirt was a darker brown than in the surrounding area. The most deeply brown spot was almost round and about twice the circumference of a man's head. I didn't have to be a CSI expert to know what had stained the weeds and soaked the ground. I needed only to remember where I'd smelled the sickly sweet odor. I'd smelled it in my Uncle Eddie's hearse the night it had been used to steal Antonio Batista's body.

The stain was blood. The odor was death.

Ten yards away was another depression in the vegetation. A third lay a few yards beyond that. My hand went lax and the flashlight slipped from my fingers. I wasn't looking at miniature crop circles. Someone very terrestrial had turned this deserted graveyard into a killing field. And I thought I knew who it was.

"Sammy?"

My heart was beating in my throat—but at least it was still beating—when Chaiya came up behind me. She'd seen me drop the flashlight between the gravestones and had come to my rescue.

"Sammy?" she repeated softly. "Please tell me you saw a ghost."

I wished I could. A ghost would have been a better thing to see. Chaiya wasn't afraid of ghosts, and I didn't believe in them. A ghost would have been the best thing for both of us.

"I—I thought I saw a ghost," I lied. How could I tell her what I saw was dried blood, and lots of it?

I picked up my flashlight and turned toward the far street. We had to get back to Chaiya's car—fast. I'd taken two steps in that direction when I realized Chaiya was moving the other way. Despite the offensive smell, she'd seen something on the sepulchre that caught her eye and drew her forward.

Or maybe she hoped to see the ghost for herself.

"Look at the carvings on this," she said. Nearing the platform, she used the beam of her flashlight to caress the coffin-sized granite box. "It's decorated with birds and flowers and even a man's face." She leaned forward to run her fingers over the bas-relief. "He was hot!"

"Let's go," I said. "We have to get to the police."

Chaiya was rounding the chest-high tomb to see more carvings when my words registered. "Police?" Before she could make her way back to me, something else—this time something on the ground—caught her attention. She turned for a better look, her back to me.

I watched Chaiya's slender shoulders begin to tremble. Buffeted by the autumn wind, the few scant leaves on the trees overhead swayed and shook in much the same manner. In the next moment, Chaiya's quakes became massive heaves. She bent over double to vomit.

I rushed to her side, but I didn't ask if she was all right. I knew that she wasn't.

Shaking, still sick, Chaiya moved backwards until she leaned against the sepulchre. Though ashen and speechless, she managed to point toward a spot inches from my shoe.

I trained the beam of the flashlight on the ground. The bloody pool at my feet was viscous on the edges, but red and wet in the center. A smear led toward the sepulchre and stopped.

I stumbled to the side. As I did, my flashlight swung to the left and I saw something else on the ground about five yards away—a crumpled, lifeless pile of flesh in an NYU sweatshirt.

It could only be Carlos Diego.

Chapter 27

"Is he dead?" Chaiya whispered.

Or maybe I didn't hear my cousin at all. Maybe what I heard was the sound of my pulse pounding in my ears, the wind shushing the trees, or the tombstones murmuring, *Is he dead? Is he dead? Is he dead?*

I lurched forward and dropped to my knees next to Carlos Diego's prone form.

Is he dead? Is he dead? Is he dead?

I wanted to scream, "Of *course* he's dead! Can't you see the blood on the ground? Can't you see his body?" I knew if I turned his pale, peaceful face into the dirt it would prove to Chaiya (and the trees and the tombstones) what I already knew—that Brother Simon was missing the back of his skull.

I wanted to cry, "Where were his saints when he needed them? How could this have happened?" Carlos was brave. He was good. He wanted to spend his life serving God.

My fingers trembled as I reached for a lock of hair that had fallen over his right eye. Thank goodness the eye was closed. I couldn't have borne it if Carlos's eyes had been open, glassy. I brushed back the hair a fraction of an inch—scarcely enough to show where the bullet had entered his skull.

Except that Carlos's forehead was unblemished and his skin was warm to my touch. "He's alive!" I ran my hand under his hair and pulled it all back, just in case. There was no bullet hole. My fingers flew to the top of his neck. There *was* a pulse. "Chaiya, he's alive!"

Averting her eyes from the pool of blood, Chaiya knelt next to me. Her voice wavered when she said, "Are you sure?"

"Yes!" I cried, giddy with relief. "He's breathing. He has a pulse. He's alive!"

"What happened to him?"

"I don't know."

"I know," Chaiya said a moment later. With the tip of her flashlight she nudged a jagged piece of gravestone that lay near Carlos's head. It was about the size of a brick, and bloody.

Ever so gently, cradling the side of his face in one hand, I rotated Carlos's head until I could see the wound at the side of his skull. I might have shrunk back from the matted, bloody mess over his ear, but it was so much less ghastly than what I'd expected, it almost made me smile. "You're right," I said. "Somebody hit him." I scooted a little closer on the cold, litter-strewn ground, close enough to rest the monk's head in my lap.

Meanwhile, Chaiya reached into the pocket of her jacket and pulled out a small plastic bottle of antiseptic. She extended it wordlessly. I shook my head. Carlos needed an ambulance, a doctor, a hospital—not a squirt or two of Bactine—but Chaiya applied the whole bottle anyway.

Carlos didn't move.

"Harry Potter would have had iodine," Chaiya said. "That would have worked better."

Harry *Price*. Harry Potter would have had a magic wand (which is what we needed), but I didn't correct her this time. I was thinking. Minutes earlier, my only thought had been to get out of that cemetery and go for help. I think I *could* have gone with Carlos still missing. I could have convinced myself that we couldn't find him if we were dead. But we *had* found him and he was hurt. I couldn't leave him now, not under these circumstances.

"You have to go for help," I told Chaiya. I knew she wouldn't argue this time and I was right. She had already begun to rise when I reached for her elbow. "Don't drive back to Nightshade. It's too dangerous."

She looked at me as if I were daft.

"He might be waiting for you there." I knew it made no sense to her, but I couldn't waste precious seconds in an explanation. "Drive to a police station. Don't stop for anything. Don't even stop at traffic signs. Speed. Maybe somebody will stop you. Tell the first officer you see where we are. Tell him someone was killed here. Get an ambulance."

I delivered the instructions so fast my words tumbled over one another. But rather than spurring Chaiya to action as I had hoped, they paralyzed her with fear.

I was about to say it all over again when there was a flash of light at the far corner between the tenement and the graveyard. A car would soon turn onto the deserted street.

Instinctively, I grabbed Chaiya's flashlight and flicked it off. In the next second I did the same with my own. "Get down!"

"Sam—"

I pulled her down with me. "Don't move."

There was now too much light to suit me, but it was a large cemetery and, fortunately, we were in an area with a lot of statuary and still-erect tombstones. If whoever was in the car did look our way, it was unlikely they would catch sight of us.

The car sped around the corner fast enough for us to hear the squeal of tires, but then the driver slowed rapidly, apparently at the sight of the two cars parked on the street.

Chaiya started to sit up for a better view, but I pushed her back down.

"Sammy!" she said. "I think that's the same car." The width of her green eyes told me she meant the car she'd seen on Saturday night. "Do you think Blue Guy's here looking for you?"

"No," I said. I owed her the truth now for sure. "If it's the same car, the same guy—and if he's here looking for anyone, Chaiya—he's looking for you."

I had figured it out when Chaiya told me Blue Boy was one of the "partiers" she saw at the graveyard Saturday night. If she'd seen him well enough to recognize him, then he had seen her too—dressed in my clothes—and remembered where she worked from their meeting at Nightshade. (Veronica had assumed from his description of the "babe in black" that he'd meant me—and, yes, I should have known nobody would call *me* a babe.)

Blue's reappearance didn't have anything to do with Uncle Eddie's hearse. It had everything to do with what Chaiya had seen and misunderstood. She hadn't seen Blue Boy and three of his friends out for a party. The shiny bottle neck she thought she saw was the muzzle of a gun. She'd seen three assassins and their latest victim—the kid Chaiya thought they were holding up because he was too drunk to walk. They'd arrived at their usually deserted slaughterhouse unaware of the "ghost hunters" who had parked at the tenements and walked across the street. When Delano appeared and they saw they had another witness nearby, they put their victim back in the car and took him to the canal where, according to what Thom had said, somebody spotted his body about ten hours later and called the police.

Blue Boy had gone back for the witness.

I told Chaiya this as we watched the car stop next to hers. I wondered if it would be the last thing I ever told her. She looked like she might die of shock.

Two men got out of the car, and I could make out the outline of a third still in the driver's seat. They examined both cars for a couple of minutes then stood on the sidewalk looking out across the cemetery.

"They see us!" Chaiya whispered.

"They don't," I said. "They couldn't." One of the things I appreciate most about the night is the way it neutralizes the world into black, white, and shades of gray. At noon, Chaiya's purple leggings could have been seen by low-flying aircraft. This close to midnight they looked almost as black as the pants I wore.

"Are they leaving?" Chaiya whispered when the two men got back in the car. She'd crossed her legs, her fingers, probably her toes, and certainly her arms. The last were crossed in prayer.

I didn't know if they were leaving or not. Maybe they were arguing about what to do because at first the car didn't move, but then it made a wide arc in the street and went back the direction from which it had come. I wished we could count on it staying gone, but I knew better. There'd been too much hesitation for me to believe they wouldn't change their mind and come back to complete whatever mission had brought them there in the first place.

Carlos moaned and I looked down in concern. He was so still and so pale. How much blood had he lost? How long ago had he been hit? Shouldn't he have come to by now? What if he was in shock? What if the blow had caused bleeding in his brain?

What if you stop obsessing and try to keep thinking? I told myself. *If only my thinker was a faster, better model.*

"I'll go back to the car," Chaiya decided aloud.

"No! They might be watching the street."

"We can't stay here. They might come back." She looked from one tenement to the other. There were almost no lights on now. Besides, it would be impossible to get inside either building without being seen from the street. "If we scream for help, someone might hear us."

"Who? The only people we know for sure are awake are the killers."

Chaiya amazed me. I'd told her enough in the last ten minutes to cause anybody to fall apart, but she was holding together brilliantly. Now she was looking the other direction for an escape route. "What's on the other side of that wall?"

"I think it's a freeway," I said, wishing there *were* such things as ghosts. I'd hire one to haunt whoever had had the bright idea to build that wall. It was the only thing that separated us from civilization as we knew it—and the help we desperately needed.

"Okay then," Chaiya said. She looked back at the street, then stood cautiously.

"Chaiya, we can't get over that wall, if that's what you're thinking."

One of her eyebrows rose. "Maybe *you* can't, but I do rock climbing at the gym three times a week."

"That wall is over ten feet high!"

"The one at the gym is twenty."

"The one at the gym has handholds, and a rope and pulley if you fall."

"I never fall. I am indelibly fragile."

Even if she meant "incredibly agile," she couldn't climb that wall. Spider-Man could. Batman would make it with the help of his utility belt. But Chaiya? No way.

She headed toward the wall.

I removed Carlos's head from my lap as gently and quickly as I could and followed.

My cousin was dwarfed by what might as well have been the Great Wall of China. "Thanks for coming over to give me a boost," she said.

Oh, sure. A boost was all she needed. Not. I am 5'2" and Chaiya is only a quarter inch taller. If she stood on my head she still couldn't see over that wall. We had no idea what was on the other side.

But she had already kicked off her shoes and was flexing her bare toes.

"Chaiya, don't," I said. "Even if you can climb it—and you can't—you don't know what's on the other side."

"You said it was a freeway!"

"But I don't know *where* the freeway is. It's not very close because the traffic sounds aren't loud. And the ground must slope down on the other side or else the lights would be more than a dim glow." I pictured a high wall, a steep embankment, and traffic whizzing by in the dark. The thought made me reach for Chaiya's arm. "Even if you make it to the top, what if you fall and roll out onto an access road or something?"

"Then before I draw my last breath I will tell the driver who hits me to send help for you and Carlos."

I didn't doubt it. And I didn't doubt that she was going to try to climb that wall, no matter what I said or did. Maybe she was right.

Maybe it was better for her to be anywhere but here if the killers returned. I put my hands into a stirrup and gave her a boost.

Batgirl isn't as "indelibly fragile" as my cousin. Chaiya was at the top of the wall almost before I'd had time to unclasp my fingers.

Straddling the slump block, she looked toward the lights of the freeway. "You're right, it's a long way off," she said. "And there's at least one fence." Before I could respond she added, "Don't worry, Sammy. Fences are easier to climb than walls." I watched her look down at me, at Carlos, and at the far street where the thugs might still be parked. Her full lips trembled. "I'll see you again *really soon*. Right?"

"Right," I said.

If only it were true.

Chapter 28

With my cousin gone and Carlos still unconscious, San Rafael's burial grounds were an even lonelier and more eerie place. I huddled among the tombstones with his battered head in my lap and listened to the sound of the wind in the trees and the occasional rustle of small, foraging animals on the ground. I prayed for Carlos to be all right until help came. I prayed for Chaiya to be protected on her errand of mercy. I prayed for the killers to stay away and/or for a patrolman to be inspired to check out these streets for no particular reason. I even prayed for God's will to be done, but mostly because I was certain He could see the wisdom in what I wanted.

Then I sat and waited. And waited. And waited.

When I couldn't look at Carlos's pale, motionless face another second without losing my mind, I tilted my head back to stare at the heavens instead. The moon had set, but sunrise was hours away. Hence, the sky was as dark as it gets in Phoenix—dark enough to reveal a smattering of stars overhead and to the east. When I found the brightest one, I made the first wish that came to mind—that something would happen. Anything. It was a thoughtless, stupid wish born of anxiety, depression, and desperation.

So of course it was granted.

All at once and without benefit of seismic activity the earth moved. I felt it before I heard it, and I heard it before I saw it. It was a noise that could not be attributed to the wind or the trees or an underground rodent, at least not a rat smaller than a rhino. It was the sound of one large stone being scraped across another—the low reverberation of a tomb opening from below.

Believe it or not, I wasn't afraid. (No, I wasn't petrified, terrified, or any other synonym either.) Fear requires input from the brain. A little synapse somewhere has to raise a cry of alarm to activate the flight-or-fight response. That didn't happen. When the beautifully carved sepulchre began to move off its base, every one of my synapses either froze in surprise or fainted dead away. I might as well have been sitting on the couch at Nightshade watching *The Grave Guardian Presents Tales of Mirth and Mayhem.*

The grave guardian?

Almost before I thought, it he was there, peering out from a crack in the ground that was now almost as wide as a tombstone.

I hadn't dared turn my flashlight back on in case the killers returned, so the only light was from the stars and the seemingly distant city. It wasn't enough for him to see me, or for me to make out more than an outline of wild, snowy hair above a lean and craggy face. Mesmerized, I leaned forward.

He must have noticed the movement. With a howl of anger, outrage, or dismay, the man's face sank from view. Seconds later, the gap began to close.

I will never know why I did it, but I slid out from under Carlos, grabbed the first thing I saw on the ground—a remnant of an iron cross—and shoved it into the crack between the sepulchre and its base.

The synapses in my brain were awake now and active. *Flee!* they screamed. *Fight!*

With nothing to fight off except panic, and nowhere to flee, I ignored the dizzying rush of adrenaline and turned back toward Carlos. At the same moment, the car of my nightmares reappeared at the corner. This time, though it once again slowed to a crawl when approaching the two parked cars, it didn't stop.

Fight! Flee!

I watched the car, but I didn't move. It proceeded slowly—very slowly—to the end of the street. There was little doubt in my mind that the men within were carefully searching the cemetery for witnesses before they returned to the scene of their multiple crimes. When nothing moved, they would grow increasingly confident. That meant that in another two corners and one long block they would arrive where I was. There was no way they would overlook me up close and personal.

Flee! Fight!

Fight? I looked around. I had rocks and the bar from the rusted iron cross. The peaceful Papagos had been better armed when the Spanish arrived—and look at how that turned out. The invaders I faced were fewer but better armed. The men coming for me had guns—with silencers.

Flee? Even if it was the better choice, there was no place to go.

Of their own volition, my eyes cut to the crack between the sepulchre and the platform upon which it rested. I pulled my eyes away.

The car turned the first corner and my eyes went back to the crack.

Flee!

Say I *did* decide that slipping into the ground to face who-knew-what in the darkness below was better than staring down three armed assassins up here. What chance did I stand of moving that heavy stone sepulchre, even if I wanted to?

It moved easier than I expected. Before I had decided whether or not to try, I found myself taking advantage of the adrenaline rush I'd just experienced and using the iron cross for leverage. It wasn't effortless, but it was easier than was reasonable. Whoever had designed the doorway to Hades must have been a brilliant engineer.

When the crack was as wide as I was, I dropped to my knees and stared into the gaping black hole. I glanced back at Carlos and wondered what to do. Even if I managed to drag him to the entrance in time (and I didn't think I could), I knew I couldn't do it without injuring him worse than he already was.

But if I left him there, the men who were coming might kill him.

Flee!

This time, the voice in my head was too loud to ignore. It was insistent, but not panicked. In fact, it was calm despite its force. That's why I obeyed it.

"I'll stay close," I promised Brother Simon's prone, unconscious form. Then I squeezed into the blackness of an open tomb just as the car turned the second corner.

Chapter 29

Advance planning is not something at which I excel. That's why I often end up in situations like this one: I'd chosen to hide from bad guys in Hades itself, but I had no idea how to close the gates of heck behind me. I was pretty sure the assassins would notice a me-sized crack in the ground where a sepulchre used to be. I was less sure I could convince them I was a gopher when they looked in it.

I hoped I had been prompted rather than impulsive in acting on the belief that it was safer below than it was above. There *was* a grave guardian down here, but surely he'd be more hospitable than the fiends who would soon arrive up there. Besides, he had gone deeper than I would ever venture. I would go only deep enough to be out of sight of anybody who peered in the crack I'd left behind. Still afraid to attract attention by turning on my flashlight, I ran one hand over the wall at my side while one foot searched for my next possibly foolish step.

This will probably surprise you, but the slope leading down to the underworld is not as steep and slippery as we've been led to believe. (It *was* paved with good intentions, however—my intention to survive.) Rather, the steps were wide, only about six inches high, and dry.

I went down one stair. Then another. On the third step my hand encountered something long and hard set into the wall. It was too dark to see it clearly, but it felt cool and metallic and was about as big around as the crosses above.

A lever?

This will probably *not* surprise you, but I have a lot of Alice in me. If there is a bottle of something purple and fizzy lying around, I will probably sip it. If there is a red, magical mushroom left on a table, I will probably nibble on it. If there is an unidentified lever in the wall of a passage underneath an ancient graveyard, I will probably pull it.

Forget *probably*—I pulled.

Above and behind me, the sepulchre ground back into place, obscuring the stars and causing me to gasp for breath despite the fact that the air was still as cool and fresh as it had been the moment before.

Although I could see that no light came in from outside, I wasn't as sure that no light could escape from within to give me away, so I groped my way back up the stairs in the blackness. When I found the crack, I sat down and leaned against it. I'd stay there until one of two things happened. Either enough silence would pass to assure me that the killers hadn't stopped after all—or I would hear them come and then go again. Either way, when the coast was clear, I'd turn on my flashlight, find the lever, and go back out with Carlos to wait for Chaiya's return with the police.

The second thing was what happened. (Well, part of it happened, at least.) I hadn't been sitting there for more than a couple of minutes when I heard voices. The killers had arrived. I couldn't believe how close I'd cut it. The sepulchre must have quit moving about the time they pulled up on the street.

I pressed myself against the rock with my ear at the crack, but they were too far away—or the stone was too thick—for me to make out what they said.

Do our ears adjust to sound the way our eyes adjust to light? I don't know if it's a scientific fact, but it seemed to happen to me. At first the voices were distant rumbles, but after a minute or two of concentration, I could make out most of the words. That wasn't a good thing. It wasn't even a helpful thing since most of the words were of the nondescriptive, noninformative, can't-be-published-in-an-LDS-book variety.

After a long, vehement string of profanity, a voice muttered, "He took it already? He took the (words deleted) body *already?*"

Another said, "Goodness gracious."

You know I made that last line up. There was nothing good or gracious about the language these men used.

There were a few words from yet a different man—bad words? good words?—I don't know because I couldn't make them out. Then the first guy said, "How was I supposed to know he's a cop? You said take him out and I did. When *that* body turns up . . ."

I didn't hear the rest of the sentence. I didn't hear anything but a crackle of ice in my veins. My body temperature had taken an immediate drop from 98.6 to 32.0—or whatever temperature at which blood freezes.

They'd murdered a cop. I'd seen the blood myself, not ten feet from where Carlos lay. Father Rodriguez's housekeeper told me Brother Simon went to the cemetery to meet somebody—presumably somebody he knew. Carlos knew exactly one cop: Thom Casey.

I must have screamed out the *"No!"* that reverberated through my head because one of the thugs said, "You hear something?"

"Gotta be the crazy guy," somebody else responded. "Let's get outta here."

"But he musta got the cop's body."

"He can have it. Let 'em chalk one more up to the Marigold Murderer."

"But—"

"Come on!"

"What about *him?*" Whoever said it obviously meant Carlos.

"He don't exactly see us," another replied. "And look at the cross. I ain't killing a priest."

"I didn't say kill him," the first guy responded. "But that's gotta be his car on the street. When somebody comes looking for him, he better not be *here.*"

"Bring him," a third, more authoritative voice said. "Get his keys outta his pocket, and we'll take him and his car to a cliff and run him off it. It'll look like an accident."

"I ain't killing a priest," the second guy repeated.

"You won't hafta kill him. If he don't die before we get him there, it'll be the crash that kills him."

It was logic only another thug could appreciate.

"What about the cop's body?" the worrier whined next. "We just gonna forget it?"

There was a pause. "We got any choice?"

Seconds passed, then minutes, hours, days, weeks, months, years. It seemed I passed my whole life sitting in indescribable darkness, unable to move, listening to silence thrum and whine in my ears.

Thom was dead. Carlos was as good as dead. I thought I should be screaming or crying or vowing vengeance against their murderers or . . . *something,* but I felt dead too. I was as senseless as the hundreds of other people with whom I shared the ground beneath San Rafael.

I don't know how long I sat there until I saw a flicker of orange. It looked like a single birthday candle. As I watched and tried to process what I saw, the faint orange glow increased in circumference and grew yellow. It was another few seconds before my brain engaged and I recognized it for what it was: the flickering light of a candle-powered lantern coming toward me through a stone passageway.

The grave guardian must have heard me scream and knew he had company.

I fumbled for my flashlight and found it quickly, but I didn't turn it on. With my eyes now long accustomed to the dark, the dim candlelight was enough for me to be able to make out the wide stairs that led past the lever and into a small chamber below. I didn't look around. I had no curiosity about my surroundings. I'd use the flashlight for a weapon if I wasn't quick enough to reach the lever and move the sepulchre in time to escape.

As I've mentioned before, I'm pretty fast. I was down the stairs with the flashlight raised and my free hand on the lever when the man in black robes entered the room. His gray hair was wild, and the light from the lantern emphasized the hollows of his cheeks, dark circles under his eyes, and sallow, craggy skin. I froze in horror.

Then I saw the cross.

In the center of the "grave guardian's" chest, glowing in the candlelight, was a hand-carved wooden cross on a long, golden chain.

I looked again at the older man's face, closer this time, and gasped in shock—and relief. "Father Rodriguez!"

At the sound of my voice, the priest's contorted face seemed to soften and melt like a waxen image held too close to the lantern's flame.

"Father Rodriguez?" I said again.

"I . . . yes?" It wasn't an affirmation as much as it was a question—as if the man wasn't sure who he was himself and hoped I could confirm it for him.

I lowered the flashlight and released my grip on the lever at the same time. "Father, it's me. Samantha Shade."

"Do I . . . know you . . . Samantha?" he asked, squinting in the flickering light. His eyes seemed glazed and haunted as he tried to focus and remember. "Are you . . . in my parish?"

"No," I said gently. It was as if I had awakened him from a long sleep. In another second or two he would be himself. "You asked me to work for you—to help you at San Rafael."

"San Rafael?" Father Rodriguez was at once surprised and pleased. "San Rafael? I . . . asked for . . . your help?"

"You did," I said. "And I've been trying to help. I've—"

"Samantha," he said. "Yes, I remember Samantha. And here you are." He raised the lantern a little higher and it shone bright on his wide, expressionless eyes.

I leaned forward. The father's eyes looked like glass marbles. Then, within them, the blue contorted, wavered, and was still. I gasped and fell backward. This was no TV special effect. I didn't know *what* it was.

"You are a godsend, Samantha," Father Rodriguez said. "I've tried my best—the saints know I've tried my best, but . . . " His words trailed off.

"Tried your best at what?" I asked. Gooseflesh rose on my neck and arms. This *was* Father Rodriguez . . . and it wasn't. I reached for the lever.

"Come, Samantha," the priest said. He turned back toward the passageway from whence he'd come. "There's much for you to help me with at San Rafael."

I pushed down on the metal bar. Chaiya would be back with help before much longer. I'd wait for her above and send somebody down here who could really help the father—somebody with the right medications and a degree in psychiatry.

I pushed again on the bar, this time with the added force of most of my weight. The sepulchre didn't move. I pulled up on the lever, but with the same effect.

The priest paused at the entrance to the tunnel. "It latches itself, Samantha."

"Please show me how to unlock it." It was both a plea and a prayer.

"We won't go out that way," Father Rodriguez said. "With your help, I can finish in time. When we're done, we'll leave through San Rafael. Come."

I didn't know what to do. I could stay there and try to find the latch to move the lever—or at least scream for help—or I could follow the priest and hope he led me to another exit.

I'd decided to stay and scream when Father Rodriguez came back for me. As he ascended the stairs, his free hand—the one I hadn't yet seen—appeared from within the folds of his vestment. In its grasp was a long, wickedly sharp knife. On the knife was blood. Bright red. Sickeningly fresh. Blood.

"Come, Samantha," the black-robed man said. "We have much to do."

Chapter 30

"I brought you here once before," Father Rodriguez said as he led me through a tunnel that I thought must lead from the graveyard to the mission itself. "You've met my predecessors."

The priest drifted in and out of lucidity. He remembered taking me on a tour of San Rafael, but he forgot that these long-abandoned tombs had not been on that day's itinerary. Also, while his tone was calm and solicitous, he fingered the carved handle of a bloody knife with the same attention he might have paid a rosary. I didn't know that he would use the knife on me if I resisted, but I didn't know that he wouldn't, so I followed along, praying I was not a lamb being led to the slaughter.

"You *have* met my predecessors," he repeated.

I didn't know what to say. I didn't want to upset the father, but I certainly didn't want him to go out of his way to introduce me to anybody else who might be down there.

"Or have you?" he said, slowing his pace. "I don't remember anymore. There are many things I don't remember."

I didn't respond. I kept walking—and breathing. The second was harder. The air in the tunnel was cool and dry, but almost unbearably close. I held tight to my flashlight, keeping it off to save the battery, and counted each step to myself. I was determined to find my way back to the stairs at the sepulchre where I knew help would eventually arrive to look for me. I hoped I wouldn't lose my flashlight and have to return alone and in the dark, but if I did, I would know how many steps it would take to get me there.

Ahead was a door of very old wood, splintered at the bottom and along one side. In the center was a carved cross, outlined in iron nails. As Father Rodriguez neared the threshold, he crossed himself with the hand that held the knife and mumbled something I didn't understand—probably a Latin prayer. He hesitated as if reluctant to enter, then pushed the door open and moved forward.

I followed with even less enthusiasm.

In this room, lantern light was worse than any darkness I could imagine. Before my wide and terrified eyes, firelight licked the walls. This caused the spectral shadows of the forms lining those walls to convulse upon their beds of stone.

We had entered the crypt. There were no ornate marble stones or finely chiseled coffins here. The crypt of San Rafael was an austere barracks for the dead. Narrow stone recesses had been carved into the chamber walls, one atop another, two or three niches high. On these bunk beds of clay lay generations of priests who had served San Rafael in years long past. Because of the intense heat and dryness of the Phoenix area, most of the bodies had mummified. They grinned up toward heaven or out into the room, still attired in rotting vestments and clutching ancient crosses and rosaries in blackened, leathery hands.

My head spun as I prayed I would not be sick. These weren't the first mummies I'd seen. I'd been formally introduced to one from Egypt, but it was still decently ensconced in its sarcophagus at the time. I'd seen others in the pages of *National Geographic*, on screen at the movie theater, and even one behind glass at the Heard Museum. But these were the first real-life mummies I'd encountered up close and personal, in the middle of the night, in a crypt I feared I might never escape.

Believe me, there's a difference.

"I fear these men are disappointed in me, Samantha," Father Rodriguez said. I thought he was probably eyeing the remains as we passed them, but I didn't look up to see. I'd seen enough— more than enough to give me nightmares for the rest of my life.

"My little flock trusted me, and I failed them. I will never earn a place here."

Not only did I not understand why anybody would want a place here, I didn't understand how Father Rodriguez thought he'd failed his flock. And frankly, I had a hard time whipping up empathy. I could remain upright only if I looked at my shoes and filled my head with numbers. I knew that if I looked anywhere else or thought about anything else (read: *Thom*) I would scream in horror. Once I started screaming I might never stop.

It took us 112 of the longest steps of my life to traverse the crypt. I let my mind take the briefest of side tracks—still number-related, of course—as I wondered how far we had come. Stairs. Chamber. Tunnel. Crypt. And now we faced another, narrower tunnel. When we got to the end of it, would we have gone far enough to have crossed under the cemetery, the street, and the tenements? Walking by way of city sidewalks, the sepulchre was almost two blocks from San Rafael. But as the crow flies—or the peasant digs—it was probably less than one block total.

We should be almost below the mission.

What then?

Father Rodriguez had to bend nearly double to pass under an iron gate that came halfway to the ground from the ceiling and stretched from one side of the burial chamber to the other. I bent my head and followed, grateful to be anywhere else but in that crypt.

"We are almost there, Samantha," the father said as if to confirm my calculations. He'd led me through the tomb slowly, thoughtfully, reverently. But now that we were in the final tunnel, he walked briskly, his thoughts apparently turning to the tasks ahead.

I couldn't even speculate about what those tasks might be without losing my supper. I continued to count, whispering the numbers out loud, to keep my mind from the conversation I'd overheard in the graveyard. Despite my best efforts, awful bits and pieces kept returning to my brain.

"One. Two."

How was I supposed to know he's a cop?

"Three. Four."

Gotta be the crazy guy.

"Five. Six."

He's got the cop's body.

Counting couldn't shut out the horrifying, mind-numbing words. I could no longer deny—as much as I wanted to—that Father Rodriguez was unbalanced. (And that's putting it nicely.) I had learned just enough as a psychology major at ASU to convince me that I am poorly qualified to diagnose anybody with anything. Still, I would have sworn that whatever mental illness the priest displayed was a new development. Sometime since the day he'd taken me on a tour of San Rafael, Father Rodriguez must have stopped taking medication or perhaps had a severe psychotic breakdown.

What any of that had to do with Thom's murder, or his body, I didn't know. I didn't want to know. Knowing something is true and seeing that it is true is like the difference between reading about mummies in a glossy magazine and encountering them in a crypt. Somehow I had survived that. I would not, however, survive corporeal evidence of Thom's death. Physically overcome by dread, my steps slowed and then stopped.

Father Rodriguez walked eight or nine steps ahead before he noted the silence behind him and turned. I knew I could outrun him back to the sepulchre, but I also knew the race would lead back through the crypt and to a locked stone door I could not open.

"Samantha?"

I drew a deep breath. The air that had been stale and unpleasant in the tomb seemed distinctly foul here.

"I need you," he said, extending the knife. The manner in which he held it toward me wasn't as threatening as it was pleading, pathetic. "I have done the others, but this one—this *one*—I could not finish. You came to help me, Samantha. That's what you said."

I shook my head.

"You must!" he cried. "We have little time!"

Before my eyes and without a drop of Dr. Jekyll's potion, Father Rodriguez underwent a transformation. He blinked and rolled his eyes, then he raised a hand—the one with the knife—to his ear. I feared he would hurt himself, but instead he stuck his index finger into the ear canal as if to bore from there through to his brain. The lantern in his other hand rose as well, and with the greater illumination on his eyes I once again saw unnatural, impossible movement there. I took a step back, and then another.

All at once the priest brandished the knife, lunged forward, and let out an animal-like screech of fear, pain, and despair. Now I knew for certain who had made the unearthly sounds in San Rafael. They had come from Father Pedro Rodriguez: shepherd, priest, tortured soul.

For a man his age the priest possessed great strength. He grasped me by the wrist to pull me down the tunnel, deeper into the bowels of San Rafael's underground. There was no use resisting. His fingers were long and agile enough to hold my wrist and the hilt of the knife effortlessly. As he dragged me along, I forgot to count steps and concentrated instead on keeping the veins in my arm away from the razor-sharp blade.

"I must have your help," the priest said as we reached the end of the tunnel. He pulled me into a cell-sized chamber. "There isn't much time."

Out of breath and shaking, I stared at the mercurial priest, astonished that he had once again turned docile and melancholy—and in the brief time it had taken him to drag me here. He released my wrist, shook his head sadly, and said, "While you do your work I will take the officer where his friends can find him."

Thom. I didn't say it. I couldn't even think it. His name never made it out through the blinding pain in my heart. I closed my eyes so I wouldn't see his body.

"Poor Antonio," Father Rodriguez said. "How glad he will be that you came to us."

Before I could process the bizarre words, Father Rodriguez had pressed the hilt of the knife into my hand. Startled, I opened my eyes in time to see him pick up a beautifully carved onyx box about as long and as wide as a shoe box, but flat. This he pressed upon me, too. Then, with one palm on my shoulder, the priest turned me toward a block of granite that abutted the far wall.

I should have kept my eyes closed. On the makeshift table was a body in a more active state of decay than those I had seen in the crypt.

Mystery solved.

I had found Sully's dearly departed client—the stolen corpse of Antonio Batista.

Chapter 31

Perhaps you recall my first experience with a corpse. That one had been pulled from a refrigerated storage locker still safely encased in a body bag. I had fainted dead away. Imagine then my reaction upon encountering a corpse outside a body bag—a cadaver that hadn't been embalmed but had been deprived of refrigeration for about a week. A corpse with a gaping hole where its stomach once had been.

Horror and wooziness times a thousand overcame me, but this time there was no one to catch me when I fell. Nor did I lose consciousness all at once. When the back of my head hit the unyielding clay wall, I heard the thud. When the side of my face impacted with the stone floor, I saw the blood. I thought I had died and was having an out-of-body experience.

Or maybe I just hoped it.

Unfortunately, some time later I came to. I was bruised and bleeding, but still alive—and still in the room with Antonio Batista. The only difference was that this time I knew instinctively that I was the only living thing in that room.

To make sure, I turned my throbbing head to one side. The knife, the box, and the lantern were laid out neatly by my side, but enough time had passed for the fat candle to burn down to only a couple inches of wax. Even with my head pounding and my brain scrambled I was lucid enough to worry about how long the light would last. I turned my head to the other side, looking for my flashlight. It was there, but the bits of glittering glass around it told me I had broken the lens and bulb at the same time that I broke my skull.

"Father?" I called, trying to push myself up. The sharp pain and pin pricks of light that floated before my eyes convinced me that sitting was a premature decision. "Father Rodriguez!" (Yes, I considered a crazed lunatic better company in a crypt than none. Like you wouldn't have?)

But Father Rodriguez was gone. I shut the thought of his errand—returning Thom's body to the city streets—firmly out of mind. I *couldn't* think about it, couldn't touch it with even the tip of my consciousness, because there madness lay.

And I was halfway to madness already.

Time passed. The candle burned lower. Father Rodriguez did not return. Ignoring the pain and lights and swaying of the room, I struggled up until I was leaning against the wall. I gagged on the smell of the rotting corpse and vomited onto the floor at my side. At least I hoped it was the smell rather than the movement that sickened me. It seemed I'd learned in a first-aid class somewhere that brain injuries and nausea can be a deadly combination.

I swallowed repeatedly and willed the sickness to pass. I had to get out of that chamber where Antonio Batista's body was— where Thom's body had been. I had to get help before it was too late for me too.

I left the bloody knife and onyx box where they were, but I picked up the lantern. After several attempts, I struggled to my feet and determined that my legs, though wobbly, would hold me.

There was only one way out, but that was okay. All things considered—and nothing personal against Antonio—I'd liked the mummies better. For sure they hadn't smelled as bad. I would go back through the crypt to the stairs that led up to the sepulchre. Maybe Chaiya had found help by now. If so, Delano and Knute were probably tearing the cemetery apart looking for me. Even if I couldn't figure out how to move the sepulchre to open the door, I could scream for help and let them know where I was.

I held the palm of one hand to my head to try to staunch the flow of blood. I held the other, the one with the lantern, before me and made my way out into the tunnel. As much as I wanted to run, I could scarcely hobble. Every ten or twelve steps I had to pause to steady myself against the wall. More than anything, I wanted to lie down. Knowing it was the worst thing I could do kept me moving.

The passageway seemed interminably long. I had almost given up hope of ever making it when at last there was a glint up ahead. The iron gate! I moved a little faster but was still twenty feet away when I stopped, stared, and screamed.

Yes, a real scream. A scream that would have made the San Rafael ghost—if there had been one—sit up and take notes. I screamed so loud and so long and so thoroughly I have no doubt that half the people out in the cemetery rolled over in their graves.

Father Rodriguez had lowered the gate. I knew without trying that not only would it be impossibly heavy, but it too would have been designed with a hidden latch I would never be able to find.

I tried anyway.

I couldn't budge the gate. I couldn't unlatch it, and I certainly couldn't go through it—even if I fasted for the rest of my short life. I had no doubt that Father Rodriguez had lowered the gate on purpose. In fainting I had failed him. He'd left me there alone and he wouldn't return.

At least he wouldn't until he was sure I was as dead as everybody else down there.

I screamed again, but since this scream felt even more hysterical than the first, I cut it off by clasping a hand over my mouth.

If you lose it now, you will die here.

I didn't know if the words had come from the Spirit of God or the spirit of despair. Either way they were true.

The blood from my head continued to seep down my cheek, and I realized I would probably die there either way. I looked down at the sputtering candle in despair. And I would die in the dark with nobody but a madman ever knowing what had happened to me—or to Thom and Carlos and poor Antonio Batista.

I didn't scream again. It had suddenly occurred to me to save my voice for the only place left where it might do any good.

As I turned and stumbled back down the tunnel toward the chamber of horrors, I prayed. It was a sincere prayer of the Thy-will-be-done variety because I honestly didn't know what I wanted to happen. I wanted to live, of course. I wanted to be saved. I wanted to be found eons before my body was as wrinkled and thin as those of the mummies beyond the gate. But I didn't know what miracle to ask for specifically. With my head battered and throbbing and my sanity stretched very near the breaking point, I couldn't think of any way salvation could come to me. That's why it was such a good prayer. If I didn't find a way to save myself, at least I would know all the way to the dark, terrifying end that my death was the fulfillment of a plan better than any I could devise.

My eyes filled with tears and overflowed. I didn't cry because I lacked faith, or because I was hurt, or even because I thought I would die. I cried because I'd just remembered the last thing Thom had asked of me—he'd made me promise to stay out of San Rafael.

I'd broken that promise, and betraying Thom's trust seemed like the worst thing I'd ever done. I cried harder. How could I face him in the hereafter? Then the voice of reason in my head (the one I thought had been killed in the fall) said that maybe I hadn't broken my promise. I wasn't in San Rafael, after all—I was under it. Perhaps when I died and Thom and I discussed the semantics in person, he would understand.

This brought on a new onslaught of tears. I loved Thom. It wasn't supposed to end like this. How had we managed to get all the way from "once upon a time" to "the end" without even one real kiss in between? More importantly, how could we be sealed in eternity when we hadn't had enough time together in mortality for a first date?

* * *

I smelled the chamber before I saw it. But my last, best hope lay therein, so I reached down and yanked the neckline of my shirt up over the lower half of my face. The muffler effect on the odor was probably negligible, but the psychological effect carried me back into the room.

I took inventory: onyx box and bloody knife on floor. Check. Body on table. Check.

Now that I had forced myself to look, I saw that there was another granite slab near the one where Antonio's body lay. It was empty, but slick with blood. Thom's blood.

The room turned a rotation and a half and I grasped the only thing nearby, a splintered wooden table, for support. It was the first miracle granted—I remained upright.

Since the vertigo was worse when I closed my eyes, I forced myself to stare down at the table in front of me. It held a box of disposable plastic gloves and an assortment of knives. Carved into the wall next to the table was an oval basin filled with bloody rags. Below the basin sat a five-gallon plastic jug, still half full of water. (Or maybe the jug was half empty. I certainly wasn't an optimist at that point.) Next to the jug lay a crushed orange flower. A marigold.

The single bloom was all it took for the puzzle pieces to fall suddenly into place. I knew then that I was standing—if barely—in the laboratory of the Marigold Murderer. Not the killer himself. There *was* no deranged serial killer. The "sicko" sought by police was really just a case of serendipity gone horribly awry.

If I were Adrian Monk, this is the place in the story where the video would cut to flashback footage as I said confidently, "It happened like this . . ."

The thugs Chaiya interrupted must have been vigilantes like Thom said. They had taken their first victim to the secluded cemetery for reasons of their own. (What reasons I couldn't imagine.) After the execution, they'd left the poor man where he fell. Father Rodriguez had found him and brought his body down into the crypts. Here he had removed the tongue before cleaning up the corpse. Then he used the tunnels to transport it to an above-ground location where it was sure to be found. When the press—and the police—made a bigger thing of the mutilation than they did the murder, the "Marigold Murderer" was born.

The real killers must have known a good deal when they saw it on the evening news. Not only had someone cleaned up after them, he'd diverted suspicion. Perhaps hoping they could count on the same mysterious help they'd received before, they chose the same spot to kill again. And again. And again. And . . .

But WHY did Father Rodriguez do it?

I held onto the table while the room revolved around me. When at last I decided I was as steady as I was ever going to get, I scanned the cell again. I hadn't missed much on my first inspection. There was a single wooden chair and beyond that an unadorned wall of adobe brick. This was as far as I could go.

I set the lantern with its almost-spent candle on the table and cleared the tears from my throat. I had one chance to live to see another sunset. I would scream for all I was worth and hope that someone up above heard my cries and was smart enough to figure out that ghosts say "boo," and not "help me!"

One chance. I staggered to the chair and sat down. If this didn't work I might as well be as comfortable as possible when I died.

Chapter 32

I screamed my head off.

What an apt turn of phrase. Considering how much it hurt, that was certainly what it felt like.

Trying not to sound like the "ghost" of San Rafael, at first I screamed, "Somebody please help me!" After a while I forgot my manners and screamed, "Help me!" About the time the candle began to flicker alarmingly I was croaking, "Help?" at a decibel that couldn't have been heard across the room.

As plans go, it wasn't a brilliant one. Mine seldom are.

I leaned back in the chair and stared at the wall because, let's face it, the view beat everything else in the room. Besides, it was a fine wall. A massive wall. A plain, unremarkable, and cracked wall. *Cracked? Right there in the middle?*

Ignoring my pounding skull, I leaned forward. The crack didn't waver and it didn't disappear. Maybe it wasn't a hallucination after all. I grabbed the lantern from the table and fell on my knees in front of the adobe bricks. It *was* cracked. The crack led up from the floor about three feet, over another three feet, and back down to the floor.

A door! I couldn't believe I hadn't seen it before.

It explained a lot. Another chamber on the other side of this one explained why nobody heard me from the street and came to investigate. I was still too deep for sound to escape. And it explained the sudden disappearance of the mystery noises I'd heard, too. When Thom and I first heard the scream—and later when

Chaiya and I heard the moans—I'd thought they sounded like they had been cut off in the middle, as if someone had closed a door.

Someone had. Father Rodriguez, agonizing over the dead from his parish, had been opening and closing *this* door.

What do you want to bet it was locked like all the others? For sure it didn't have a doorknob. I pushed with all my might (which wasn't much at that point), then searched the room for a lever. There wasn't one. At least not one I recognized as such.

I went back to the table and gathered up all the knives that were on it. I had water and, thanks to the now-comforting supply of fatty deposits upon my hips and thighs, it would be days before I died of starvation. Maybe weeks. If I didn't bleed to death or lose consciousness because of the concussion, maybe I'd have time to chisel my way through the adobe wall.

In case you don't know, adobe is mud and vegetable matter that has been formed into bricks and baked in a kiln or dried under the sun. Not exactly high tech. You would think it could be crumbled with little effort, right? Let me be the first to tell you that Arizona-sun-baked adobe, scooped from the vast clay reserves of the Salt River Valley, is possibly the hardest substance known to man. Within an hour the candle had gone out and my hole was not yet big enough to service a spider.

I threw down the knife and cried again—this time in frustration. And fear.

The darkness was the worst. It was even more oppressive than the smell. I knew what caused the smell. Somehow, knowing where the body was but not being able to see it was worse than seeing it in the first place.

I had been thrust into the worst nightmare imaginable. I was buried alive with a corpse.

While I sobbed out my terror, I must have scratched at the wall and beaten it with my fists. For sure it was the dawning awareness that my hands were beginning to hurt as much as my head and my throat that finally restored sanity. Or what would have to pass for sanity at that point.

I cradled my torn and bloody knuckles in my lap and leaned my uninjured cheek against the wall. It felt cool and comforting—cooler, the sensitive skin of my face told me, by the crack.

Fresh air?

I choked back the last of the sobs and forced myself to think. If the air was fresher at the crack then there *was* something—maybe even outdoors—on the other side of that stupid door. I *had* to get there.

I couldn't get there.

Okay, I couldn't make a hole big enough to climb through, but maybe I could make one big enough to holler through. I fumbled on the floor until I found the knife. Next I traced the crack with a swollen finger until I found what seemed to be the widest space. I stuck the knife blade in the crack. I'd been using it as a chisel, but this time I sawed vigorously back and forth. That's when something told me to try up and down instead.

I pulled the knife blade toward the floor. It wasn't as easy as cutting butter, but it wasn't difficult either. Then, when the handle felt as if it was about three quarters of the way to the floor, the blade hit something that stopped its progress. I applied more pressure, but couldn't get past whatever it was. Raising my free hand to the spot where the blade had stopped, I felt around. The crack wasn't any narrower at that spot. If anything, it was a little wider. With more hope than I'd had since entering this awful place, I pulled the knife out, felt around again, and inserted it at the bottom of the crack near the floor. When I pulled it back up, it hit the same obstacle, but from below.

I'd found the latch.

I soon learned that I hadn't missed my calling as a lock-pick. It took me forever to spring the latch, even after I figured out how it worked. (If you want a more accurate measurement of time, consider this: three minutes in a dark crypt is roughly equivalent to three hundred years above ground.) At long last I heard the click. Then, like the sepulchre in the graveyard, the brick door swung out and away.

The opening didn't lead outdoors as I had hoped. It didn't even lead to a place that was any lighter. I could only assume it had opened into another tunnel or chamber—one with who-knew-what-horrors lining its walls.

I couldn't cry anymore, but I still had a little despair left in me. How big *was* this place? I might as well have been in the crypts underneath Rome for all the progress I was making back to aboveground Phoenix.

On the other hand, this corridor at least smelled marginally better than where I had been. I took big gulps of air and crawled forward. Within moments my hand hit another wall.

No, not a wall, or my head would have hit it first. It must be a stair.

Stairs! If there were stairs maybe there was a lever on the wall, and if there was a lever . . . it would be latched like the one that opened the sepulchre and I would never find the latch in the dark, or be able to work it if I did find it, and I would *still* be lost.

The power of positive thinking isn't very strong in people trapped in crypts.

Out of ideas, out of energy, and finally out of hope, I dragged myself along the floor just far enough to slump onto the bottom of the staircase. The rough-hewn rocks felt blessedly cool and welcoming against my swollen cheek as I at last lay down and gave up. I'd given escape my best effort, but I had failed three times over. I had nothing left to give. My hands bled, my throat screamed in pain from screaming, and my head was simply too heavy to ever lift again. I couldn't see the room spin in the darkness, but the nausea that was coming in increasingly frequent waves told me it did.

I didn't care anymore. Now that I was away from the corpse I could lie down and rest.

I could sleep.

I could . . . die.

I woke with a start.

"Help!" I cried. (Except that it was more of a bleat.) "Help me, please." The second plea wasn't even a whisper. Nobody could have heard it, but *I* heard an answering voice from above.

Not that the voice was talking to me.

"Bring me that sledgehammer," he said. "And a crowbar. The entrance has to be here."

I turned on the stair and pointed my face toward the voice as I stared into the inky darkness. There was one thought left in my battered, exhausted, terror-addled skull. That thought was, *Impossible.*

There was a grating sound of stone on stone, an exclamation of triumph, and another grating. "Never mind!" the voice called. He pushed or pulled a third stone and I heard the *click.* "I got it!"

Ten or fifteen feet above my head a door opened, and light flooded the narrow stairwell. I used my swollen hands to shade my eyes as I looked up in awe at the first heavenly being I'd ever seen. In the midst of a rectangle of impossibly bright light stood an angel.

It must be true what they say about our bodies being made perfect in heaven. Thom Casey was more perfect than I'd remembered. He was tall and broad shouldered, and the ethereal backlight that always accompanies angels lent streaks of gold and bronze to his hair.

In the next second I realized that if he had come for me I must have died. *But when?* Had it happened on the stairs, or earlier when I saw Antonio Batista's corpse and fell and hit my head? The last was more plausible. I'd even suspected as much at the time. Everything after that—the gate and the screaming and the door in the wall—must have been an out-of-body experience.

Except. I looked down at my hands. Raw hamburger would have looked more appealing. The damage to them could only have happened when I was still inside a physical body and had the ability to pound them to shreds. When had I done it? I couldn't remember, but then I couldn't even remember when I'd died.

"Sam?" Thom sounded pretty unsure himself, especially for a seraph.

I *must* have died on the stairs. I could see by the look on his face that's where my body was. Huddled at the base, dressed all in black with a blood-encrusted head and swollen face, I must have looked more like a demon than an angel novitiate. Probably Thom would leave me there and go back to paradise were there was a whole heavenly host of better dating material than me.

Go toward the light. That's what all the near-death-experienced people tell you to do. Too bad I couldn't move.

In the next second Thom descended into the darkness towards me.

Now that I could see him better, I realized that the former Detective Casey was a little frowzy for an angel. His tie hung around his neck like a noose, and his shirt certainly wasn't white, at least not anymore. What's more, he had a day's growth of beard. But maybe beards were all the rage in heaven and he was just trying to fit in.

Regardless, he looked incredible. *I* didn't even look human. What's more, after the company I'd kept, I knew I smelled worse than I looked. Like any creature of the night, I shrank away from the glorious being and tried to melt into the shadows.

Thom knelt at my side, said my name again—this time in a way that brought tears to my puffy, bloodshot eyes—and gathered me into his arms. "You're okay now," he said.

"But I'm dead!"

"You're not." Thom lifted me as easily as if I'd eaten more carrot sticks than powdered-sugar donuts in my life.

"You're dead too," I told him. That would account for his superhuman strength.

"No."

"And Carlos."

"He's at a hospital," Thom told me. "Hush, Sam. You'll be all right."

I *wasn't* dead? I was alive and in Thom Casey's arms?

I didn't believe it for a second.

Chapter 33

Thom carried me out through the sacristy, holding me a little tighter than I think was technically necessary for a police rescue, and set me down gently on the only remaining pew in the sanctuary at San Rafael. Sunlight poured through the high windows, bathing the saints in light and whitewashing the walls. It was pretty, but not exactly celestial. Maybe I *hadn't* died. Probably I hadn't. Your body is supposed to stop hurting when you're dead. I hurt all over.

I was vaguely aware of several people besides the saints looking on, most of them in uniform, but I only had eyes for Thom.

"Where's that ambulance?" he asked one policeman. Then he nodded toward the open sacristy and said to another, "Get CSI in there."

"Please not Amber," I moaned. Fortunately, nobody heard me.

"They're on the way," an officer told him. "The chief, too."

Thom reached for his cell phone. He tossed it to the nearest guy and said, "Push six. Her partner's still searching the cemetery. Tell him she's here and she's okay."

Either "okay" was a relative term, or I was going to have to take his word for it.

Thom took one of my hands in his. I didn't know if he wanted to hold it or take my pulse, but I pulled it away. What would he think when he saw those dirty, broken fingernails? Besides, there was so much to say and I couldn't hold hands with him and talk at the same time.

"Carlos," I croaked. "I heard them plan to push him over a cliff."

"Fortunately, this is Phoenix and we're real short on cliffs," Thom said. "They left the car abandoned in a parking lot. Thanks to Chaiya, every cop in town was looking for the car. They found him at dawn. He was hit pretty hard, but he's going to be fine."

I slipped my hands into Thom's after all. He held them, maybe even tenderly. "I thought you were dead too," I whispered. "They said they'd killed a cop."

"They did," he said soberly. "An INS—Immigration and Naturalization—agent. It was the guy Brother Simon said looked like a flying monkey. Thanks to your favorite monk, he was getting close to the ring of smugglers. Too close."

"Smugglers? You said vigilantes at the party."

"I was wrong. They're coyotes, Sam. INS has been on their trail for months."

I leaned forward. I needed to share all the shocking and horrible things I'd learned before the paramedics arrived to haul me off to the hospital. "Thom, they murdered all—"

"I know," he said to save me the words. "They probably killed the first victim because he talked to the authorities. The other executions were to frighten everybody else into silence."

"You've caught them?"

"No, but we know who they are thanks to the drawing in Chaiya's car and José's statement. It's only a matter of time."

"You found José?"

"He found us." Thom released my hands to take my shoulders and move me carefully back until I was once again resting against the back of the pew. He was looking at my blood-matted hair, and the dimple on his cheek was as deep as I'd ever seen it. "Sit quietly, Sam," he said. "We can talk about this later."

"Now," I begged. "Please."

Probably because he figured it would be the best way to keep me quiet, Thom agreed to elaborate. "Brother Simon found José and convinced him that police protection beat a bullet in his forehead. He and the Batistas came in Sunday afternoon. That's why I broke our date for that evening."

I wanted to nod happily, but it made my head spin.

Thom put a thumb under my chin to halt whatever motion I'd managed. "The killers have been running a human smuggling operation for years now, but recently they added a twist. They began using their human commodities to smuggle in drugs as well." The dimple appeared in his cheek. "They've been giving them cocaine in balloons. They force the Mexicans to swallow as much as they're able, then . . . return it to them in a few days when they're inside the state. It's a new condition of their 'immigration.' If somebody goes back to Mexico for a family member, like Antonio Batista did, they have to do it again."

The spinning in my head increased, but I didn't think it had much to do with my head injury. "A balloon broke. That's what caused Antonio's drug overdose." I thought of the gaping hole in the stomach of the corpse and wanted to cry, but all my tears were spent. "That's why they took his body," I realized aloud. "They wanted their drugs back."

"That or to keep the mortician from finding them," Thom said. "They had no way to know Sully wouldn't embalm the body."

But that was only half the horrific equation. I shuddered. "Father Rodriguez . . . " I began. I could have sworn I didn't have another tear left, but one coursed down my dirty cheek just the same.

Heedless of his fellow officers, Detective Casey gathered me back into his arms. "I know, Sam. I'm sorry."

"You *know?*" I sniffled into his chest. If his shirt wasn't dirty before, it was now. "You couldn't possibly know."

"Father Rodriguez has been gathering the bodies," Thom said quietly into my ear. "He removed the tongues and cleaned them up. It explains why the one body turned up with the tongue intact. With Chaiya at San Rafael on Saturday night, the killers took their victim elsewhere." He shook his head. "But it doesn't explain why Antonio's body is still missing. I'd have bet they'd take it to the graveyard like the rest."

"They did," I whispered. "It isn't missing, Thom. It's . . . down there. Father Rodriguez couldn't . . . fix it. And I don't think he wanted to return it the way it was."

"I'm sorry, Sam," Thom said again, holding me closer.

So he *did* know about Father Rodriguez. But how?

"You told me," he said when I asked. "It would never have occurred to me to look into Father Rodriguez if you hadn't remembered him wearing a Franciscan cross. A background check showed he was a monk before he entered the priesthood. It was *his* cross Chaiya found in San Rafael."

Which didn't prove anything. If I'd had the energy, I'd have pointed that out.

"It's where she found the cross that's significant," Thom continued. "But I wouldn't have known that if you hadn't believed there were important clues in Sarasate's diary and given it to me to read."

He was giving me a little too much credit, but I didn't point that out either.

"You found the wax and marigold at the base of Saint Dymphna, the patroness of the mentally ill," Thom said, motioning toward the statue. "The priest has been lighting candles there."

I moved my head enough to see the woman with the rose of stone. "Then Father Rodriguez knows he's sick?"

"Probably not anymore," Thom said. "But he knew at first. His housekeeper thinks he contracted a very rare parasitic illness on his last trip to Mexico. She's a native, so she's seen it before. Essentially, microscopic eggs are ingested, and the bloodstream moves them throughout the body. When they lodge in the brain they hatch. You can see the larvae move in the victim's eyes and—" He stopped himself at the look of horror on my face. "Sorry. Too much information. At any rate, we'll find Father Rodriguez soon and get him to a hospital."

"There's a cure?"

"There's a treatment," Thom said. "With Phoenix being so close to the border, the doctors here have seen a few cases of cystercosis. It's distinctive in that it affects the frontal lobe first."

I knew from psychology that the frontal lobe is the part of the brain that controls rational thought. I also knew that when the ability to reason is compromised, the sufferer often acts upon a random idea, then fixates on it to the exclusion of all else. That must be what had happened to Father Rodriguez. "But do you know *why* he cut out the tongues?" I asked Thom.

"I believe he's put them in a reliquary for Saint Anthony," he said. "You found the cross at the base of his statue."

This saint, Thom told me, was also a Franciscan, canonized as a miracle worker. It is said he was such a gifted teacher that when his body was exhumed 336 years after burial, the flesh was consumed, but the tongue was as red and fresh as in life.

"Father Rodriguez came to believe that if he could preserve the victims' tongues and offer them to the saint with enough faith," Thom concluded, "Saint Anthony would give the tongues life on All Saints' Day to testify against the killers."

My heart thrummed in my chest. Today was All Saints' Day and the priest *had* led us to the solution in the case. In a way it had happened just as the faithful, devout man had hoped. I looked up at Thom and wondered if he saw the same significance I did.

"Yes," he said to my unasked question. "But it worked out this way only because of your intuition, Sam. And courage."

Thom's eyes were soft and warm and his lips were incredibly close. For one of the sweetest, most delusional moments in my whole life I thought he might kiss me. Instead, he glanced toward the door and pushed me away. Ivan Lasovik, the chief of detectives, was just coming in with everyone from Nightshade and half the Phoenix PD.

As Lasovik approached the pew, Thom stood. His boss gave him a curt nod on his way up to the sacristy and then, I presumed, into the crypt. "Not half bad work, Tennyson," he said as he passed.

In the next second Chaiya was beside me on the pew, Knute and Delano in the background. She threw open her arms for a hug but considered my battered form and patted the top of my head instead. Her eyes cut toward Thom, and she leaned forward and whispered in my ear, "You look awful."

"You look wonderful!"

Chaiya made a face. "Do you see my pants?" Her purple leggings were in shreds below the knees, and the sweatshirt tied around her waist probably hid worse damage above. "Whose bright idea was it to put garbed wire on a fence?" Then she brightened. "But, hey, I *told* you no problem. I am indelibly fragile."

"You're indelible, period!"

I'd avoided Knute's eyes to that point and hoped to avoid them longer. I knew there would be a lecture—a very long lecture, no doubt—regarding the stupidity of (a) leaving Nightshade when he'd told me to stay put, (b) leaving Nightshade without a cell phone, (c) going to an abandoned cemetery without backup, (d) going *anywhere* without leaving a note, (e) . . . You know, never mind. Suffice it to say that a lecture on my stupidity could have continued right on through the alphabet to *z*.

But the next moment I was encompassed in a hug by the biggest bear of a man you'll ever run across. "That was stupid, Sam," Knute said, but his heart wasn't in it.

"Sure," Delano growled. "Just because you're 'the boss' you think you can have all the fun while the rest of us work." I'd never seen Delano glad to see me before. If he'd had a tail (and of course he doesn't), it would have wagged. "I solved the mystery of who left the note on the door at Nightshade. Not that anybody cares."

"I care!" I said.

"Veronica!" Chaiya guessed.

"No, Kayak," Delano said with a grin. "The note arrived on Friday and Veronica didn't worry about Sam until Monday." When Chaiya stuck her tongue out at him, the grin got toothier. (Negative attention is better than no attention.) "It was Count Creepazoid."

"No!" I said, but even as I said it I knew I'd recognized the handwriting from Trey's poems. He's a vampire, but he's also a poet. "I don't believe he stole Sully's keys!"

"Nah," Delano admitted reluctantly. "He knew who let 'em in, though. He heard his bigot father talk about how much he disliked working for a Jew and how he'd made a few bucks from some guys messing with Sully. Trey was worried that his dad might go after you Mormons next."

"But the marigold?"

Thom said, "Maybe he has a crush on you. To the classical poets, the 'Mary Gowles' symbolized devotion."

Oh, right. I'd been planning to work that tidbit into conversation myself but had forgotten. I'd forgotten a lot, in fact, and felt like I was forgetting more and more with each passing second. There were more things I wanted to know, but I couldn't remember what they were. If only the room would stop moving, maybe I could get a little sleep.

As if on cue, two men approached with a gurney. I struggled to my feet to stumble toward it. I wanted to lie down for a very long time.

"They're from the coroner's office," Thom said, putting an arm around my shoulder and steering me toward a second gurney—this one manned by paramedics.

I scowled at the first pair as if they'd tried to trick me. I didn't want to lie down *that* long. But I did deserve a rest. I'd solved The Case of the Screaming Specter *and* The Mystery of the Marigold Murderer. That was pretty good for one night. And I wasn't done (or done for) yet. There were more mysteries to solve, wrongs to right, and . . . things were getting a little hazy . . . what was that last thing . . . Gotham City to save?

I looked up at Thom's face. Both of them. "How many more carrot sticks do I have to eat before I can ride a Bat Cycle?"

It's the last thing I remember saying, but I have since been told that everything that came after was worse.

Chapter 34

On Wednesday night I was back in the cemetery near San Rafael. The late autumn moon bathed the tombstones in otherworldly light and caused the iron crosses to cast long shadows across the graves.

Fortunately, that is where the similarity to the last night I had been there ended.

It was Dia de los Muertos, and a celebration the likes of which I'd never seen was in progress. The sweet roll in my hand looked good enough to have come from a Cinnabon shop, but I knew it hadn't; instead of frosting on top it had bits of sugared bread shaped into a tiny skeleton. It was pan de muerto—bread of the dead—and Marina Batista had brought it to me herself with tear-glistening eyes and a grateful smile.

I passed Thom Casey the bun but held onto my pink sugar skull. Somebody had carved "Sam" into its forehead. I loved it. I loved everything about the night. Especially I loved being alive and celebrating Dia de los Muertos from the top side of the ground. I scooted a little closer to Thom. "How's this for a first date?"

And it *was* a date this time. After Carlos called to invite us both to the impromptu celebration, Thom offered to pick me up. I found a green silk blouse at the back of my closet and put on blue jeans instead of black. I washed my hair despite the emergency room doctor's orders not to, and Chaiya pulled it into a twist that mostly covered the stitches. Then I scrubbed and buffed my nails until they were clean—if almost as sore as when

I'd used them to try to scratch my way out of the crypt. I couldn't do much about makeup besides a little lip gloss. They just don't make foundation in the shades of blue and yellow I'd have needed to match the side of my face.

"You mean *our* first date?" Thom asked.

"Yes," I said firmly. Prescription pain relievers are a wonderful thing. They had not only quieted the jackhammers in my head, they made me brave enough to say things to Thom that I'd wanted to say for weeks. Things like, "Now we are officially dating."

I was gratified—and relieved—when he smiled.

Further conversation was impossible when a mariachi band and troupe of dancers in brightly painted calaca masks moved closer. Overhead, strung between the trees, intricate and fragile papel picado banners cavorted in the breeze, mimicking the dancing below. All across the graveyard candles glowed, marigolds bloomed, children played, and storytellers passed the three-thousand-year-old traditions of their ancestors to the next generation. Dia de los Muertos was nothing like the strange and macabre rites I had imagined. Instead, it was warm, hopeful, and very touching.

There was still one part of the cemetery cordoned off, of course, but even the officers who stood guard over the crime scene seemed to be enjoying the celebration going on nearby. And why not? Their post was mostly a formality. The killers—plus three others in the drug-smuggling ring—had been apprehended on Tuesday.

The news had flashed through the barrio at the speed of sound. By midafternoon on Wednesday, dozens—probably hundreds—of people had gathered at the San Rafael burial grounds with rakes, hoes, scythes . . . and marigolds. More marigolds than I'd thought grew anywhere in the world. I knew these humble people had emptied the shrines in their homes to bring so many flowers and candles—and emptied their thin wallets to buy the garbage bags that were now stuffed with the litter and debris that had long defaced the graves. It was a spontaneous, joyous celebration of justice. And it was a fitting, heartbreaking memorial to the men— husbands, fathers, sons, brothers, friends—who had been slain here.

As we listened to the music and Thom watched the masked dancers, I watched him. Tonight his clothes were freshly pressed, his face clean shaven. He didn't look as heavenly as he had standing at the top of the stairs in San Rafael, but he looked plenty good.

The mariachis moved off and Brother Simon approached. He'd donned his robe for the occasion, and he looked good too—even though he'd lost more hair than I had to the razor-happy nurses in the emergency room. Thom extended his hand, and Carlos shook it warmly. I jumped up for a hug. We'd talked twice on the phone, but this was the first time I'd seen Carlos since he lay unconscious beside the sepulchre.

"How is Father Rodriguez?" I asked after we'd chatted about the celebration, the weather, everything except what was on the mind of everybody there that night—the dead men and the troubled priest.

"He's heavily sedated," Carlos said. "He doesn't remember clobbering me when I followed him to the graveyard. He doesn't remember anything right now, but the doctors say that's a good thing." We sat down and Brother Simon said to Thom, "I found those records you asked me about, Detective. They ended up at a church archive in California." He grinned. "You have no idea how excited they were to hear about that journal you found. One of the curators told me he'd work on your request himself. If there's a record of where Manuel Sarasate is buried, they'll find it for you."

"If we can convince them he didn't commit suicide, can his body then be moved to his sepulchre?"

"I don't know if you have 'channels' in *your* church," Carlos said, "but we have more hierarchy than heaven has angels." He shrugged. "The short answer is maybe. I hope so."

"Thanks," Thom said. "It was a wild hare of an idea to start with."

"Didn't I say you have St. Jude in you?" Brother Simon said. "I'll toss in a few extra candles and good words to the patron saint of lost causes and maybe he'll help this one along."

I'd been out of the loop as long as I could stand. Longer. "What are you talking about?"

Carlos pointed to Thom. "It's the detective's idea. Ask him."

Thom was embarrassed, but at last he pulled the old journal out of the pocket of his jacket. "You asked me to read this, Sam," he said. "My Latin is mediocre and I didn't recognize all Sarasate's archaic Spanish, but I got the gist of it."

"What did you find out?"

"That Brother Vincent was a gifted artist, a brilliant engineer, and a good man."

"He designed the entrances to the crypt," I guessed.

"He did. And he carved the sarcophagus that led there. He hoped it would be his final resting place. Unfortunately, I think the records will show that Sarasate was buried outside hallowed ground because Father Sebastian was led to believe he committed suicide when in fact he was murdered."

"Then *he* was the tragic friar?" I gasped. "Manuel Sarasate is the one haunting San Rafael?" It took me a couple of seconds to realize what I'd said. "I mean, he's the one who *inspired* the ghost stories?"

"It looks that way," Thom said. "But a girl wasn't his love, his vocation was. And I don't think he killed himself. He wrote in his journal that he feared harm from another friar who he had observed in what he called 'an unspeakable act.'"

It was a murder mystery more than a century old. I couldn't wait for the records to come from California so we could solve it at last. If anybody deserved to rest in peace, it was the man with the heart of a poet and the hands of an angel.

I thought of what a miracle it was that we had found the journal in the first place, and the hair rose on the back of my neck. I leaned toward Thom. It would be the silliest question I'd ever asked, but I couldn't resist. "You listened to the recordings Chaiya made at San Rafael. Did you hear 'Sarasate' and 'book' in them?" I was giving myself goose bumps, but it *was* Dia de los Muertos, the day the dead are supposed to return to earth to tie up unfinished business.

"'The most beautiful thing we can experience is the mysterious,'" Thom said. "'It is the source of all true art and science.'"

"Longfellow?" I guessed. After Shakespeare, Thom is very big on quoting Longfellow.

"Albert Einstein," he said. He didn't say if it was a "yes" or a "no" to my question.

That was okay because I had another question. I wanted to know why, with everything else he had to do, he had taken time to pursue a centuries-old homicide. Talk about a cold case. There hadn't been anybody to arrest for more than a hundred years.

"I feel like I owe him," Thom said. "If it hadn't been for Manuel Sarasate's journal, I would never have known about the crypts beneath San Rafael, let alone known how to open the passageway to them."

I drew in a breath and held it. He might be grateful because that's how he solved the case. On the other hand, he might be grateful to have saved me. I was hoping Thom had meant that second thing when Carlos reached for my scratched and bruised hand and held it gently.

"There's something I want to tell you, Sam," he said. "Seeing you again after all these years brought back a lot of memories." He looked toward the sepulchre. "And almost losing my life the other night made me think about how I want to live out the rest it. I . . . I've decided not to become a monk."

I glanced at Thom. I was almost certain the guy who couldn't come right out and admit that he was glad I hadn't died had just stopped breathing.

"I'm going to enroll in seminary," Carlos continued. "I've received a call to become a priest." Seeing that he now had my full attention, he smiled. "I wanted you to be the first to know. Remember back in high school? You were always after me to go to seminary."

"That's not the seminary I had in mind," I said. Then I hugged him. "But I'm so happy for you—and happy for all the people you'll bless."

Across the cemetery, near the long stripe of yellow police tape, a woman began to wail. In the minutes that followed, others joined her. La llorada, the weeping, had begun. It would go on for some time, I knew. Here were a people with a great deal to mourn.

Brother Simon stood and excused himself to tend his flock. Thom and I rose too. The public portion of the ceremony had come to an end. It was time to give the mourners privacy.

For the first time that night my heart was heavy. "Those poor people," I said as we walked toward Thom's car. "They have almost nothing. How do they survive?"

"With faith, hope, and the help of God and people like Brother Simon," Thom said. He looked toward the tenements as we passed. "Emerson wrote, 'There is no great and no small to the Soul that maketh all: and where it cometh, all things are; and it cometh everywhere.'"

The peace and warmth that come with the Spirit replaced the heaviness in my heart. The beautiful words were true. Our Father sends His Spirit everywhere with all the comfort we truly need to meet any circumstance. I had felt its influence, even in the crypts.

I couldn't resist a final glance back at the cemetery. If not for the intelligent, in-tune man at my side, I'd still be down in those crypts. I moved close enough to nestle my hand in Thom's. His hand was strong and warm and exactly the right size to hold mine. I said, "Thank you for coming to look for me."

"Always."

Always? My heart grew two sizes.

But then Thom changed the subject. "Has your uncle come back yet?"

"He was supposed to," I said. "They were at the hotel packing when he got a call from a man he'd worked for years ago. Now the guy is head of one of those cruise lines that keep turning up with passengers missing. Uncle Eddie said a free month-long cruise on the French Riviera was too good to pass up."

"So you're still interim head of Nightshade."

"Yes! And I have a new case."

Thom chuckled. "In the few weeks I've known you, you've been on the trail of a mummy and a ghost. What is it this time, Sam? A zombie?"

"No," I said, "a vampire." Thom stopped in his tracks, but that was all right. We were at the sidewalk beside his car by now, alone and under enough moonlight to make me hopeful. "A friend of Trey Tucker's has gone missing," I explained. "The police won't look for him because they say he's a 'troubled kid' who ran away."

"But you can find him."

"Of course I can. I can find anyone or anything." From where we stood on the corner, I could just see the bell tower of San Rafael silhouetted against the stars. All was quiet there tonight. No one moaned or screamed or haunted the once-hallowed halls. The only one left with unfinished business was me.

I smiled up at Thom. "I have a quote for you, Detective Casey. The author of *Ghost Hunting for Dummies* wrote, 'True love is like a ghost. Many people believe in both, but few find either.'" I moved closer. "*I've* found both."

"You have, have you?" Thom put one hand in the small of my back and used the other to cup my chin. He was either going to kiss me or examine my skull for brain damage.

"Yes," I said. "And you can quote me."

He kissed me instead. Would you believe that man kisses better than he quotes? Better than he detects? Possibly better than he reads? In short, if he has a flaw, that isn't it.

Don't worry. I won't leave you hanging. I'll find out what's wrong with Thom Casey and get back to you. It might take a while, however. Quite a while. Fortunately, I'm willing to stay on that case forever.

Since two of the great loves of my life (aside from Thom) are crosswords puzzles and hot fudge sundaes—and since the former is much easier to slip into a book than the latter, consider this an added treat from me to you. All the answers to the puzzling questions can be found somewhere in the book. Happy sleuthing! When you finish the puzzle, write to me in care of www.kerryblair.com and I'll send you a prize!

—*Samantha Shade*

ACROSS

1. Religious haven established by Catholic emissaries to New World; San Rafael

5. IV; how many types of hauntings there are, according to Chaiya

7. Sphere or globe; when caught on film, glowing object thought to indicate presence of a ghost

10. Abbreviation for police field technicians who gather forensic evidence; popular TV show

11. Anger; wrath; a cause of "unfinished business" from the hereafter?

13. Underground vault; worst place to spend the night

14. Pad used to absorb shock; what I ought to take with me when viewing cadavers

15. Crossword puzzle dictionary word for whirlpool or trap; going down the drain—like my cases sometimes

16. Form carved in stone; object of art in San Rafael sanctuary

18. Pronoun; objective case of I; from my perspective, the person who wrote this book

19. A losing; what both Sully and the Batistas suffered when Antonio's body was stolen

20. The patron saint of lost causes (Roman Catholic)

22. Jane ___: Brontë's heroine who also heard strange sounds coming from a mysterious room

23. Spanish for dead

24. Away or forth from a place or position; I was ___ of ideas for how to get ___ of the crypt and running ___ of time.

28. Another word for corpse; what Sully never calls his clients

29. Two words: 18th-century Spanish mission (fictional); patron saint of healing and singles (Roman Catholic)

31. Loosely, fate; Chaiya's mother; one of my many aunts

34. Spanish word for fried bread; scone

36. Small wolf of western North America; unscrupulous person who smuggles people across the border from Mexico

37. Harry ___, father of modern ghost-hunting techniques

38. Seaport in west central Florida; place my uncle often vacations when he should be running Nightshade

40. Four words: Dia de los Muertos; festival celebrated in October/November in much of Central America and the Southwestern U.S.

45. Unlawful and malicious and/or premeditated killing of a person

48. To accustom to pain, trouble, etc.; what life in Mexico and illegal immigration to the U.S. had done to many of the people in the barrio

50. A religious ceremony; what would have to proceed without Antonio Batista's attendance unless I found his body

51. Crossword puzzle dictionary word to hush or rebuke; what I wished somebody would do to the ghost of San Rafael

52. Mineral element; most common of all metals; what 55 ACROSS was often made of in the absence of wood in the desert

54. The evening of October 31, followed by All Saints' Day on November 1; a great reason for a party

55. An upright post with another across it; something often used to mark graves

56. A sound made to express disapproval; what ghosts are said to cry out (Because they disapprove of death?)

57. Alfred ___, an English poet (1809–1892); what the chief of detectives called Thom because of Thom's fondness for literature

DOWN

2. Water frozen solid by cold; what seems to form in your veins when you're scared to death

3. Persons officially venerated for having attained heaven after a holy life (Roman Catholic); latter-day people of a certain church doing the best they can (LDS)

4. Done openly with evident intent; the Marigold Murderer's efforts to harass and terrify

5. Swipe, steal, pilfer, purloin; what somebody did in the morgue next door

6. Likewise; in addition; I should ___ exercise and drink a lot of water if I want to lose weight.

8. English rectory where Harry Price garnered most of his fame as a ghost hunter in the 1920s

9. A feeling that what is wanted will happen; that thing that springs eternal when you're me

10. Without needed facts; the perfect name for our dumb dog

12. A small difference, as in a ___ of gray; our family name

13. Graveyard; place for burial of the dead; not a place I'd go on a first date . . . or second . . . or hundred-and-fifth

16. __ ye ___, so shall ye reap (second word); one of the creeds by which Brother Simon lives (see 17 DOWN)

17. __ye___, so shall ye reap (first word); one of the creeds by which Brother Simon lives (see 16 DOWN)

20. A daily record of happenings; a priceless artifact found in San Rafael

21. A man who takes vows to join a religious order

25. Plant of the composite family with yellow or orange blooms; blossoms traditionally scattered on Dia de los Muertos to guide the dead back to their earthly homes

26. A vehicle used to transport a corpse in a funeral procession; the car I often drive when mine is in the shop

27. A vault for burial, usually above ground; a place you don't want to take your body while it's still alive

28. Spanish word for artistic mask associated with Dia de los Muertos

30. An oily or greasy material found in animal tissue (yuck!); something I intend to have less of by the beginning of my next book!

32. Abbreviation for pseudo-scientific method of recording audible ghostly phenomena

33. Primate; slang for man of a simian nature

35. Anything that appears unexpectedly or strangely; a ghost

39. Very nearly; all but; I ___ lost my mind

41. Three words: Spanish for "I don't know" (Don't forget the little mark over the *e*.)

42. See 21 DOWN and make him a Roman Catholic, and he's probably one of these

43. To visit often or continually (whether you're alive or dead)

44. A regimen of special or limited food and drink (Carrot sticks and pencils surely qualify.)

46. The chief evil spirit; someone who can't really make you do anything

47. The house of a minister or priest; where Father Rodriguez lived

49. The supposed disembodied spirit of a dead person; a pale, shadowy apparition; how much of a chance I thought I had to find Antonio Batista's body

53. Abbreviation for the largest international women's organization in the world (two words)

55. A prefix meaning with or together

ANSWER KEY

MISSION FOUR AL
ORB H CAV CSI LS
O O E IRE L L SS
CRYPT N R U CUSHION
WEEL E STATUE H A
ME LOSS L JUDE E
M EYRE W MUERTO E
OUT M H S U S
N E CADAVER SANRAFAEL
KARMA R A E N AT P
Y I I R V A A T U
L A G SOPAPILLA A L
COYOTE E PRICE
TAMPA L P HR
L DAYOFTHEDEAD E
MURDER O R A I R
O E E N INURE IG H
SERVICE O A N TUT H
T I T S R T IRON
HALLOWEEN CROSS S
R BOON N T
TENNYSON N

About the Author

Kerry Blair and her writing partner, a spooky black cat named Chakotay, live in a disappointingly unhaunted house in central Arizona. Also in residence are her husband, Gary, their two children, Kerry's mother, and more pets—who will just have to be offended that they haven't been mentioned by name like Gary and the cat. The other two of her children serve in the Armed Forces and are currently stationed in South Korea and Iraq.

Kerry has never been ghost hunting, but thinks it sounds much more compelling than searching for her glasses—a task that occupies much of her time these days. She enjoys her new calling as a Primary teacher and loves to speak at firesides, conferences, and Enrichment meetings across the Southwest.

Ghost of a Chance is the second book in the Nightshade series and the eighth of her novels published by Covenant. Kerry loves to correspond with her readers. Contact her at her website, kerryblair.com, through Covenant email at info@covenant-lds.com, or through snail mail at Covenant Communications, Inc., Box 416, American Fork, UT 84003-0416.